THE LAST LAUGH

By Linda Wiges

"The fool doth think he is wise, but the wise
man knows himself to be a fool."
—William Shakespeare. As You Like It, Act v.
Sc. 1

ISBN-13 9780692960035 (Fallen Oak Publishing)

ISBN-10 0692960031

Cover art by Andrew Bouska

The town of Haven in this book is entirely fictional. It bears no resemblance to the tiny settlement of Haven which actually can be found in Tama County, Iowa. Too, all businesses referred to in the book are fictional as are the characters. Any similarity to real persons, living or dead, is purely coincidental.

DEDICATION

To the talented and committed members of the clown community who have recently suffered unfair attacks on their integrity and have lost their jobs due to changes in the modern public's perception of humor.

1

Nebraska 2016

Clown Alley *originally described the area inside the main circus tent where clowns and other performers gathered to put on costumes, apply their makeup, or just relax. The area was a dark one along the side of the big top and resembled an alley. Today Clown Alley is the name given to any organized group of clowns whether associated with a circus or not.*

Reflected light from the center of the big top reveals wide eyes full of alarm. The usual laughter has become an anxious murmur. In spite of an effort to speak quietly, the voices rise in nervous anticipation.

A firm but subdued speaker interrupts the chaos. "Okay, now! Give Lola your attention. I don't like to order people around, but somebody needs to take the lead right now. We have just a short time to make a big decision. I propose we leave, strike out on our own." Gasps are heard in the close quarters. "I can't force you to do anything. I'm just saying what I believe. We've given our lives to a profession that can't protect us. In fact, it's becoming clear we could be in mortal danger here. Some of us have even had death threats. I don't know about you, but it's hard for me to be funny when I'm wondering what the crowd is intending to do to me."

"Yeah! Somebody broke in my trailer and cut up my costumes. Makes me scared of what's coming next!"

"That isn't what clowning is supposed to be. It looks like our occupation is going the way of the elephants – out of here. If we want to stick around we're going to be doing menial jobs like cleaning the animal pens. You might not mind that, but I would."

"I sure don't want to make a career out of horse manure. But what choice do we have?"

"We must discover our choices," states their temporary leader. "Thanks to the impersonators, circus goers don't feel the same about clowns as they used to. And the owner of HAPPCO is definitely not on our side. It seems to me it's time to find new lives. Or at least take a break."

A young man in the back of the area speaks up. "I don't have a place to go. Haven't heard from my mom in a long time. And I haven't got savings to live on."

"Don't worry, Pike. You won't have any trouble finding work. And don't stress about where you'll live. For now, we'll stay together."

"Who's going to take in five unemployed people? I wouldn't."

"My dears, you need to trust me. I have a lead on a place not far away that will fit our needs perfectly. The only catch will be keeping a low profile. We must live off the radar so those who want to wipe out our community won't know where we came from."

Ms. Sofie can't help but shed a tear. "It'll be hard to hide me. I should stay here. It'll serve me right for eating so much these past few months."

"And Gordy? What about him?"

"He goes where I go. We're family. Nobody stays behind unless they want to. Just give me a few hours to contact my cousin Monique. She's our best hope. Now I know some folks believe we can all pile into any little car, but this is the real world. We'll need to carry along some belongings, so we'd better take the van. It's pretty noticeable, but we can travel at night."

There is a stunned immobility among the generally animated group. These instructions are far different from anything they've been prepared to hear.

"Won't the circus send out the police or detectives to track us down? I don't think they'll just let us disappear!"

"I'm not sure they'll be that concerned. They'll just be happy they can keep our paychecks. When we get to where we're going, I'll write the owners of HAPPCO and tell them not to worry. I won't say where we are but just tell them enough to get the circus off the hook when people ask. That should keep them from trying to follow us."

"After so many years, you wouldn't think it would be that easy to get the circus to forget."

"We cost them more than we bring in. That makes us liabilities. Now go ahead and pack only items you can't live without. You can keep a few costumes, but you'll also need to take along any clothes you have that're plain and drab. We must blend in when we're out in the community."

****

Midnight on the midway is a quiet time, and the frightened friends have gathered once more. "What did you find out?" is the question of the moment

Lola is ready with answers this time. "I talked to Monique, and let her know about the threats we've endured around here. When she heard that attempts were made on the lives of two of us, she was eager to help. She told me about a property she's recently purchased on the outskirts of a little town called Haven. She says it looks like a typical haunted mansion. But there's no history of that. It's huge. Big enough to accommodate all of us plus a few paying customers. Monique is willing to take us in until it's safe to come back here or until we can all find other homes."

"But it sounds like she bought the big house for a money-making business. And we don't have money to pay her. Unless we stay here until after payday. And that would only cover a month of rent."

"We can't wait around for paychecks. The idea is to get away soon without anyone catching on. As far as us paying Monique, she's made a generous offer. She said I could be her apartment manager and can have one assistant. She was going to have to hire those anyway. But, still, she'll be losing money if she lets us use three or four other apartments for free. We'll have to find the money one way or the other. Legally, I hope."

"What are you saying? We might have to turn into thieves? That isn't who we are!"

"That would definitely be our worst case scenario. But extreme circumstances call for extreme actions. We'll do what we must. I'm not worried. You're all smart and have plenty of marketable skills."

There is a short silence while the friends try to decide what skills she's talking about.

"I don't think I like the idea of living in a house that looks haunted. What if it is?"

"Beggars can't be choosers. Besides, it won't appear that way when we're in it. We'll make the building smile!"

No one answers. No one smiles. The group isn't convinced.

2

Six Months Later - Iowa

Vanessa Martin's inner excitement is out of proportion to her ordinary surroundings. She learns that Doug's Diner, Haven, Iowa's only downtown eating establishment isn't the place to go if you're expecting anyone to make a big fuss over your good news.

In the middle of a Saturday afternoon she's one of just three customers in the diner. A man is reading the newspaper and a woman sitting by herself appears to be playing Solitaire on her phone. Much to Nessa's disappointment, neither person notices that the young woman who has recently entered is wearing the glow of womanhood, a look that says, "I'm an adult now. On my own and beginning a new career!" The room is quiet except for noise from a small TV sitting on a shelf behind the counter. The local weather is on, but no one seems interested. A skinny, frowning waitress with a nametag reading MAVIS approaches and asks for Nessa's order. "Whad'llya 'ave?"

Bursting with her recent success, Nessa can't resist sharing it. "I'm new in town. I just found out I'm going to teach English at the high school. I'll probably be coming in here a lot." Maybe the girl felt a similar sort of pride when she got the job in Doug's.

Mavis looks at her blankly, then asks, "Ya want water?"

"Yes, please. And what entrees do you have for a vegetarian?"

"Uh... nothing, really."

"Do you have soups, salads...?"

"Oh. Yeah. Sure."

"Give me your soup of the day and a garden salad."

"Fries?"

"No thanks."

The constant sizzle of a griddle explains the waitress's unfamiliarity with Nessa's type of diet. She doesn't let it spoil her mood, however, even when Mavis calls out, "One bowl-a meatball soup!"

"Do you know anything about the Fancy Tramp boarding house?" She's determined to get something useful out of the droopy girl before she gets away.

"You mean the old haunted house on the hill everybody's afraid to go near? No."

"It's haunted, you think? Nobody believes that, do they?"

"It's what I hear from kids who sneak up there at Halloween. A witch runs it."

"Oh, great. Well, thanks for the information." Nessa decides to ignore the rumors. *Kids always say that kind of thing about old houses where no one lives.*

Nessa finds herself hoping the students in her classes are more cheerful than Mavis. Even if they are, she'll likely have to face some challenging ones. Her mother has shared some horror stories from her teaching days, and Vanessa can't forget the trouble-makers in her own class in Chicago. *It won't matter, though*, she thinks. *I'm up to it. The worse they are, the more difference I'll be able to make. I'm going to change this town, one student at a time. Some people find a way to make a difference even in darkest Africa. I should be able to create a ripple in Haven.*

Her cell phone rings just as she's blowing on her soup. It's her mom, of course. Tracy Martin has probably been waiting for a call all morning so is finally making the first move. "Hello, sweetie! How'd it go?"

"I got it! Mr. Bingham the principal said I'm just what he's been looking for and offered me the job without even meeting with the superintendent and the board. He told me they do whatever he says, so they'll take his word when he tells them I'm the best English teacher who applied!" At last she's telling someone who'll be impressed by that fact.

"Well, sure you are, honey. Mr. Bingham sounds like a smart man to have for your first boss."

"He's really impressive, I think. If I were to draw a picture of the ideal school principal, it would look like him. So far all signs are good for Haven High."

 When do classes start? Are you coming back home for a while first?"

"It's three weeks until the teachers have to report to work, so I'll be home for a week or so. Right now I have to line up a place to live."

"Didn't you ask the superintendent or principal for some ideas?"

"Actually, Mr. Bingham really pushed me to visit one particular apartment complex. He almost sounded like he owns an interest in it. It's an old Victorian house called The Fancy Tramp. I love the name. Sounds like it has personality."

"Ew." Her mother can convey a lot of distaste with one syllable. "Sounds like a brothel."

"I asked a lady at the gas station about it. She told me it's not particularly fancy anymore, but it's cheap. That's good, right?"

"Well, check for bed bugs and don't take anything on the top floor. Old apartments are usually fire traps."

Count on her to think of the worst possibilities. "Don't worry. One good thing is, it's furnished. I won't need to buy anything new. And it's run by an older motherly-type woman. I'm sure she'll take good care of me. After all, I'm a respectable school teacher now. The perfect renter."

***

Scarred blue paint on the front door of the Fancy Tramp and on the matching loose shutters speak of past glamour and present neglect. The picture of a woman in a floppy hat and boa adorns the hanging sign to Nessa's right. It would be a cute welcome if the letters weren't badly faded. It makes her wonder if the manager won't be a bit faded as well. A hand-written paper taped to the door invites guests to COME ON IN. Nessa has visions of Mavis's witch beckoning with a long, crooked finger, *"This way, Dearie!"*

Standing just inside on a mat covered with various pairs of shoes, Nessa is reassured other people are inside. She clears her throat, hoping someone will notice. Sure enough, a tall lanky woman appears from what could be an office door. Fiery red hair piled into a messy top knot and a robe decorated with large orange poppies catches Nessa's attention before she can take in the lined but heavily made up face. The face is smiling, a positive sign for a young teacher who is hoping to have found her first home away from home.

"Greetings and salutations, my dear!" comes the woman's high raspy voice. "I'm Lola Lang. I hope you're looking for an apartment."

"Actually, I am. Do you have one you can show me?" Nessa knows enough not to make any arrangements without a thorough inspection. Even if this is the only show in town, she can't help having a few misgivings. Maybe the old house should be condemned. Maybe Mr. Bingham has never actually been inside its doors. She attempts to channel her mother. "Hopefully, your vacancy isn't on the top floor."

"Oh, no. Even though you look like you have good knees for climbing stairs. The one that's empty is where Marvin died. Right down here." And she takes off down the hallway to her right, bright yellow house slippers flapping. "I couldn't understand it. I always thought there was plenty of fresh air when you opened the windows, but the paramedics thought he suffocated. He was a vagrant so there wasn't a lot of explaining to be done."

Vanessa decides her mom won't be hearing about Marvin. The word *suffocated* conjures a picture of the man with a pillow being held over his face.

Lola opens the door of the last apartment in the dimly-lit west wing. A quick walk-through gives a favorable impression. Nessa is especially taken with the spacious bedroom. Paisley wallpaper and an iron bed tend to fit her expectations for the Fancy Tramp. And, thankfully, the pillows appear new. The area is charming in an old-West-boarding-house kind of way. Another nice surprise is the smell. Or lack thereof. Not what she feared. Judging from the remnants of a strong perfume she detected on Lola, she's expected a heavy flower-scented room deodorant, covering who-knows-what. "I'm sure the rooms have been cleaned since Marvin lived here," she comments hopefully. Who knows what the routine is in this unconventional apartment complex.

"Oh, of course! I couldn't wait to have Monique dig in and de-Marvinize."

Nessa ignores the woman's rather dehumanizing verb and gets to the details. "Do you check for bed bugs?" It sounds impolite, but her mom is sure to ask, and frankly, Nessa wants to know, too.

"Monique would track down and kill any bug that found its way in here. Or she'd set fire to the place. I call her our Clean Queen. She don't allow critters of any size. Except for the cats."

Cats plural. That could be bad. "Cats?"

"My tenant on second has … three very talented ones. Monique puts up with them. Says cats are clean animals and kill any mice that show up. Whatever. I don't let them roam the house."

Marvin's former kitchen, bathroom, and sitting room all have outdated furnishings but seem to be adequate for a single woman with few possessions. Nessa reminds herself the new teaching position is temporary, a resume builder, a place to gain experience before she finds her dream classroom in a progressive school. Hopefully, her next job will be in a thriving community with attractive houses to choose from. This spooky-looking monstrosity will do in the meantime. "How much is the rent?"

Lola quotes a very reasonable price. "Due after your payday. I know the first check of the year is a long time coming for teachers. I've had a couple of them living here."

Nessa fleetingly wonders why she's had "a couple" of teachers who aren't around now. Do people not stay long at the Fancy Tramp? "Have any of your other renters… suffocated?"

"Naw. That was a first. The closest we ever came to a tragedy, besides Marvin, was a woman who slammed a window down on her own finger when she thought she saw a creepy clown looking in at her." She flashes her red lipstick-lined smile. "Oh, and one elderly man claimed he was chased off the porch by a rabid squirrel. Never a dull moment!"

Having ambitions to write fiction, Nessa can't help being intrigued by the bizarre goings on in this quaint old building. And the fact that a cleaning fanatic works here gives her some comfort. Knowing the size of the town, she could be looking at her only choice, so with the faint sound of her mother's sure-to-come, "What do you know about Lola?" echoing in the back of her mind, she finds herself saying, "I'll take it. Can I move in a week from Monday?"

After an oral agreement that leaves her feeling a bit uncertain, Nessa exits. The front porch steps are so rickety as to make one wonder if the place is up to code. Surely apartments must comply with certain requirements, but judging from a quick look around, she has a feeling the safety police haven't caught up with Lola.

As she starts down the front walk, she nearly collides with a tall young man. All lingering doubts fly out of her head when he flashes a perfect smile, gives her an intense look, and says, "I don't think we've met. Have you looked at the empty apartment?"

"Yes. I just now told Lola I'd take it." The handsome guy is still smiling. "Did I make a mistake?" *Please say no.*

"Oh, no. It's an okay place as far as I can tell. You'll be my neighbor. I'm on the opposite end of the downstairs. My name is John. John Smith."

Of course it is. And I'm Martha Washington. "I'm Vanessa. You'll have to fill me in next week when I come back."

"Give me a holler if you need help moving in." He continues up the front steps.

An afterthought causes her to call him back. "Oh, er…John! Could you answer something for me?"

"Sure. If I can."

"The Fancy Tramp. I know what everybody's going to think when I tell them where I live. Is Lola a … you know?"

John laughs. "Maybe in another lifetime. Now she's just an eccentric. And so are most of her tenants from what I've seen."

Nessa is relieved. She wouldn't expect her new boss to point her in the direction of a bordello. "I'm the new English teacher. Reputation is important."

"Don't worry. Nobody in Haven will think less of you for living here. I'm pastor at a church in town." He pauses a moment and then continues, "They're building me a house. The

12

church council arranged for me to live here in the meantime. If it passes *their* conditions, it can't be a house of ill repute." Vanessa walks to her car trying to reconcile the various stories that have already come out of the Fancy Tramp. She's sure she hasn't heard them all.

3

The week with her mother goes fast. There are tasks to be done and good-byes to be said. Her best friend from high school is sticking around the Chicago area to do her teaching at her alma mater. "I couldn't stand to go off to some one-horse town that doesn't have running water. You probably won't even be able to get cable or any cell phone service."

"It isn't that bad," Nessa tells her. "I'll be as connected as you are. I'm sure life moves a little slower there, but I'll be busy with my job."

"Oh, groan. I sure don't want life on my own to be all work. Give me Glenview with its restaurants and theatres and men to be met."

"Well, I know Haven has Doug's Diner that serves a mean meatball soup, and I saw a movie theatre that says they only charge three dollars. *And* I met a gorgeous guy who lives in my building."

"Well, the gorgeous guy sounds promising, but I'm guessing he's taken. Truly single ones don't hang around small towns from what I hear. And what will you do to expand your mind? To stimulate your thinking? Am I going to see you in a year and find out you have the same hair style, the same clothes and listen to the same music you do today? Time stands still in places like Heaven."

"Haven. And you're wrong. I'm sure there're lots of fascinating people here." Nessa thinks of Mavis, the waitress. "I just have to find them."

After going through her belongings from high school and college, she decides only a few of them need to be moved. Everything seems to belong in the family home of her previous life. Selecting mostly clothes and books she'll definitely be using, she loads her car.

"Thanks a lot," says her mom when they take a break to have iced tea. "I was looking forward to having some extra space here after you leave, but you're packed, and I can hardly tell the piles of boxes are any smaller. What am I, the Goodwill drop off?"

"I'm sorry, but my apartment is small, and the whole arrangement feels kinda shaky. I could find out it's a basket of crazies and have to move out. The less I have with me, the better."

"If your instincts tell you that, maybe you shouldn't even bother with it."

"Well, I'm also kind of attracted to the house. It looks like something out of some gothic mystery. Definitely more appealing than most rental properties I've been in. I'll give it a month."

"A month could be a long time with crazies."

"At least that John Smith seems sane." *And very muscular. Beautiful blue eyes.* "It helps to know he'll be down the hall."

"You know nothing about the man. I hope you checked the apartment's security. You'll want dead bolts on your doors."

"It's a small town. I'll be surprised if they even lock the doors."

15

"Oh, my gosh! You're throwing yourself to the wolves! Haven't I taught you anything about survival?"

"You always think of Chicago. People in Haven don't live in fear of each other."

"It only takes one pervert to put you in danger. I'm sure I wouldn't want to leave my safety in the hands of Lola the tramp."

Vanessa sighs. Now her mom is getting carried away. The more the woman thinks about it, the more dire scenarios she'll come up with. Just the same, Nessa makes a mental note to check the locks when she returns to the Fancy Tramp.

Her cell phone rings. The number is unfamiliar, but Nessa recognizes the area code for Haven. *Maybe they changed their minds. The school board has met and decided to withdraw their offer of employment.* "Hello. This is Vanessa."

There are a few moments of silence. She is about to hang up when a woman speaks. "Vanessa, my name is Beverly Birch. I'm the secretary at Haven High School. I got your phone number from your file." Silence again. Is Nessa supposed to know what a call from her means?

"Good to hear from you," she finally responds. "Do you need more information from me?" *I knew it was too easy.*

"No. Everything is in order from your end. I just...well, I know you'll be looking for an apartment to rent, and I got to worrying that you'd chose the Fancy Tramp."

Good guess. "You're right. I've already made arrangements with them."

"Oh, dear. I should've spoken up sooner. I'm afraid there's something you should know."

Doesn't sound good. "Okay." Nessa waits. *That apartment house has been condemned or it burned down overnight.* Only an emergency would warrant this call.

"My niece Jodi was the last English teacher. She lived at the Fancy Tramp, and she fled in terror before the end of the school year."

Vanessa can't believe her ears. "Terror of what?" she manages to ask. "Are the students that bad?"

"No. Jodi seemed fine here at school. It had to be something else. She never told me. She said no one would believe her. She moved to Ohio, and I haven't heard a word from her. I do know from my sister that Jodi's been in therapy since she left."

"Well, I appreciate you letting me know, but if she didn't confide in you, how can you know she was terrorized? Maybe the job just wasn't a good fit for her. Not everybody can teach." Nessa could think of other people her own age who would be scared silly in front of a classroom. "It's hard to know what it's like until you try it."

"Jodi wanted to be a teacher ever since kindergarten," Beverly responds. "She loved her student teaching. I think if she'd lived with me everything would've been different. There was something about that apartment. I went over to visit her one evening and met her running out the front door looking like she was being chased by the devil. I'll never forget the fear in her eyes. She didn't even seem to see me."

That definitely sounds like terror. "What are you thinking I should do? I already accepted the position. I'm moving tomorrow."

"Go ahead and take the job but not the apartment. Find another place. Maybe a motel for now. Listen, I have to get off the phone. I just had to warn you. I couldn't live with myself if anything happened." And the phone goes dead.

Thankfully, her mother wasn't nearby to hear the ominous conversation. She'd never let Nessa leave Chicago. Tracy Martin is a good mom but a protective one. Ever since Nessa's dad died of a heart attack when Nessa was five, Tracy has taken seriously her dual parental roles. "Now you've got to give me a full report on this old place after one day. If that Lola isn't normal, tell me right up front. I'll help you relocate."

"I'm sure she's just an ordinary older woman. About your age. And she seems very upbeat and optimistic." Her thoughts go to the school secretary. "I think I'm going to appreciate that."

In spite of her daughter's crack about an older woman, Tracy is still in her forties and hardly looks that. Vanessa has heard comments that she and her mom look exactly alike. Dark brown hair worn straight, dark brown eyes, and fit bodies. Vanessa is aware her mother has had several chances to find a new love and life partner. There have been dates, but none has lived up to the woman's requirements. Nessa is sure Tracy would be easier to please if she were childless. It's always come down to being too big a risk allowing someone else to interact with her baby. Tracy feels, right or wrong, that she's the only person who knows what's best for her daughter. Nessa has always believed that if her mother ever actually falls in love again, the man will have to be the next thing to God.

A relationship might have a better chance now with Nessa on her own. Her mom's loneliness is a constant source of concern for her only child. When she's out socializing with friends, Nessa is often plagued by visions of her mother sitting at home alone, tearfully drinking tea and working crosswords. A widow in her forties can have friends at work, but in the evenings, most of them are involved with their families or out doing the singles scene which hasn't so far worked out for Tracy. She's concluded that most men who aren't married by midlife are undesirables. Of course, that isn't always true, but so far she hasn't been interested enough to give any of them a chance. Her daughter tries to encourage her to join clubs, but Tracy isn't much of a joiner. "You won't meet Mr. Right in a bar," Nessa advises her. The statement is the same one her mom has used on Tracy in the past.

This week has been fun for both of them, eating out, going to movies, doing a yoga workshop. All things neither of them get around to doing by themselves. Knowing their time is limited, the two have refrained from the usual bickering that can get in the way of mom/daughter time, so the days have flown by.

Nessa's last overnight on the home place promises to be a sleepless one. Car packed, good-byes to everyone but her mother over, she lies with her eyes open wondering whether she's going to be driving to her doom early the next morning.

Should she listen to a woman she doesn't even remember meeting about a niece who might or might not be mentally ill? The two people she's met so far at the Fancy Tramp don't seem threatening, especially not John Smith. She hasn't signed a lease so maybe she should stay a night or two before she does just to give herself time to look into Beverly's story. Perhaps someone in one of the apartments remembers niece Jodi and can assure Nessa there was a good explanation for the young lady's abrupt exit.

4

By the time she approaches the driveway of the Fancy Tramp, it is late Monday afternoon. The sky is cloudy and a breeze has picked up. Rather than offering a cozy retreat, the house on the hill looks down at her with suspicion. This young upstart of a teacher from Chicago may not know how to act in its dark musty interior. Nessa could be someone it should scare away – like Jodi. In spite of her uncertain impressions, Nessa is determined to make the old building accept her. The Tramp reminds her of an aging but mysterious woman. Like Lola. Nessa can't wait to get acquainted.

A young gangly Afro-American guy with an abundance of hair standing out around his head and wearing baggy jeans comes out to meet her. "Hi!" he says. "I'm Pike. I live upstairs. Lola says to pull up onto the yard to unload. It won't hurt anything." And he takes off walking down the gravel lane with a bounce to his step. No sign of terror in that renter. Pike appears totally carefree. He's done his good deed for the day by relaying a message. Veering into the grass at the side of the road, he turns one-armed hand springs down to the corner. Apparently, it hasn't occurred to him the lady he just met might need a hand carrying in boxes.

Nessa doesn't take offense. She considers herself anything but a helpless female. She opens the trunk of her aged Honda and lifts out a large suitcase. It takes both her hands to carry it. She's scolding herself for putting too many books in one container when the front door opens, and she's greeted by the handsome preacher. "May I help?" he asks as he approaches with his hand extended.

Nessa gives him a thank-you worthy of a delicate weakling of a woman. "Oh, yes, kind sir." She hands him the suitcase she's been carrying, then goes back to the car for more. Rev. John Smith proceeds to her apartment.

They meet again at the front entrance. "Your apartment door was unlocked," he said. "I guess Lola was expecting you. You'll want to get a key from her, but I don't think she's at home right now. She has a habit of riding off on her bike and being gone for hours."

"I wouldn't think the gravel lane would be very good for biking."

"No problem for Lola. She whizzes down that road spraying dust until you can't see her."

"And leaves her place of business unattended?"

"Yep. Guess she figures we can each lock our own apartments if we're worried. I don't have much anybody'd want."

Nessa thinks about her meager possessions. "Right. My rooms could only attract a burglar who likes to read. He wouldn't find any money or jewelry. I'm not a Kardashian. "

"Me either. My intruder would need to have a curiosity about … religion. Most of them don't."

"Do you own a gun?" Vanessa inquires. "I don't like them, but one might come in handy if this turns out to be a home for homicidal types."

John Smith laughs. "A gun-carrying pastor is usually frowned on. I'll have to rely on my training in Tai Kwan Do.

Don't worry. After all, we have Ms. Sofie's attack cats and Lola's fly swatter."

Nessa isn't sure if he's serious. "You're kidding about Lola."

"Nope. I've seen her when she hears a noise at the window or it sounds like someone is coming in the front door late at night. She grabs the fly swatter." He gestures toward a bright green one hanging on a hook by the door. "Guess she must figure she won't get in trouble if the intruder is a legitimate customer because a swatter looks very non-threatening. Like they caught her in the middle of going after an insect. Kind of like answering the door to a messy house with one hand on a vacuum, I guess."

Somehow Nessa doesn't think her mother would be impressed. "How long has Lola survived up here?"

"The story she told me was that she's lived here just long enough to know some of the house's secrets. I didn't let myself ask what they are. Maybe it's better not to know."

Speaking of the devil, the front door opens, and Lola Lang enters pushing her bicycle. "Greetings! I'm so glad you came, Vanessa. And I was hoping Preacher Smith would be around to help you. I went down to the grocery to pick up something for supper. Now, though, I'm so shaken I couldn't possibly eat!" Her striped blouse is hanging out of her bell-shaped skirt, and her eyes are wide like she's just witnessed some frightful sight.

Nessa wonders if the woman has seen the same thing that scared Jodi, the school secretary's niece. "Did you have an accident, Lola?" she asks when she notices the woman has somehow lost one shoe.

"No, no. That is, I don't think it was an accident. I believe someone deliberately stepped from behind a tree and stuck a long pole into my spokes. It sent me flying! My eggs, too! Guess I should go back and clean them up, but I just fled, I'm embarrassed to say."

John Smith seems very concerned. "Did you get a look at who it was? It'd have to be a very disturbed person to do something like that for no reason."

"They must've *thought* they had a reason. I could have an enemy. I might have made someone angry, but I try hard not to do that. I didn't get a good look except I had the impression the figure in the trees was an adult wearing camouflage." She stops talking and looks momentarily confused. Then the smile is back. "Or maybe I just thought that's what I saw. Never mind. I'm none the worse for wear. I'll go back later and look for my groceries and the shoe."

Nessa glances at Lola's remaining one and sees it is more of a boot than a proper shoe and not very attractive. She doubts even a one-legged woman will want it. "The deal is, we need to solve this. You shouldn't have to feel unsafe biking to the store. Has anyone else in town been accosted or just you?"

"I haven't heard of anything happening lately. There were several strange stories going around over the summer. People were threatened but couldn't identify the suspects. Just that they looked like. . ." Lola busies herself propping her bike against a wall and neglects to finish her sentence.

"Looked like what?" prompts John Smith.

"You know – like clowns. They appeared all over the country – even overseas in France! You must've heard about them on the news."

"Oh, yeah," he replies. "But I thought all that had kind of died down. And the clowns never actually did much besides scare folks."

"Yes, but I don't think I ever heard if the ones around here were caught."

"I don't think they made many arrests. The so-called clowns were mostly teenagers trying to have fun. What happened to you doesn't sound like a joke."

"That's very true. And it couldn't have been a real clown. One of those wouldn't cause me to crash unless he knew I was going to land on a padded surface."

"You should report this incident to the police. If there're no consequences, the person will probably try again." Nessa feels strongly they shouldn't ignore an assault on an elderly woman.

"It won't do any good," says Lola. "Several mysterious things have happened that felt like somebody is trying to tell me to go away – leave town. I've reported some of them, but the police are always short with me. They think I imagine things. Which I don't. I know when I've been attacked and when I haven't. So far no one has managed to maim me. I'm kind of like the Road Runner. I just get up and keep on going!"

Nessa looks at John to see if the manager's story sounds as incredibly unfair to him as it does to her. Rev. Smith is obviously taking Lola much more seriously than the police have. "If you want, I can call it in. Maybe the dispatcher reacts better to men."

"No, thanks. I'll just pick a different time of day to ride my bicycle. High noon should be safe. I can__"

Their conversation is interrupted by the opening of the front door. It's Pike, returning from wherever he's been. He's smiling from ear to ear. "Hello again!" He looks at Nessa. "Hope you got moved in okay. Sorry I didn't help, but I needed to get to the library before it closed."

Nessa is glad he has a good excuse for not offering. "That's okay. Have a nice evening!" She watches him go up the stairs. "What do you suppose he carries in the bag? It doesn't look heavy enough for books."

"I don't think Pike reads," laughs Lola. "He just pretends he does. He sacks groceries at Fair Foods. It's probably his work shirt. He'd never want to be seen in it anywhere besides the store."

Nessa can understand that. She used to work at a drive-in burger place and had to wear a dorky short skirt she'd never walk home in.

Eager to start her unpacking, she breaks away from the little group to go to her apartment. When reaching for her door knob, she remembers to ask Lola a question that has gained importance in the past few minutes. "Do you have a key for me?" A dead bolt is obviously out of the question.

A momentary look of bewilderment crosses Lola's face. Perhaps she is trying to remember in which drawer she last saw the pesky keys. "Of course! I'll find you one. I usually lock the outside door at ten in the evening so I don't think much about the inside ones."

Usually? Vanessa vows to double-check every night to see how dependable Lola is. If necessary, Nessa can volunteer to do regular night duty. She doesn't want her rooms open to creepy clowns from off the road. And especially not to one in camouflage.

It is meat and drink to me to see a clown.
–William Shakespeare, As You Like It

5

Vanessa's first evening at the Fancy Tramp goes quickly. It turns out to be satisfying work, arranging her clothes in the small closet and her books on the shelves. Both tasks have been enjoyable because she didn't bring every piece of clothing she owns nor every book. What she has now is a manageable collection of her favorites. She vows that when she brings any new item into the apartment, she'll purge one old one. Or at least take it back to her mom's. *Poor Mom*. Stuck with all Nessa's extras and lonesome besides. She really should call her.

"Hi! I'm all settled, and the apartment looks … sweet. You're going to have to come visit."

"I'm being invited to my daughter's place, the Fancy Trollop. I can't wait. What about the key?"

"Lola will special deliver it to me later tonight."

"Sounds like she isn't prepared at all. She probably has to get one made downtown."

Yeah, probably. "I won't let her get by without giving me one, so you can relax."

"Have you talked to the preacher some more?" Nessa already regrets mentioning that man. Her mom is sure to inquire about him regularly and expect some kind of progress report. When it comes to locking doors, Tracy is diligent. In matters of romance, Nessa is careful compared to her mother who is the product of a more innocent age. "We've just exchanged a couple of words. I think he's older than I am and probably engaged or gay. But he does live on the same floor as me so you can be happy I have a non-molester looking after me."

"That *is* nice. Now if you will just decide you have room for more of your stuff, I'll be a happy mama."

Nessa is glad she called her mother. Being twenty-two and on her own is great, but it's still comforting to know the one person who truly cares about her is just a phone call away. And she trusts her mom. The jury is still out on the integrity of the citizens of Haven and the lodgers at the Fancy Tramp. Of course, they may feel the same about her.

To finish off her night of accomplishment, Nessa takes out her copy of *Macbeth*. She plans to teach a unit in Shakespeare sometime during first semester so feels the need to read some of his works again before grading compositions takes all her free time. She turns out the overhead light and switches on the floor lamp by the couch. *Not bad* she thinks as she basks in the cozy glow of the room.

The television turned off, she makes herself comfortable and gets absorbed in reading the play. After a few minutes, an uneasy feeling comes over her. She looks up and around the room to be sure she's alone. Her breathing stops when she realizes she isn't. In the corner shadows behind a chair, a man stands silently, watching her. Her heart is beating so hard and fast, she's afraid he can hear it. How did he get in? Through the door, of course. No mystery there. When one's door is unlocked, some people take it as an invitation. This silent guest didn't even close the door behind him.

Nessa prays her landlady will stop by. She doesn't know whether the gentleman in the corner is a renter or someone off the street, but it doesn't matter. He's an intruder and lucky she doesn't own a gun. He appears to be elderly, but that doesn't mean he's harmless. "Wh-who are you?" she ventures. Her voice sounds unfamiliar in the dark room. "Please go away." She's sure it would be best to be firm and commanding, but Nessa can tell she's coming off as more pleading and frightened. She wonders if this is the kind of thing that sent Jodi off into the night.

Instead of obeying her request, the man creeps closer to the sofa. She wishes he'd speak. But then maybe he's a sleep walker. Maybe he doesn't even know where he is. She wonders if sleep walkers ever unknowingly assault women.

The man comes closer. His steps are slightly wobbly. Could he be drunk? She can see he has gray hair and needs a shave. His mouth turns down in a sad, droopy way. She tries smiling, but gets no reaction. He isn't asleep. He appears to be watching her with a questioning expression on his face. The man advances to within inches of her as she lies awkwardly on the couch, trying not to make a sudden move. She wants to scream but hates to startle him.

"Gordy!" It's Lola. Blessed Lola, standing in the open doorway. The man turns slowly toward the voice. "Come on, Gordy. Time for bed. Leave the nice lady alone."

Nessa is appalled. Lola doesn't even sound surprised. Gordy might do this kind of thing every night. Her mother's horror is coming through loud and clear. *This is unacceptable! You have to find another place to live. Tonight.*

"Don't let Gordy give you bad dreams," Lola throws over her shoulder as she guides the man out. "He was my sweetheart, but now there isn't much left of him. He lives in the basement. At night he comes upstairs and tests the doors, and if they open, he makes sure people are sleeping safely. He sometimes makes the rounds two or three times. Here's your key so he won't be able to check on you." And Lola places a door key on top of the TV before going out. Nessa doesn't waste a second locking herself in.

Oh, my gosh. I can't believe John Smith didn't tell me about Gordy. How am I ever going to sleep in a house where a mindless old guy tries to come into my room every night?

Resuming her reading doesn't do much to help. She's on her own now, like she's always wanted to be. But there are strange people ready to cross her path, ready to threaten or at least alarm her. She swears she won't run like Jodi did at the first sign of trouble. *"Screw your courage to the sticking place..."*

But later in bed, words of Shakespeare come to her again, *"Sleep no more! Macbeth doth murder sleep!"* At the moment, she is troubled more by a man named Gordy than by some old Scottish king. She can almost feel a pillow covering her face.

The next morning, after a nearly sleepless night, Nessa emerges from her room and is happy to spot Lola, bent over in concentration. The manager is doing bookwork at a desk in one corner of the large entryway. Her hands fly as she apparently adds columns of numbers without the aid of a calculator. Nessa wonders what the totals are telling the woman. It seems unlikely that profits add up very fast in this business. And now winter is coming. What an impossible task it will be to heat this monstrosity. Being cold blooded herself, Nessa hopes the owner won't be forced to play freeze-out with her renters in order to keep costs down.

"Excuse me," she dares say to the busy woman.

"Why, Nessa. I was so lost in these numbers I didn't even realize you were here. Can I get you anything? I hope you didn't have any more scares from Gordy. He gets restless at night and feels like he has to be watchman for everyone in the house. He was always the caretaker type in his good days. I guess that hasn't really gone away with all the rest he's lost."

"It helps to understand. You might want to tell new renters about him first thing so they don't panic. Like I did."

"You're right, of course. Part of me still sees Gordon as my handsome and devoted lover, and I forget that man is pretty much gone. He might even seem dangerous to a stranger, I suppose." And Lola's face briefly reveals the heartbreak she must feel every day.

"Some people might not want to move in if they know. I don't think he'll be a problem for me though." Just the same, Nessa has decided to keep her ears open for a less depressing place to live. "I'm wondering if you can tell me anything about a former renter. Do you remember a young woman named Jodi? She had my teaching position last year."

Lola closes her eyes briefly as though forcing herself to go back in time. "I do remember. She was about your age. Nice enough but didn't stay long. I'm not sure why."

"She didn't tell you why she was moving out?"

"No, she didn't. I received cash in the mail for the rent that was due, but she didn't come to collect her things. Very puzzling. I don't think I'd had a chance to warn her about Gordy, but anyway, I don't think she ever ran into him. Maybe the house was just too dreary for her. I have no idea. Young people these days don't seem to feel bad backing out on something that isn't exactly to their liking." And she goes back to her figures.

Nessa is disappointed. She was hoping for an exciting story about Jodi's breakdown, some particular incident that triggered her flight. "Did she have the same apartment I do?" she prods Lola.

"No, she was in the one John Smith has. I think Marvin was still living in the other one."

Now the real situation is coming to light. "Was Jodi living here when Marvin passed?" She avoids saying *suffocated* – that sounds too much like foul play.

Lola pushes her chair away from the desk as she gets serious about her recollections. "I'm sure she was. In fact, Jodi was the one who came and told me. She was panicked-could barely speak. I went and got Monique, and we looked into the whole thing, but … as I remember, Jodi was nowhere to be found by then. It hurt our efforts because she was the closest person to being a witness. Hmmm. I've almost forgotten how that went. Jodi found him, but then we couldn't find Jodi. Bad memories. I try to shut them down. Nothing will bring Marvin back."

"And the police didn't conduct an investigation and try to track Jodi down?" This town seems to be the place to come if one is thinking of committing a capital crime.

Lola shows signs of lost interest. "I think maybe they told us to find her and said they wanted to question her. But they never came back, and we got busy and sort of forgot. I mean, we didn't have names of family members to call or anything. Now we do better about taking down phone numbers for a renter's next of kin and stuff like that. If you or John or anyone else suffocates, we'll be ready."

Nessa has the depressing mental image of her mom receiving a call from Lola. *"Something unfortunate has happened to your daughter. But don't ask me what it was because I've already forgotten the details."*

6

By afternoon, Nessa has shaken off the effects of Gordy's visit and is looking forward to becoming familiar with her classroom. In order to lock her apartment, she sets a large box down by the door. It contains supplies for bulletin boards and for otherwise adding her personal touches to the school space she's inherited. Just before opening the large front door to leave the Fancy Tramp, she encounters Lola.

"Hello, again!" The landlady is as cheerful as if she hadn't had to escort an old man out of her new renter's living room or tell her about the mysterious death of a tenant. "I hope you aren't in too much of a hurry. I promised Ms. Sofie I'd let her meet you."

It is the first Nessa has heard of Ms. Sofie. Sofie must be the name of the cat lady on second floor. Again, Nessa sets her supply box on the floor. "I can take a few minutes. Is she coming soon?"

"Oh, yes. She's probably getting on the lift as we speak." ola looks at a sliding door that Nessa has so far not had reason to investigate. "Sofie's on the large side, so she uses the freight elevator. I can't vouch for its construction, so we don't encourage visitors to ride it to second."

Surely, Ms. Sofie's safety is worth considering also. Nessa is wondering if *on the large side* is a literal description, when the door opens to reveal a remarkably hefty lady.

"Good morning friends!" the startling Sofie says. She practically fills the space inside the elevator and is holding three cats across her front. Little black heads peer at Nessa over the mounds of flesh that are the woman's arms. Lola has slipped away for a moment and returned with a contraption on wheels that turns out to be Sofie's chair. After a ballet of movement that places the woman in the seat, a plump hand reaches toward Nessa.

"I'm pleased to meet you," Nessa greets her, trying not to sound as astounded as she is. "I see you have cats." A stupid observation, but she feels she has to say something.

"I do, indeed!" Sofie replies proudly. "They insisted on meeting you. Eeeny, Meeny, and Miney are my constant companions."

Nessa just has to ask. "There's no Moe?"

"Oh, there was, but poor Moe jumped. From the second story window. I think the confinement just got to him. But we never found him, so I'm pretty sure he survived the fall. Cats can do that, you know."

"Well, I'm glad he didn't … er…perish." Nessa feels like she should chat more but is still a little speechless at the mere sight of this renter. She'd like to ask, "How do you manage living on the second floor?" "Do you ever want to jump like Moe did?" or "Do you eat a lot or are you just naturally fat?" but, of course, those questions aren't appropriate. She looks at Lola, hoping she'll hop into the conversation.

Lola obliges. "Sofie, meet our resident school teacher, Vanessa Martin. Vanessa, meet Sofie Potter. Ms. Sofie and I have been friends for a long time. She sort of watches over me.

In fact, she and I are co-managers of the Fancy Tramp. So you can direct any complaints to her as well as to me!"

"Oh, I doubt if I'll have any complaints," Nessa assures them, pushing Gordy to the back of her mind.

"You probably have a computer, but until now, Sofie owned the only one in this house, so she keeps us up to date on what's happening in the world. It's easy to lose touch when you ... don't get out much."

"Well, the internet usually tells us more about the world than we really want to know," says Nessa in an effort to make conversation. "Have I met everyone now?" She's already dreading her mother's first visit to her apartment.

"You've met all the renters. And you'll probably run into the maid soon, Monique."

"Oh, yes. The Clean Queen. Well, you sure have an... interesting group here." She addresses Ms. Sofie. "I'll probably be pretty busy in the evenings with class prep, so I may not see you often, but look forward to catching up with you every once in a while." Nessa has never heard of such a close knit bunch of neighbors. *Aren't most apartment dwellers lucky if they know even one of the people living in their buildings?*

"I'll have you come for supper soon," Sofie offers. "Monique or Pike will deliver the invitation since I only rarely venture downstairs. It will be an honor to host a school teacher. I don't think I ever have."

Nessa can't imagine how the lady intends to cook supper for her. Perhaps it will be catered. "I look forward to it," she says politely. She pictures the cats sitting in their own little booster chairs at the table and wonders about the smell in Sofie's rooms. *I hope the Clean Queen doesn't mind emptying litter boxes.*

Lola is chatting with the obese woman when Vanessa exits the building. It occurs to her that the red- haired landlady does more than collect the rent at the Fancy Tramp. She seems to have a certain amount of personal involvement with everyone. Perhaps she has no family and regards the people in this house as substitutes. Nessa remembers Jodi. Where did Lola go wrong with her? Maybe the girl had an unnatural fear of cats.

Clown Alley

The refugees from the circus have become meeting in Sofie's apartment over the noon hour on Monday mornings.

"Sofie has been looking for us on her computer," Lola explains to the group. "So I'll let her report her findings." Lola is happy to relinquish her leadership position when it comes to discussions about the internet.   She's always shunned technology. "I grew up Amish", she always says as though that explains her fear of electronic media, including cameras.

"We've been wondering if we aren't famous online. I keep thinking surely one of the administrators or one of the performers has been looking for us, even if it's just out of curiosity!"

Sofie finally reports. "I've just learned how to get onto the circus's web page. I've found that we were quite the news item for a while. It sounds like some people were concerned that we've turned into a band of gypsy thieves. They wonder where we will surface! People have been warned not to hire anybody off the street who's comes to their door looking for work and to keep a close eye on their kids if they're playing outside. "

"Ha. That's pretty funny really. Some people wanted to kill us and now they're the ones who are scared. As if we'd ever hurt a child – or even intentionally frighten one!"

The room is abuzz with comments. They aren't used to being suspected of anything bad.

"I think that's all calmed down now though since nobody has reported any incidents in several months."

Lola has to caution them. "I'm sure it has, but be sure not to do anything that draws attention to yourselves. It won't take much to start more rumors."

"Lola, do you think our new renters, John and Vanessa, are to be trusted with our secret?"

"I haven't decided yet. I like both of them so much, that I'd like to think so, but we should wait a little while before we get too close with them. People aren't always who they seem to be."

7

The school is a welcome sight after the unusual happenings at the apartment. Here at work, Nessa will be allowed to interact with regular people like herself. She won't have to look askance at each one, wondering if he or she is sane. Surprisingly, the front door is unlocked. Perhaps daytime security precautions aren't in place yet.

The first person she encounters is Beverly Birch, the school secretary. Her desk is located behind a glass partition which looks onto the lobby of the high school. Nessa gives Beverly her friendliest smile. She's fairly sure she should pretend the woman didn't recently call her at home with a dire warning about housing arrangements.

"Hello, there, Beverly. I guess it's time for me to get my classroom in order. Do you have a key for me?"

"Yes, of course," the secretary responds formally. She goes to the office safe, opens it, and removes an envelope with Vanessa's name on it. "You'll probably want to buy a lanyard so you can hang it around your neck. Just one minute. I'll record the number and it's yours." When that's done, she looks up at Nessa and gives her a pointed stare along with the key. "For as long as you remain on the job."

"Well, then, I'll have it 'til May. I intend to do a lot of my work at school instead of at home."

It seems obvious the secretary wants to say more. As Nessa starts to walk out into the hallway, Beverly stops her. "Where are you living now?"

Unaccountably, Nessa hates to admit she didn't take the woman's earlier advice. "I'm at the Fancy Tramp. So far so good, but I'm staying alert for any problems."

A look of anger flashes across Beverly's face. "Well, I warned you. It's all I can do."

"And I truly appreciate it. Really. I'm pretty hard to scare though. I might be able to stand things your niece couldn't."

"I'd have said Jodi was tough, too." Beverly snaps. "But the people who live at the Fancy Tramp are odd. Surely you've noticed that."

"Oh, yes," answers Nessa with a little laugh. "But I've always been partial to odd folks. They're so much more interesting than ordinary ones, don't you think?"

Beverly gives her a look that says *you have to be kidding.* "I think *odd* spells trouble. And Mr. Bingham agrees with me. Who knows what those weird types are capable of? You'll remember my words later when it's too late." Then she picks up some papers, indicating an end to the conversation. Nessa leaves feeling like she's lost her chance to secure the school secretary for a friend. From all she's heard, that was a bad move. Maybe there's a chance for her and the custodian. That person is another good ally to have if older teachers can be believed.

Nessa soon has her opportunity. As she approaches Room 106 she notices the door is standing open. She steps cautiously inside and right away sees the custodian mopping in a corner. "Hello! I'm Vanessa Martin, English Literature and Senior Composition."

"Cotton Downs," comes the gruff reply. A head of heavy white hair that stands out like a giant puff ball must be the reason for the nickname. The fact he even has one of those indicates he's regarded with affection by the students and staff.

"I noticed a puddle back here," he tells her. "Got some kinda drip going on. Must be coming from the bathroom upstairs."

"Lucky for me you noticed. We could have been wading in here on Monday!"

"Probably not. I'll be in tomorrow, too. I'll do a walk-through of all the rooms before things get started. Plenty will go wrong later, so I want to see that things are at least working to start with."

"It sounds like we're in good hands, Cotton. Let me know if I neglect any part of the cleaning that's my responsibility."

"I'll let you know alright." And the man smiles. Vanessa sees he isn't old like his hair color suggests. And there's a sense of humor behind his twinkly blue eyes. She's going to depend on that. Cotton continues, "Just don't let those kids leave food 'n pop cans around. Tell them, 'I'm not your mother so I won't pick up after you.' "

"I'll put that in my opening speech. Thanks."

While Cotton works diligently around her pipes, Nessa goes into the hall to see if another teacher is around to answer some trivial questions that have occurred to her. *Do you advise me to eat school lunches or bring my own? Are the hallways usually pretty quiet or will I want to keep my door closed at all times? Are there any trouble-makers I should be ready for*? Things that aren't in the handbook.

Not surprisingly, Beverly is the only human in sight. She is coming through the door from the principal's office. Nessa isn't eager to hear any more of her opinions. The woman doesn't seem to have a positive comment about anything. "Excuse me. I was just looking for any other teacher who happens to be around today."

"None of them are. This isn't a school day or a work day. The teachers know they're going to have plenty of time to make whatever preparations they need to make. Most of them are probably doing something relaxing with their final hours of freedom." The implication is that she wishes Nessa were doing the same.

"Well, by next year, I'm sure I won't come to work before I have to either. Teaching is so new to me now. I can't wait to find out everything I possibly can."

"If you really want to learn, you shouldn't ignore what you're told by people who've been here longer than you have. You should welcome any information."

Well, I must've asked for that. "That's what I try to do. However, I have to weigh the importance of any advice I get. And whether it applies to me or not. I like to think for myself when I can, and I'll teach my students to do the same."

"That's a fancy way of saying you're a know-it-all. But nobody does – *know it all.* Every person needs to listen closely or suffer the consequences."

"Words to live by," Nessa offers as a way of keeping peace. "I'm surprised you aren't having some fun today, too."

"I am." And the woman's eyes travel straight to the principal's office door. She seems to catch herself then and changes the subject. "And my contract started two weeks before the teachers' first day, so my year has been underway for a while." There's a definite tone of pride in those words. Beverly wants it known that she was here first and knows the ropes.

Suddenly, Nessa understands. This school is more than just a job to Bev, and the principal is a big part of her feelings. When it comes to any relationship between Birch and Bingham, ignorance on her part may be the best policy. *I think I'll go into my classroom and stick my head in a book. No outside silliness is going to interfere with my teaching. Nose to the grindstone, eyes straight ahead. A true educator doesn't get caught up in petty staff concerns.* "Thanks for your help, Bev."

8

$\mathcal{A}$ new morning brings promise of another quiet day in the school. This time next week she'll barely remember what it was like to hear an echo in the spacious building. Peace and anticipation will have been erased by the noise and disrespect all around her. She's been in enough high schools she doesn't have illusions about a quiet workplace.

This weekend, the high school hallway emits the same clean, waxy smell Nessa remembers from her own student years. That smell has always made her excited for the start of classes. New notebook, new pencils, waxy smell. She supposes those things will always bring back the magic for her.

Being a teacher isn't quite as thrilling as being a third grader, but she still considers herself blessed to get this fresh start. And she can look forward to many more in her career, with slight changes. New class lists, new schedules, but always, hopefully, the waxy smell.

Even though she's completed her bulletin boards, she has some computer charts she wants to prepare. The teachers will have two days to work in their rooms before classes begin, but she has nothing better to do this Saturday morning. And poor Cotton might like knowing he isn't the only staff member who's on the job.

Though her new key is ready for service, she finds the door opens easily without it. Cotton must have found another puddle. There's no sign of him, so Nessa goes to the far corner where she met him for the first time the day before. She's making sure things are dry when she stumbles on something behind the last row of desks. Cotton lies sprawled on the floor, the impression being that he's unconscious – or worse. She drops down beside the man. Using the emergency training from her lifeguard days, she manages to find a pulse. She makes sure his head is turned to allow him to breathe and then calls 911. "Man unconscious. Haven High School. Room 106. Hurry!"

While waiting for the EMTs, she looks around for a clue as to what happened. The floor is again wet, but she can't believe Cotton hasn't navigated wet floors before. Glancing around nearby desks, looking into the corner and under a large table, she searches for clues to what has taken place. No heavy objects or bullets are in view. Presumably, whatever happened to the man was natural. She's relieved it was probably an inevitable occurrence and not something she could've prevented.

Help is quick to arrive, and in no time Cotton is loaded into an ambulance. She's tempted to ask to ride along, but since she isn't family, she opts to follow them. The ambulance driver explains the closest hospital is in the neighboring town of Arbor City, ten miles away. Nessa doesn't mind the drive. She gathers her purse and starts for the front door.

Glancing toward the reception area, she's surprised to see Beverly is there. She's getting something out of her desk. "Cotton collapsed in my room," Nessa tells her. "Can you notify his wife?"

Beverly's face registers surprise. "He isn't married. Was it a heart attack?"

I'm not a doctor. "I don't think so. But he wasn't conscious when I found him."

"That's very odd." Nessa knows what Beverly thinks of *odd*. The secretary gives a look of reprimand. "You were the only person in the room with him." An accusatory tone can be detected, but there's no reason the woman should blame her for anything.

"Actually, I wasn't in the room when it happened." Those words are flung over her shoulder as she turns toward the exit. Nessa chooses not to hang around to defend herself further. She makes a quick dash to her car, one of three parked in front of the school.

While driving, she contemplates the information she may be asked to provide. The cops will want to know what she witnessed, how well she knows the janitor and maybe if she can tell them what he was doing in her room. She'll be no help. If he's found to be okay, she may be asked nothing. She wishes she had John Smith's phone number. Cotton could use his prayers, and she could use the company. As she approaches the turn off to the Fancy Tramp, she decides to take it. Hopefully, the preacher isn't on duty because she doesn't have time to locate the church.

"Let's go!" Is John's immediate answer when Nessa relates the story from outside his apartment. "We can take my car. I know a shortcut to the hospital." Almost as an afterthought, he goes back inside for a Bible.

Riding with John Smith would be thrilling for Nessa under different circumstances. She knows this trip is a necessity and that she can in no way be flattered. Ministers always go to the aid of people in distress and probably take along anyone who wants to go.

Linda Wiges

"I have no idea if it's serious. I thought he was dead at first, but by the time they got him on a gurney, he seemed to be coming around. My impression was he'd been knocked out."

"I hope you're wrong about that. That would mean you have a dangerous person with access to the high school. Did you notice any dislodged bricks or plaster that could've fallen on him?"

"No, and I did look around for something like that. I just hope he's okay. I only spoke to him once, but I liked him right away."

"Maybe he had a stroke or an aneurism."

"He seemed healthy to me, but that doesn't really mean much. Anybody can drop over at any time. I'm just glad he did it in my room. I think Beverly and I were the only other people in the building. We could both have left without ever finding out he was in trouble."

'Hmm. What do you know about Beverly? Is she a teacher?"

"No, she's the principal's secretary. I'm surprised she works on Saturday mornings."

9

Cotton is in the ICU when they arrive but is propped up and looking alert. His speech is slow and soft, but his sense of humor seems intact. "Hello!" He tries to smile. "Ask me if I'm going to do any more work in the English room."

"Oh, Cotton, I'm so sorry for whatever happened to you! What *did* happen?" Nessa has meant to hold back her question, but she can't wait.

"Can't tell you. I don't remember anything. I guess my brain's damaged." He smiles again, weakly.

"Well, I feel so bad about it. You were in *my* room trying to fix *my* drip, so I feel sort of responsible." She remembers John then. "Cotton, I want you to meet my neighbor from the rooming house, John Smith." The men acknowledge each other, and Nessa continues, "Rev... Mr. Smith gave me a ride here." She doesn't want to give the janitor the idea she's brought a man of the cloth to give him last rites.

"Has anybody contacted your family?" John asks Cotton. "If not, I'd be glad to make some calls."

"You don't have to. Nobody's worrying about me, and I don't think I'll be here long."

"Has a doctor been in? Did you hear anyone say what they're treating you for?" asks the minister.

"I think I overheard something about *head trauma.* Must be why it hurts so much and why I can't think straight. I wasn't much help to the cops right after it happened."

"You'll have to stay at least overnight so the doctors can watch for signs of a concussion. And the police will probably come back later when you're thinking more clearly," says John Smith like he knows about those things. Nessa, thankfully, has no experience with head injuries or cops.

A nurse comes in then and asks the visitors to leave. "Your friend needs to rest," she explains.

"Of course," says John. They exit the room, then he right away darts back in to tell the patient, "God bless."

It dawns on Nessa then that Reverend Smith must not think Cotton is so bad off. He didn't even offer a prayer or a Bible reading on his behalf.

Being much more relaxed on the way home, she even allows herself to take note of John's profile. He looks like a model. Not in the least effeminate, but perfect none the less. He reminds her of the princes in Cinderella and Beauty and the Beast.

Nessa reprimands herself for such frivolous ideas when Cotton is still in a hospital bed. At least, there doesn't seem to be any risk he'll die. "We do have to worry though," she realizes. "Head trauma sounds like he was attacked. Maybe somebody hit him before he turned on the light, and they were meaning to hit me!"

"I don't think so. Doubt many people know you well enough to want to hurt you – yet."

"You wouldn't think so. Maybe just to meet me is to hate me," she teases. She's thinking of the snarky secretary who hasn't even given her a chance.

"I haven't found that to be true, myself." And John turns her way and gives her an engaging smile.

Nessa is self-conscious now so changes the subject. "I don't think Cotton will be in school by Monday. Or even when the students start on Wednesday."

"Nope. Doubt it. You'll have to empty your own waste cans."

"We can get by. He's been working all summer so the place is really clean right now."

"That reminds me, have you met the delightful Monique at our apartment complex?" John's articulation of the word *delightful* makes it sound more like a joke than a compliment.

"Not yet. Am I in for a treat?"

"Depends on what you expect. I was imagining your typical French maid— short skirt, cute accent."

"I don't really watch those kinds of movies," Nessa replies, wondering whether the good Reverend should be that familiar with French maids himself. "I can't wait to see how she compares to the rest of the Fancy Tramp cast of characters."

"Well, she fits in. I can tell you that much."

Nessa's curiosity is satisfied soon after they arrive back at the apartments. They're met in the front foyer by none other than Monique, armed, not with a fly swatter, but a feather duster. "Bonjour!" Her greeting is appropriate, but her appearance is atypical. The woman could be as old as eighty. Her wrinkles have wrinkles, and her gray hair, up in a tangled pony tail, does nothing to hide her age. She's wearing green cropped pants and thick-soled tennis shoes. A frilly apron adds a French-maid touch. "I try to keep the cobwebs out of the hallways but the ceilings are pretty high and that ladder is getting a little hard for me. If I missed any, be sure to let me know. I live in the tower room way at the top! You can ask Pike to fetch me."

Nessa and John are shocked that someone of her years has to stay three flights up. "If you'd rather live on first, I can trade with you Ma'am," offers John Smith.

Monique laughs gleefully. "Thank you darling, but I'm fine where I am. I chose that apartment. I can look out the windows and survey my property. It's quite impressive and will be even better when I've saved enough money to have the house transformed into the painted lady she once was."

"You're the owner, then?" asks John.

"As a matter of fact, I am. The owner *and* the cleaning lady. I don't pay me much, so I'll probably keep my job even though I'm slowing down."

"Lola told us you're the best," says Nessa.

"Well, isn't my cousin a doll? For an old gal, she's a good manager, too."

Nessa can see the family resemblance between the two women. Neither looks anything like anyone else she's ever seen. Monique and Lola appear to belong on the stage of some bizarre burlesque show.

"We just got back from the hospital in Arbor City." Nessa explains. "The janitor at the school where I teach was injured this morning, but I think he's going to be alright." No need to cause fear that some other maniac in camouflage is on the loose.

"Goodness! That must be Cotton! You're sure he's okay?" Monique is surprisingly distressed by Nessa's news. "He's one of our friends. He lived here when we first came. But when he found a fulltime job, he was able to rent a room close to the school. Which was good because he doesn't own a car." Monique looks so worried, John feels obliged to reassure her. "He's a good worker, I'm sure. They'll want him to stay."

"I hope you're right. Poor Cotton. His job is really important to us...him." And she turns to ascend the stairs, lost in her thoughts, her feather duster hanging forgotten at her side.

Ness plays back the maid's words, "... he doesn't doesn't own a car." Who's was the third car at the school when Cotton was hurt?

My mom used to say I didn't run away from home. My destiny just caught up with me at an early age.
Red Skelton

10

Vanessa arrives at school early on Monday. There's to be a short faculty meeting to get the year started. Not surprising, Beverly looks settled in, as if she's been at work for a couple of hours already. "How did Cotton come out?" she asks as soon as she sees Nessa.

"I think he's going to be okay. He's lucky though. Head injuries can be fatal."

"Oh, yes," agrees Beverly.

"I haven't reported the incident to Mr. Bingham. Did you have a chance to tell him?"

"Of course. I called him from home."

"He must feel terrible to have something like that happen right at the beginning of the year."

"Mr. Bingham doesn't like disturbances at any time of the year. Hopefully, Cotton will be able to continue his full duties. I mean, he won't be crippled or forgetful or anything will he?"

"Gosh, no! He's as good as new. The doctor just wanted him to stay home a couple of days as a precaution. Do you have any idea what could have happened?" Vanessa asks her. Most long-time secretaries would be very concerned if a staff member were injured at work, and would've spent time over the weekend trying to find answers.

"None," answers Beverly. "If it happened in your room, and you know nothing, I'm sure I don't."

"Okay. I guess we have another mystery to add to your niece's fright at the Fancy Tramp."

The teachers meet in the auditorium. The superintendent and the school board president both give welcomes. There are reports of building improvements that have taken place since last year and, of course, introductions of new staff members.

The school superintendent gives what are to be the most words the teachers will hear from him all term. He indicates his hope they'll have a productive year and then turns the business over to Principal Bingham. "We are very lucky to have Mr. David Bingham at the helm of the high school this year. He comes from an acclaimed situation in Missouri bringing us his new and innovative ideas. Because I have so much confidence in his leadership, I'll feel you're in good hands while I'm spread thin between governing duties at both Arbor City and Haven Schools. Any concerns you want to address to my office can be routed there starting with Beverly Birch, the secretary in this building." In general, the man gives the impression of being very inaccessible. He takes his leave, assuming everything is under control.

Nessa feels young and green. It seems like only yesterday she was a student in high school. Now she's supposed to automatically be mature, poised, and full of knowledge. She's probably expected to call fellow teachers by their first names. Maybe there's been a misunderstanding. Maybe she heard wrong and she's been hired as a teaching assistant, not someone in charge of anything. She did okay with her student teaching in Chicago, but she always had a superior to refer to. This afternoon she is going to be thrown off the pier to sink or swim.

Beverly's esteemed supervisor takes the podium then. "Good morning, teachers. I am David Bingham, your principal. I'm here to charge you with taking the reins of the only school in the state to adopt a Superior-at-all-Costs policy. The details of that method will unfold gradually as the year progresses. But for now, suffice it to say we do nothing in a second-rate way. You've all been selected for being the cream of the crop among instructors. Keep this in mind every minute you work with the minds of our exceptional student body. Good luck. Don't be surprised if I drop in on your classes unexpectedly. It's important I know how you conduct yourselves and present your material. Then I hope to see all of you at our January meeting when we evaluate your success. Until then, stay strong and don't let up. Your very jobs are at stake."

The staff leaves the room unsmiling. Even veteran instructors appear tense. Vanessa's impression is that she's going to have a surveillance camera on her every day, making sure she's living up to Bingham's standards. She would gladly trade places with her students. They are responsible only for themselves. The worst that can happen to them is they have to repeat a class.

Her first full day at Haven High is less traumatic than the opening meeting. The students are much like those she remembers. Being called *Ms. Martin* instead of *Nessa* will take a little getting used to, but being addressed that way does give her a certain amount of confidence. She's glad she chose to wear a skirt for her first day. She even put her hair into a messy bun which gives her height and a little dignity.

By the time the final bell of the day rings, Nessa is ready to morph back into jeans and sweatshirt and wipe off the lipstick, but she must continue playing the role of experienced professional for another half hour. Teachers are expected to be available in their classrooms for any student who has questions.

She suspects they are all running for the hills after this first day. The weather is still beautiful and they aren't anxious to give up their freedom for one extra minute.

Though she's been under some stress since she came this morning, the work itself hasn't been difficult. Everything is introductory so far, but she's as exhausted as if she's done something physical. Getting acquainted with one hundred and seventy high school students who have a lot of catching up to do with their fellow classmates, is not for the faint of heart. Little do the lively teens realize their teacher is experiencing her first day of being a head instructor. Of course, they may have figured it out. In spite of efforts with her appearance, she suspects she appears much the same age as the sixteen and seventeen-year-old pupils. "Don't worry," her mom had comforted her last week. "You'd be surprised how old you'll seem to the students." Nessa tries to feel good about that idea.

She's busy trying to memorize the names on her seating chart when a sensation of being watched overtakes her. She turns around to see the youngest renter from the Fancy Tramp. "Pike! I'm surprised you're here. Is anything wrong at the house?"

A shy grin tells her nothing's amiss. "I forgot to deliver a message to you this morning before you left."

Nessa is curious.

The young man recites his invitation as though he's been practicing all the way from the apartment. "Ms. Sofie says to tell you she requests the honor of your presence at dinner in her suite on second floor. Six o'clock if that works."

"Why, of course. Are you coming, too?"

Pike is surveying the room and answers absently, "Yeah, I'm bringing the food. From the grocery store's catering."

"That's super," says Nessa. "I can't wait."

"The other reason I came by is to see inside." The young man is pacing now, looking in desks and even picking up a marker and drawing a funny face on the whiteboard.

Nessa is puzzled. "You mean, you wanted to see what the school looks like? Was yours a lot different?"

"I haven't been inside my school since I was ten. I kinda forget."

"Ten? Haven't you taken any classes since then?"

"Nope. School and me didn't get along so good. I couldn't really read, so I got bored, and then I just horsed around and made the other kids laugh. I could tell the teacher wanted rid of me. So ... I left."

"But there are laws. Were you home schooled?" That practice has gotten pretty common. Much as she loves her mom, she wouldn't have been able to stand her for a teacher all day every day. Maybe Pike's mom is more the type to do the job.

"That would've been the worst. Home was so scary for mom and me, and when my dad drank, I couldn't have learned anything. I don't think he knew how to read himself so he didn't think I needed to. "

"That's too bad." Nessa would like to ask more about his scary home, but she only has the few minutes between classes. "Did you have a mentor around after you left home?"

"No. I just had Gordon. He was a teacher a long time ago so he was a really good reader. But then he got so he couldn't remember what he wanted to tell me, so he stopped trying to help. Sofie tried to show me how to read, but I wasn't a very good student. If I could go back, I'd work harder than I did when I was ten. If I could read, I could get a better-paying job."

"Do you have any of your own books? I mean, do you get much chance to read for fun?"

"I don't. Ms. Sofie tried to find some for me, but they were baby books. Since I came to Haven I check books out of the library downtown. It's fun picking them out. I can't read them, so I just end up taking them back. But it's fun to imagine what they're about."

Nessa is sure her facial expression is registering the surprise and concern his honesty has caused her.

"Not reading didn't really bother me before because nobody I lived around noticed, but I'm scared now that people in this town will find out, and everybody will think I'm stupid." Pike has made this rather lengthy speech without looking at Nessa. He seems like such an intelligent young guy in other ways. The reading thing must be a secret that's hard for him to acknowledge. Because he's hidden it from most people, he missed out on any professional assistance.

Nessa is a sucker for young people whose education has been neglected. "Do you want me to find out if you can sit in on a couple of classes?" If Beverly or Bingham have anything to say about it, there'll be no way. But maybe she can ask another administrator, someone more sympathetic. This school doesn't seem interested in helping outsiders, and Pike's black skin would make him especially unworthy of tutoring.

Pike is running his hand along the books on the back shelf of her room. "Thanks, but I have to be at my job most of the day. And I told Melody I'm out of school. It's a white lie. I'm old enough to be graduated. But I'm not."

Nessa feels like she's missed something. "Who's Melody? Does she live at the Fancy Tramp?"

"She's my sort-of girlfriend. She works where I do – at the Super Mart. Only she's a manager. I just bag groceries."

"I guess I don't know what a sort-of girlfriend is. Does she know she's your girlfriend?" Nessa suspects this Melody has no idea.

"Well, I really like her because she's pretty, and she always smiles and says *Hi, Pike*. I try to be friendly, but I can't ask her

57

on a date because I don't have a car. Or any money once I pay Monique."

Nessa doesn't see those facts as deterrents. "You could ask her to take a walk with you to look at the fall leaves. Some girls would think that was romantic."

Pike's face lights up. "Maybe I will!" He takes a book off the shelf. "Have you read all these?"

"Most of them," Nessa responds. "I always have a book going. If you want, I can help you read sometimes in the evenings." What is she promising? Having her personal time is very important for her sanity. But Pike seems so sincere...

"Really? Could we read a Harry Potter one? I used to see lots of people reading those books and always wondered what they're about."

Nessa is eager to know whether the young man has a learning disability or if he hasn't been taught phonics. Under normal circumstances he should have already been a competent reader by the time he quit going to school at age ten. "Harry Potter books are pretty long ones, but we can give one of them a try." She already knows she'll regret her promise, remembering how addictive that series is and knowing she doesn't have the expertise to help Pike if he needs therapy of some kind. "You'd better go now. You don't have official permission to be in here. Just be careful not to let the secretary in the office spot you."

Not surprisingly, Pike must have slipped out of the school building without being detected. There's no sign of her new friend when Nessa peeks out into the empty hallway. She isn't as lucky when she finally leaves at the end of the day. The secretary is at her station. Nessa wonders how long she'd have to stay at school to cause Beverly to leave before her.

"Did you get all your work done?" the woman asks in a sarcastic tone.

"I don't expect to be *done* until school's out in the spring," Nessa answers. "That's the downside of teaching composition." She tries to sound upbeat, to create a rapport with the other woman. "I've been meaning to ask, do we have anyone who could test a student to see if he has a reading impairment like dyslexia?"

Beverly takes the opportunity to lecture. "Why? I don't think we have anyone at Haven High with that kind of problem. They're put in the building down the street. This office has no contact with those students. He or she would have been encouraged to open enroll at another school, and if that isn't possible, they go into the special education program. It's run by Area X. We only work with normal teens here."

"What's a normal teen?" Nessa asks, joking. "I don't think I've heard that expression much."

Beverly isn't amused. "*Normal* is the key word around here. Normal is what we do." And the lady glares at Nessa as though daring her to challenge the idea.

"O-kay. I doubt many schools can make that claim. Even about their teachers. Or their office personnel." *Oh, dear.* Nessa is risking an argument. *Time to leave.* "Have a good evening, Beverly." She can feel the secretary's cold eyes on her back as she opens the front door. *Normal.* She must look more closely at the school's policies. Bingham, it seems, finds ways of imposing his own policies.

11

At 5:55 Nessa starts the climb to Ms. Sofie's suite on second floor. She feels like a princess ascending the ornate staircase. She's also a little nervous about the unknown. She really isn't ready to get particularly chummy with these people, but she's also a bit curious. To her immense relief, John appears beside her on the steps. She suspects their hostess is considering this dinner a matchmaking opportunity.

"Well, here goes!" he says. "I'm pretty hungry so hope she has enough for us *and* the cats."

"She probably does. Pike's in charge, and he won't skimp."

At the top of the stairs, they look to their right and see the door to the west wing apartment is ajar. Nessa is surprised the cats aren't trying to escape. Her answer greets her when she steps inside. Eeney, Meeny, and Miney are sitting primly in high chairs at two card tables that have been pushed together and covered with white butcher paper. Paper dishes and plastic utensils have been laid out, but no food is visible yet. The only indication it is a special occasion is Sofie's bright pink silk dress which looks like it could be a costume for a tap recital. And the cats are decked out in bright blue silk jackets with their names embroidered on their fronts. Nessa fears she shouldn't have changed out of her teaching clothes for this gala event.

Ms. Sofie is seated in the center chair facing her guests and smiling radiantly. "I'm so happy you could make it! I was afraid you might have other plans."

"I never do. Have plans for dinner that is. I'm glad you asked," says John.

"Well, I think you young people should get together a lot and share TV dinners or whatever you usually have. I know from experience it isn't fun to eat alone. If it weren't for my babies, I'd probably skip meals."

John and Nessa both smile. The babies, it appears, have been present and encouraging her at every meal.

Pike seems to have been hired to be the waiter as well as the caterer. He wears a white bib apron and proceeds to dish up a scrumptious roast beef dinner, including mashed potatoes and gravy, green bean casserole and dinner rolls. Nessa is a little disappointed the kittens are served only platters of Feline Feast beef and fish. A little of the gravy for the humans' potatoes finds its way to their plates, however, so everyone is well satisfied.

The little ones are perfect examples of being seen and not heard. They almost make Nessa wish to have a cat. "It must be a little inconvenient providing three litter boxes," she comments. That problem has been on her mind. After worrying that she wouldn't be able to eat for the smell, she hasn't been able to detect one.

"Oh, my. I don't mess with litter boxes. My children have been potty trained for a long time. They sit on the stool in the bathroom just like people."

Both Nessa and John have heard of pets who do that but have never known of any who did it exclusively. "That's pretty amazing," John comments.

"I did a lot of work with them when they were very young. I haven't always been this chubby. I could get up and down and spend hours teaching them to be real children. The habits really stay with them. I can't imagine how Moe is getting along outside without a stool."

Ms. Sofie turns out to have a delightful personality for a lady who is so seldom out in public. And she has a remarkable grasp of what's going on in the world. The conversation runs the gamut from politics, to religion, to the latest movies. A pile of newspapers in one corner of the room partially explains how she stays informed. She also possesses a television with DVD player and a computer which is a click away if she only swivels her chair.

"You don't seem to get out much, Sofie. Do you have a family somewhere nearby?" Nessa realizes she knows nothing about the woman's life.

"No, there's nobody for me to visit. I was married once but have no children except for the ones you see here. My husband left after ten years. He declared me to be fat enough for a sideshow. He didn't take any responsibility for the stress that caused me to eat so much."

"But you didn't let him ruin your life, right?" Nessa can see that Sofie is a reasonably content woman.

"Oh, no. His mean comment turned out to be a blessing. It gave me an idea for a career! I wasn't a sideshow but I did join the circus. I got busy and lost most of the extra weight so I could enjoy training my little ones. It was a wonderful life, but six months ago when I could see things were changing, I started packing on the pounds again. That's about killed any future for our act. It's hard to keep up with the kitties when I can't get down on the floor." She momentarily looks remorseful and ashamed. "I really must get my body back." Suddenly, her face brightens. "Oh! I almost forgot to offer you dessert! Pike get us the pie and ice cream. My diet will wait one more day."

Pike takes her wishes very seriously. He opens another large box containing three kinds of pie and is quick to get the ice cream out of the full-size refrigerator. While the door of the fridge is open, Nessa gets a view of its well-stocked shelves. Pike evidently keeps his friend supplied. He hasn't said anything about his mother, but Sofie may be the closest he's had to having one of those for years.

To be nice, Vanessa has partaken of a small slice of roast beef and done very well about sampling the other dishes as well. By the last bite of pecan pie ala mode she is almost too stuffed to sip the coffee Pike is serving from the Keurig.

The kittens are extremely well-behaved compared to any Nessa has seen. "I'm surprised they aren't sleepy by now." The cat she used to have seemed to sleep her life away.

"My darlings hate to miss out on anything when there's company here," Ms. Sofie declares proudly.

"Well, I think we'd better shove off and let them get some rest," John announces. I know Nessa probably has school work, and I have er...a... sermon to work on. Is there anything we can help you with before we go downstairs?"

Pike has already cleared the table and put away the few leftovers. John gets up and helps him fold and put away the extra table. Ms. Sofie shouldn't have any work to do as a result of her hospitality.

The thank-yous and hugs are warm when the visitors finally leave. John and Nessa have stopped outside Sofie's quarters, trying to make the evening last. "That was fun," she says.

"Yes, it really was. You know, Sofie had a good idea about you and me sharing more meals. The only trouble is the lack of food in my apartment. I can't let stale snacks be my only contribution."

"I'll have you come to my place if you can do without meat."

"Maybe we can find a pizza place that delivers. We owe Sofie and Pike, too. This place could turn into a commune."

Pike steps out Sofie's door. Before he closes it, they hear the party inside continuing.

"Go Eeney! That's the way. Easy Miney. Come to Mamma." The phrases are coming from Sofie's living room.

"Can we look?" Nessa asks Pike. She has an idea of what is going on but has never witnessed it before.

"Sure. They do this every night. Sofie puts them through their tricks even though they don't have an audience. The exercise is good for them, and they love it."

When Sofie's voice is silent for a moment, Nessa knocks. "Come in!" is the friendly reply.

"It sounds like we're missing a show," says Nessa through the crack. She doesn't want to let the cats out.

The scene is not to be believed unless one sees it with her own eyes. Nessa is surprised cats are so trainable. These are obeying Sofie's commands right and left. They can push a baby carriage, carry each other piggy back, walk a tight rope and play catch. There actually seem to be no limits to their repertoire. The partially departed guests reward the little ones with applause and shouts of "Great job!!"

"Wow!" says Vanessa. "I was excited when my dog learned to sit up and beg."

"I guess we know where to go for a show if we get bored in the evenings," comments John on their way down the stairs.

Their second-floor outing has been stimulating, entertaining and encouraging. But Vanessa is stuffed and feels like getting some fresh air. When her cell phone rings, she's happy to escape to the front porch and hear what her old Chicago friend Kyra is up to. "What excitement did I interrupt?" the voice on the phone asks. "Were you just on your way to pick up your mail and feed your fish?"

"Better than that. I've already been to a dinner party."

"No kidding? Here I was going to make you feel bad by saying I'm on my way to the opera. Who on earth throws dinner parties in Haven? The PTA?"

"No, that's next week. I went to the home of a Ms. Sofie Potter. It was a formal, catered affair." Nessa is getting too good at embellishing facts. "Mr. Handsome Preacher was there, too."

"Okay. I've officially quit pitying you. I haven't ever been to a formal dinner or met even one handsome preacher."

"Well, get out of the city! That place is holding you back."

Clown Alley

Lola calls the group to order.

"I've called you together tonight just to check on morale. Is it my imagination or are we getting a little down? Late summer blahs, maybe?"

"Not me! I had guests for dinner last night and that cheered me immensely!"

"And I helped with the dinner and then went out with Melody. No blahs for me."

"Oh, dear. I'm afraid I've imposed my moods on the rest of you. Gordon has been restless lately, and I guess I thought maybe everyone was. I know a couple of you have approached me about doing some clowning on the side. I assume that means you're homesick for your old life."

"It just seems like kind of a waste for us clowns to be concealing what we do best. A concert pianist who got out of the business would still play occasionally."

"Oh, I know you have a point. I'm selfish for shutting you off completely. I'd just feel so responsible if you were to be found out. Where were you thinking of performing?"

"Anywhere somebody needs us. We could go out one at a time. And not walk around town in costume"

Lola looks troubled. She must feel like her teenage children are rebelling, wanting to get away from her supervision. They just don't realize the dangers out there. "I'm sure you know of opportunities to entertain at parties or nursing homes. My concern is knowing what happened to the creepy clowns last summer. Somebody put a stop to *them*."

"But they weren't really clowns. They were imposters who were spreading fear. We want to spread cheer."

"The trouble is, townspeople can't always tell the difference. They think now that all clowns are hiding something, and that they pose a threat. We've already seen what kinds of things can happen when fear takes over. You could clown for the elderly and then when you're leaving the nursing home, get attacked by a worried relative. Are you willing to take that risk?"

"I am. I want to prove to the world that clowns bring joy and healing. At least they always have. There're always a few fakes who try to spoil everything. But we can't let them!"

Words of agreement follow. Some in the group are growing weary of staying undercover. They long to do what they know and repair the reputations of their white-faced brothers and sisters.

"Maybe we can just do one gig a month. It would barely be noticed."

Lola is torn. She knows how they feel but remembers the figure in the trees who caused her to crash her bike. "If you insist, you'll need to be extremely watchful, extremely careful who sees your acts. And extremely firm about not doing interviews. Another thing, if you can, ask for a little pay for any entertaining you do. We're pretty depleted and so is Monique. She'll be totally helpless if any emergency bills come up. Winter isn't far off. If the furnace breaks, we're out in the cold."

"I don't want to be called 'the greatest' or 'one of the greatest'; let other guys claim to be the best. I just want to be known as a clown because to me that's the height of my profession. It means you can do everything-sing, dance, and above all, make people laugh."
–Red Skelton

12

After a frazzling seventh hour in the company of her chatty freshmen, Nessa retreats to her apartment. She takes the time to put together a huge chef's salad which she takes in to the living room. Sitting cross-legged on the couch, she opens Facebook for company while she eats. When the salad followed by some ice cream have her satisfied for a couple of hours, she'll be more than ready for a quiet evening of reading her novel. The door into the hallway is secured against the intrusion of Gordy and his debatably good intentions.

No more mulling over the meaning of *normal.* No more stressing over a possible murder. No more noisy ninth graders. Her neighbors here could be even more restless than her students, but she doesn't care what goes on in the rest of the house. The walls of Monique's period building are thicker than modern day ones, and the renters within them are usually in bed early. This evening promises to be no exception. She takes in a big breath as though to internalize the silence, to make it a part of her.

Until the music begins. The peace is gone in a flash. Nessa listens to the loud stuff herself on occasion, but not tonight. *Please, not tonight.* Strains of a calliope tune are coming through the walls. A circus seems to have landed. The sound originates from above, second floor or higher. Maybe Pike is having a party for his friends from work. Nessa imagines she hears laughing and loud music, not bad noises but annoying at this time of night. She drags herself out of bed and into the hallway. If the racket keeps up, she'll have to go up and knock on Pike's door. It's depressing to think she'll be behaving like the stereotypical *get off my lawn* elderly neighbor, but why should she have to listen to other people's revelry? To be honest, she's a little miffed she wasn't invited. She'd have declined, but an invitation would've made her more tolerant.

A strip of light shines from under John's door. At least she isn't the only outcast. Regretting her messy hair and stretched out sweat pants, she taps lightly to get his attention. He answers the knock, looking not much neater than she does. "I knew it'd be you. We're the only people on this floor. All the fun is upstairs. Maybe it's an orgy."

Again, Nessa is struck by his worldly response. "Yeah," she answers. "At least it's Friday. If it were a school night, I'd be screaming at them. Does this happen often?"

"I haven't lived here much longer than you have, so I don't know. It sounds like the kind of thing that could go on all night. What do you want to do about it? Shall we crash the party or just suffer?"

Nessa considers her answer. "I wish there were some way to get a peek at what's going on. I'm curious to know if Ms. Sofie or Monique is there. Or Gordy, who's always so quiet."

"The volume of the music sounds like a door is open. Why don't we check it out? I don't think we have reason to be sneaky about it. We pay rent, and that gives us rights."

Vanessa agrees. But she knows she'll still feel like a gatecrasher if someone catches them.

"Try to think of it like you're at school and investigating loud noises coming from the hallway while you're trying to give a test. I bet you wouldn't even hesitate."

"Nope. I wouldn't. Let's go!" The two start up the steps, taking them two at a time. There's no need to be especially quiet since the partiers aren't apt to hear the pair's arrival over their own commotion.

They stop in unison at the top of the stairs staring straight ahead. Nessa has feared they'd have to find a ladder in order to peer through a transom at the top of one of the tall oak doors. However, the celebration is being held in a spacious ballroom. She should've known such a large old house would have one. Lola and her crowd don't seem to be the type to hold a formal ball, but the view in front of them is far from that.

John and Nessa are able to hide behind giant pillars on either side of the room's open double doors. It doesn't seem very risky to peek around them every few minutes and get their eyes full. A large colorful sign on the opposite wall explains the occasion. *HAPPY BIRTHDAY, LOLA!*

Before them is a theme party. The ballroom, it seems, has been transformed into a circus. Balloons are everywhere. There is cotton candy, popcorn and peanuts. Pike, in a multicolored outfit, his frizzy hair teased in all directions, is zipping around the room on a unicycle and at the same time, juggling colored balls. Lola has her hair in pigtails that stick straight out to the sides of her head, and she's jumping rope. Ms. Sofie, in a blue fright wig, is in her chair directing her cats to perform tricks on top of small cone-shaped platforms. All three of her pets are wearing blue bonnets. Gordy stands well away from the others, and, dressed appropriately as a sad-faced Emmet Kelly character, he latches and unlatches a suitcase. Monique carries an open umbrella, wears a tutu, and walks an imaginary high wire. Crazy as the whole picture is, the circus music pulls it together into a delightful childhood dream scene.

John and Nessa keep glancing at each other and rolling their eyes in disbelief. Where did all this imagination come from? Who has designed such elaborate festivities? Then, amid all the white faces, Vanessa spots a head of bushy white hair. Cotton. He too, has on classic clown costume and makeup and is making balloon animals. He's obviously no novice because the bears and rabbits take him only seconds to create.

The overriding impression of these varied individuals, is that they're happily entertaining an imaginary audience. Of note is the fact that no voices are heard. Not a word is uttered or sung. Yet there's a feeling of camaraderie and agreement. No fights or demonstrations will erupt during this event. Lola is being graciously honored.

Then, as if the partiers are wearing shock collars, and someone hits the button, everything stops. Nessa and John take the squawk of the music ending as their cue to sneak out the way they came. Without exchanging a syllable, they make their way down the stairs and back to their apartments. Discussion can wait until later.

Nessa is eager for tomorrow. Will any of the Fancy Tramp dwellers – or Cotton – mention Lola's birthday or the gala that took place? Will any remains be evident in the ballroom? - corn kernels, airless balloons? Somehow, she's sure most of the evidence has already been whisked away. Popcorn machine, bicycles, everything. Monique is, after all, the Clean Queen. As well as a tight-rope walker.

13

None of the partiers can be seen in the halls the next morning, but Nessa does run into John coming in with a Doug's Diner paper coffee cup. They look at each other, deciding whether to say anything about their voyeuristic time on second floor. Finally, John speaks. "Did we really see anything last night?"

"I remember plenty," says Nessa "But I don't know if it was real. It feels like a dream."

"I have a feeling we dreamed the same things. I think that's called a collective hallucination. I'm not sure the Fancy Tramp is good for our mental health."

"My mother is coming to visit tomorrow. I was going to introduce her to Cotton, Lola's white-haired friend – but he seems to like clowns, and she's scared to death of them."

"Yeah. Lots of people are. I've learned lately that the phobia even has a name, coulrophobia. If they're as gentle as Cotton, though, there's no reason for all that fuss. Trouble is, most phobias aren't reasonable."

"I don't think I have any phobias," says Nessa thoughtfully, "but maybe I just haven't discovered them yet. Something tells me, this old building could be a hotbed of buried fears."

"Those folks from last night are going to be showing up any minute. I kind of dread seeing them."

"We can't say anything about the party. Though it'd be interesting to hear whether they admit they're circus folks."

"I vote to play dumb. In fact, I vote to avoid them for now. Let's talk in my apartment. I wish I had something to offer you for breakfast, but all I can do is share this coffee."

"I'm not much for coffee. Soda is my caffeine of choice. A bad habit, I know."

"There are lots worse ones." And John leads the way into his living room. It is depressingly empty. The impression is that its occupant isn't planning to stay long. *This is a stopping off place for him,* she reminds herself. *Just until his new house is finished. It'll be a parsonage where he probably can't entertain ladies.*

Nessa isn't sure it's even a good idea for her to be here. Alone with a stranger. But then, John Smith doesn't seem all that strange. He's perhaps the most normal person she knows in Haven. If she can't trust him, a minister of God, who can she trust? No one in the town comes to mind.

"Make yourself comfortable," he orders. Nessa tentatively sits in the one soft chair in the room. Remembering his earlier comment about an intruder needing to appreciate religious literature, she has pictured a cozy den with rows of books and a desk. Pastors she's known have shown her into inviting studies where people would feel at ease making their most personal confessions. This sparsely-furnished front room seems to have been decorated by the same person who designs jail cells. However, she thinks jails have Bibles and John Smith doesn't have his in sight. For some reason, she isn't surprised.

"Do you spend all week writing your sermon?" she blurts out.

John Smith hesitates. "Not really. I just think about it a lot and then put it all together on Saturday evening. It works for me."

"Oh." She wants to ask whether he might possibly be a creepy clown rather than a sweet, intelligent man of the cloth.

No one else seems to be who they portray themselves to be. "Has Gordy ever stopped in here?"

"No, he hasn't. I wish he would. I've been trying to decide whether he could be homicidal. Lola must have told you about the mysterious death that happened here."

"Yes, but I met Gordy, and he seems totally harmless. I bet I could beat him off if he does try anything. He's just a frail old man. Lola says he used to be her good friend. She gave me the idea the man has Alzheimer's or some kind of dementia. He reminds me of a sad old dog." Another silence.

"I'm sure you're hungry. I don't usually eat breakfast. I have bread, but my toaster seems to be broken."

"Maybe we could go upstairs and use the popcorn machine."

"Where do you suppose they got one of those? I guess they could've found it in the house when they moved in. Hard to tell what all might be left behind in a place this size."

"True. But a unicycle? And face paint? The house must've once been inhabited by circus people."

"That would be preferable to a band of killers. Or folks who raised snakes."

"True. You know, of course, that our new friends could've brought all the circus paraphernalia with them."

"Because it's theirs."

Neither John nor Nessa speaks for another moment.

"I have some week-old corn curls," John offers.

"I'd love some."

They sit munching until John breaks the silence. "I'm not a preacher. And I'm sure there's a special place in hell for those who claim to be."

Nessa realizes she's been waiting for that admission. "I've wondered. But why would you lie about it? Are you running from the law?"

"No. I'm a private investigator here on assignment. Being a new pastor seemed to be a safe cover, but I'm having second and third thoughts. The pretense is requiring more lying than I'm comfortable with."

"You could've told me the truth. I don't care if you're a garbage man or even if you're unemployed. I'd only mind if I found out you're a homicidal maniac."

"I'm definitely not one of those. I often have to invent stories in my line of work. With you, the preacher thing just slipped out. I wanted so much for you to feel safe taking a room here. You seemed like such a nice person. Somebody I'd like to be around."

It's comforting to know the attraction she's felt from their first meeting is at least somewhat mutual. "You say you're a private eye. Who exactly do you have your eye on? Somebody who lives here?"

"I was hired to find out if Lola and the rest are doing anything illegal. The town has a kind of watchdog group called The Association. They dress in camouflage and give the impression they're an army of some sort. From what I gather, they want an excuse to run these lodgers out of town so they themselves can have this mansion for their headquarters."

"Hmm." Nessa is skeptical of a group called The Association. "Are you sure you're on the side of the good guys?"

"I was, but I'm starting to wonder. The man who hired me is sure that one of Lola's group is responsible for the deaths of at least one renter in the past year. And there have been other unsolved homicides in this area of the state they'd like to pin on them."

"No kidding? I know they're a little quirky, but I don't feel like any of them is the least bit dangerous. I'm beginning to think there's something off about this whole thing. The job will pay well if I come up with criminal activity, but I have a feeling the only way I'll find any wrong doing in this house is to make something out of nothing. That's probably what they want me to do."

"I'd have thought you'd ask for more facts about the Association. It sounds like mafia."

"Not in Haven. It's some small-time faction of men who want to turn the town into a utopia. I haven't quite figured it out. They claim the Fancy Tramp renters are scallywags who drifted in off the highway to bring crime and mayhem to the community. But my instincts tell me the folks who live in this building are just good people minding their own business. No signs of evil intent have shown themselves. I've done a little snooping and haven't come across any weapons."

"Nothing but a fly swatter."

"Right. I do think they have a mysterious past, but it doesn't have to be a criminal one. And I can't think of any reason why they should have to give up this place. She didn't pay much, but Monique bought the old mansion fair and square, so my client is just going to have to suck it up. And maybe try to make a deal with Monique. She might have a room where the Association can meet. Maybe that giant ballroom."

"Who do you think Lola and company really are?" asks Nessa. "They seem to be connected to each other somehow. The obvious answer is that they come from a circus, but that would've been on the news. And why all of them? Maybe the circus stuff is just their collective fantasy."

"When I first met Gordy, I wondered if they weren't a bunch left homeless when a mental hospital closed. I've heard some institutions in these parts have shut down this past year. The patients have to go somewhere."

"That's a good guess, but I think the mayor or someone would've been notified if that were the case. Unusual as they are, I haven't thought of anyone except Gordy as being mentally disturbed. Of course, that condition isn't always easy to spot. They could have *mild* psychiatric disturbances. They may stay together just to give each other support."

"Well, even if they are former patients, there's no crime in that. If the state doesn't want to provide an institution for the mentally ill, then they'll have to be allowed to live wherever they can. Most of the time, they probably can't be picked out from a group of regular folks. A lot of us have some degree of mental disturbance."

Nessa remembers Beverly's recent words. "The school secretary calls Lola and friends *odd*. She says that like it's a dirty word."

"I think *odd* is a degree or two above *flat-out crazy*. My mother used to say that only very intelligent people go crazy. Slow witted people never do. I don't know how she accounted for those who're just odd. Born that way, I guess."

"I think *odd* is a subjective term. One person's idea of odd is another person's normal."

John gets down to business. "I'm going to need to talk to some of the citizens who live nearby this house. See what they observed when the bunch moved in. As far as I can see, they have no means of transportation. Can't imagine them all hitchhiking. Especially with the cats."

"They must have looked pretty noticeable when they showed up in town. You'd think their arrival would've been on the front page of whatever paper they get here. Of course, they wouldn't have been wearing the costumes we saw last night." Nessa would like to help. "I can check at the school library."

"That's a good idea. But if some reporter interviewed them when they arrived, I'd think it would all be public knowledge. Especially in a town of less than a thousand. It doesn't seem to be. During my time in Haven so far, I've learned that no one even knows Lola and friends are in town, and they've been here for several months. They must stay pretty close to home. At any rate, I think the Association better concede the house. I'm sure I could dig up more dirt on their members than I can on these renters."

"When you tell him you've decided to give up, your client will expect you to move out." That idea makes Nessa unexpectedly sad. She'll feel very adrift without John to talk to. Even though he has been misrepresenting himself and probably shouldn't be trusted.

"He doesn't have anything to say about it, but I *will* move out of here. I have an office in Arbor City. That's not far away."

"And you showed me the short cut," Nessa answers, remembering their visit to the hospital to visit Cotton. "What happens to the church? They won't have a preacher. Have they been paying you?"

"I'm ashamed to say there's no such place. My fake story hasn't gone any further than you. Bad enough, I know, but at least I haven't been scamming any church members."

Nessa is quiet for a moment, deciding how she feels about his revelation.

"Well, that's a relief. I guess." What will her mother think of a guy who does nothing for a living but spy on people? It would've been a lot easier to introduce her to Reverend Smith.

"Is your name really Smith?"

"No. The John is real, but it's Harnden. John Harnden.

"Smith is easier to say."

"Well, take your pick. I've been called so many names, I answer to most anything. Bottom line is, I can't criticize people who pretend to be something they aren't. Most people have been guilty of presenting a false front at one time or another. At least I use that for an excuse."

14

Her couch beckons Nessa to take a Saturday afternoon nap. Partway into her dream about being chased by a bunch of circus animals, there is a pounding on her door. "Vanessa! Help! Let me in!"

She's off the couch in a flash at the sound of her mom in distress. Nessa forgot she was coming today. "Just a minute." The woman isn't used to her daughter's door being locked. This constitutes a big emergency.

Tracy Martin is standing just outside with a familiar figure close behind her. His arms encircle her shoulders and seem to be holding her back from moving. Her voice quivers. "Nessa, this man... Who is he?"

Nessa sighs. What a welcome for her poor mother. She should've met her out front and prevented this. "Gordy, it's alright. You don't have to protect me. The lady is my mother. You can let her come in."

Gordon relaxes his grip and gives her an "Are you sure?" look.

"I'm positive Gordy. Say hello to Tracy. One of the sweetest women you'll find."

Tracy, bless her heart, seems to catch on and holds out a hand to shake Gordy's. Her voice quivers as she says, "I'm pleased to meet you."

Gordy obliges by letting her touch him but then quickly turns away and disappears through the basement door.

"Good lord!" says Tracy. "Here I thought you lived with a kindly caring woman and a pastor. What is this place? It looks like the home of the Munsters."

Nessa isn't sure who the Munsters are but gets the idea. The Fancy Tramp isn't the rooming house a typical mother would choose for her only daughter. But it isn't really up to her mom to approve. She should just accept Nessa's decision to live here. "Come in and see my apartment. You'll like it – I know you will. And the lights are brighter in there."

After looking up and down the hallway for creepy men who could be lurking out of sight, Tracy steps cautiously over the threshold. Nessa watches her mom's expression brighten. "Why, honey, you've fixed it real cute. It looks a little *brothelly* but charming. If I were you, I'd stay in here and never go out among the other renters."

"Kinda hard to do, mom. But the whole house is cool. It really is. Pretty woodwork, lots of nooks and crannies. Beautiful open staircase. Kinda of old and beaten up, but not spooky in the same way an apartment in the city could be. No criminals, druggies or prostitutes – that I know of. In fact," and here she remembers her recent conversation with Beverly, "people in this town think *normality* is very important."

"Oh, dear, you might be the one everybody's going to be afraid of." Tracy jokes. "Listen, I haven't had lunch. Do you have anything in your kitchen?"

Kitchen is an exaggerated term for the small room with a table-top refrigerator, apartment-sized stove, and tiny table. "I have apples, yogurt, and granola bars. What do you want?"

"Real food. Those things are fine when I'm between meals, but don't you have any hamburger? I can cook my own."

"I'm vegetarian, remember? I have a protein shake I was saving for breakfast, but I'll give it to you. Nothing's too good for my mom."

"Let's go out. I'd like to see what else this town has to offer besides a haunted mansion with a demented body guard. We could ask the preacher to come with us."

"I think he has plans for today. Let's just go to the diner. Mavis the waitress will be happy that I at least *know* someone who appreciates beef."

Nessa was going to suggest they walk down the hill but thinks better of it when she recalls Lola's experience with the camouflaged bike basher. The two ladies go toward Nessa's car. Behind them, a loud voice calls for their attention. "Where are you rushing off to?" It is Lola, saddling up her bicycle. "Do you have a guest, Nessa?"

Nessa is thankful Lola is dressed in relatively ordinary garb. Her clownish getup of last night is only a memory. "I do. This is my mother, Tracy Martin. Mom, this is Lola. I've mentioned her before."

"Yes," Tracy says cautiously. "The motherly manager."

"That's me!" agrees Lola. "I'm so motherly you'll want to take me home with you. But your daughter doesn't really need me to watch over her. She's seems unusually mature. After all, she's a teacher and very smart."

"That's right," says Tracy with a wink for her daughter. "I keep forgetting." Then to Lola, "Don't let us keep you from wherever you were going."

"I'm off to the Humane Society. I've started volunteering to walk the dogs a few times a week. I can't stand to think of them in those cages all the time. It's especially lonely for them on weekends. Ta-Ta!" And Lola sprays them with gravel dust as she speeds away.

"Oh, wow. She seems...nice," comments Tracy with forced cheerfulness.

"She is. They all are...nice."

As expected, the diner is far from crowded. There are only a few lost souls who can't make it through even Saturday afternoon without coffee. Mavis must have the weekend off. "This place is usually hopping," Nessa explains to Tracy. She hates for her mother to think the town is a dead end. "What do you want to eat? They have a lot of different choices. Most of them are greasy the way you prefer."

"Oh, I'm not that bad. I'll just have some chili and a grilled cheese," she tells the unfamiliar waitress. "Or whatever you have on hand."

Nessa hates to make her mom eat alone so she orders a salad and crackers. "I hope you aren't trying to lose weight," Tracy comments.

It's the kind of warning Nessa has grown used to. There have been times when Tracy worried Nessa was gaining too much. But those were balanced by anorexic fears. Nessa always has an answer. "Don't worry. The carbs in the school lunches keep me from wasting away." She looks around the diner for anybody she might know. "I wish I could introduce you to some of my teacher friends." Her attention is taken then by the entry of one of the people she's been hoping to see. "Cotton!"

Nessa has never run into him away from the school. He looks almost out of place in this environment. She can't imagine why. Janitors have to eat occasionally like everyone else. "Come on over here, Cotton. You must meet my mother, Tracy!"

The usually-shy janitor produces a particularly charming smile for the ladies. "Happy to meet you." And he holds out a hand to Nessa's mom.

"I'd introduce you by your real name if I knew it," Vanessa tells Cotton.

"My name is Lionel. Lionel Downs. I haven't gone by that, though, for years. It doesn't even sound like it belongs to me."

"Well, I like it," answers Tracy pleasantly. "*Lionel* is a strong name."

Cotton smiles.

Nessa thinks of Cotton as more of a pussy-cat than a lion, but she's glad her mom likes the name. She'll be happy if her white-haired friend captures Tracy's interest just because she likes him herself.

In short order, the women make room for the white-haired man at their booth and see that he gets some chili. "How are you feeling these days, Cotton?" Nessa asks.

"Oh, I'm fine. No lasting effects except for a small lump. It'll go away."

"Cotton is the school custodian. He was hit over the head while he was working in my room. It was really strange. No one was around at the time except the secretary and me. I know *I* didn't hit him, and Beverly doesn't seem the type. It must've been a ghost."

"My. Who'd think cleaning classrooms would be such a hazardous job? Maybe a hunk of plaster fell from the ceiling. Is it an old building?" asks Tracy in an effort to offer an answer.

"Not that old, Mom," responds Nessa. "If it had happened at the Fancy Tramp, we could've believed that, but my wing of the school is almost new. We just hope it was a freaky thing that won't happen again. I enjoy having a man around who takes care of things without complaining. Cotton is a friend of my landlady. Didn't I hear that right?" she asks him.

"Yes, I am," he answers but doesn't elaborate except to say, "I lived at the Fancy Tramp when I first came to town, but it's a six-block walk to school. I have to be at work pretty early, so I decided to find another house."

An hour later the trio is still chatting. Much of the time, Vanessa feels like an eavesdropper. Her mother and the custodian find out they're the same age and both love to listen to jazz. Cotton, it seems, is one of nine siblings so he left home as a teen to earn money and give a little relief to his family's budget. He has never been married. Nessa considers that to be a sad fact. The man is soft spoken with a kind manner and a sharp sense of humor. He'd be a sweet husband and kids would love him. Here she goes getting ahead of herself like her mother tends to do with every guy *she's* ever dated.

Throughout the luncheon conversation, Vanessa is aware of two men in suits at a nearby table. It appears they are having a business meeting, but she doesn't notice either man uttering a word to the other. She does, however make accidental eye contact with first the older one and then his younger companion. The men are very aware of the people at her table and could be listening in on their dialogue. *You aren't very paranoid, Nessa,* she scolds herself. Why would complete strangers care about the conversation of a janitor, a teacher and a Chicago mom?

On their way out of Doug's, Cotton appears to work up courage to ask Tracy, "Do you think you'll come to Haven often? It's a pretty comfortable little town."

Nessa is amused, listening to the older generation flirt. It's obvious to her that her companions are taken with each other. She might as well help them out. "Not really that much to do around here, but it's the safest and friendliest place you'll find. Not like Chicago where a woman alone has to be so careful."

Tracy smiles. "Right. The only thing scary I ever hear from little towns these days is that sometimes they have creepy clowns skulking around, lurking in the trees. That would be enough to keep me away if my daughter didn't live here!"

Cotton is quiet for a moment. Nessa pounces on the potentially touchy subject. "They had some of those last summer, but they're gone. No worries now about stalkers."

Tracy makes a face. "Good! I hate clowns. Anything but clowns. They're evil as far as I'm concerned. I think I have a phobia."

Surprisingly, Cotton has a response. "Clowns are just regular people in makeup. The creepy ones are only impersonating clowns."

Tracy looks doubtful at first, and then her warm smile returns. She must have decided the topic isn't worth an argument. "I hope you're right. Well, it was wonderful meeting you, Cotton. I already look forward to coming back to Haven. I should be able to get here at least once more before the snowy weather. The chili here will taste even better when it's cold outside."

Nessa offers the janitor a ride home, but he politely declines. "I need the exercise," he says. The two ladies get in Nessa's car, and Cotton takes off on foot. Nessa notices a car pull away from the curb right behind him. She didn't see the men in suits come out of the diner, but Nessa is sure that's who's in the black sedan up ahead. Not willing to risk her friend getting attacked again, she follows at a distance on her way to show Tracy where she works.

"Why are you going so slowly?" Tracy asks. "Lionel is going to get to his house before you and I even get close to the school."

"Just letting you get the scenic view of the town. There are lots of pretty little houses. Maybe you'll want to buy one."

"The Chamber of Commerce should hire you. You keep trying to sell me on Haven. Don't think I don't know what you're doing. It isn't that you'd like me to live closer. You're trying to fix me up. Just because I was friendly to Lionel doesn't mean I have my sights on him. I was only being polite."

"Sure, Mom." But Nessa's mind is now focused on their friend turning onto the front walk of his small bungalow. The black car trailing him almost comes to a stop. Someone is probably writing down the house number. The car speeds away before Cotton seems to notice. Those men are going to be back. She'd bet on it. She's going to have to warn Cotton after her mom leaves. Whoever drove away the clowns last summer must be using similar tactics on a non-violent school janitor. But why? They've put him in the hospital already. How much further will they go to make their point? And what could that point be? Evidently, men who clean schools are subversive and a threat to the town or at least to the men wearing suits. It's almost like sleepy little Haven wants to create intrigue to make the community more interesting. Let them live in Chicago a while, and they won't feel a need to manufacture excitement.

As soon as she says good-bye to her mother, Nessa takes out her cell phone. She can't wait any longer to alert their friend. "Cotton? This is Vanessa Martin. I'm just calling to give you a heads up. You know this afternoon when we followed you home? Those men in suits from the diner were following you. I felt like they were checking to see where you live."

"Thanks for telling me, Vanessa. I actually did notice the car, but it wasn't anybody I know. Do you think it's something to worry about?"

"Probably not. I don't know who they are either, but they seem awful interested in you. I think it's the same car that was parked outside the school the day you were attacked in my room. I'm not sure what we can do about them. Just keep an eye out and be sure your doors and windows are locked. I have a feeling they're trying to scare you into leaving town. Something to do with Mr. Bingham, I'm guessing. Do you have a gun permit? You might want to have some defense when you're walking to and from school."

"Sorry, Vanessa. Guns aren't my style."

"Well, I'd say, to carry *something* – a ball bat, a big rock."

So much for the *comfortable* town Cotton was describing earlier.

15

During her third hour English Lit class, Vanessa has the honor of receiving a note from the office. It is delivered by way of a student helper. *Principal Bingham wishes to speak with you at your earliest convenience.*

She doesn't know yet whether being summoned by her boss is a good or a bad thing. It's a pretty sure bet the man doesn't want a friendly chat or to compliment her on her teaching abilities. That pretty much leaves the bad possibilities.

If this meeting is to be a firing, she's probably setting some kind of record for shortest teaching career. All through the review of *Macbeth,* Nessa contemplates what she's done or said that might be getting her canned. It has to be the result of her snippy little exchanges with Beverly. The secretary is probably in a position to get a teacher into trouble if she wants to. Whatever it is, Nessa plans to plead innocent. She's done nothing so far but work as hard as she can to get her students and herself off to a good start for the year. And Mr. Bingham surely isn't miffed that she's living at the Fancy Tramp since it was his idea in the first place, and not a single alternative has shown itself. Monique's business has so far proven to be a legitimate establishment with a decent reputation.

"Thanks for coming, Ms. Martin!" greets the principal. "I know you must value your free period so I won't take up much of it. Have a seat." When she sits, he continues. "I just read something this morning that has me puzzled."

Nessa waits for him to explain.

"It was an item on my MSN feed. 'Circus Closes Down'." He stops then to let her respond.

"I'm afraid I don't know anything about a circus. I didn't think we had them these days."

"Well, actually the HAPPCO Circus has been pretty popular in these parts. It travels from city to city and has most of the usual acts. But all of a sudden it shuts down. I find that hard to understand."

"Did the article give any details?" asks Nessa. She's surely not the one to ask. Being prepared with facts about circuses hasn't occurred to her even though the subject has been finding its way into her life lately.

"Ringling Brothers is calling it quits, and that could be part of it. But also, the article indicates that attendance has slowly declined since their clowns defected." His tone says that he blames the clowns for the whole demise.

"That's . . . er . . . too bad," is her only comment. She can't understand what this story has to do with her.

Mr. Bingham stands then and turns toward the window. He seems to be thinking the situation through. "The thing is, I couldn't care less whether or not we have circuses. I'm just curious about what happened to the blasted clowns. Where did they go?"

"I actually haven't seen any around here. Your guess is as good as mine," answers Nessa. She's thinking of the pile of essays on her computer she'd hoped to have corrected by next hour. Since her job doesn't seem to be on the line, she's eager to get back to her room.

"We had some creepy ones in town last summer, but they weren't from the circus. And we put an end to their activities pretty quickly. I'm wondering now if we missed a few. Maybe there are some in town who run around without makeup and costumes. That means you could actually talk to one of them without knowing." His face shows his distaste for the whole idea.

Nessa doesn't even attempt another reply. She has nothing she dares contribute. She knows she doesn't want to rat on her new friends. Not after the party for Lola and the clowning that went on there. Hearing the town "got rid of" the summer clowns makes her fear for their safety. If she has to choose between loyalty to her Fancy Tramp neighbors and her principal, there's really no contest. Even if they prove to be suspected of murder, she'd defend them before she would many less odd citizens.

"Those folks who live at the rooming house. Where did they come from? Do you know?"

Nessa is glad she can answer truthfully. "I don't. I haven't asked about that. I don't feel it's any of my business." *And I don't see why it's any of yours.*

Mr. Bingham rises and starts to pace. He's finally succeeding in making Nessa nervous. "Well, I'm speculating that they're the run-away clowns," he says. "The timing is right and they're oddballs like you'd expect clowns to be. It's really a no-brainer as far as I can tell. They're trying to hide it, but that element is not what we want in Haven. The Association is very bothered by their presence."

"Then maybe somebody from the Association should visit the Fancy Tramp and ask them where they came from," Nessa suggests. It's probably no secret, and if it is, she sure isn't going to do their dirty work for them. During this strange exchange, her eyes have been absently traveling from side to side of Bingham's office. While trying to listen to the principal's worries, her attention is caught by something seen through an open closet door. It is a flash of camouflage. Out of place here, and certainly alarming when she associates it with Lola's attacker. Who is this man she calls her supervisor? Does the National Guard wear camouflage? Maybe he's a member.

Bingham continues his effort to recruit her for his non-educational cause. "I announced at our last Association meeting that I was sure you'd be willing to help us out. When you were applying to teach here, I saw you as the perfect person to assist our cause from within the school."

Nessa has a stab of disappointment. *And I thought he was impressed by my qualifications to teach students. He just saw me as a way to accomplish his own strange ambitions.*

"Most of my soldiers aren't paid. They voluntarily take up arms in the cause of perfection. But I can see that you're compensated for your cooperation. Just find out those renters' backgrounds. It shouldn't be a dangerous job. You can also ask the owner how much she'd sell the house for."

"I'm sorry Mr. Bingham, but I see no reason to get involved." His request is clearly not within the boundaries of her teaching contract, so she feels no obligation. "I know nothing about your association, but I assume its members are English speaking so why can't they investigate? It would only complicate things to have me in the middle."

The principal hesitates. Nessa suspects he is used to demanding rather than begging. He doesn't like to take no for an answer. The look he gives her is intended to be intimidating. "They would be more forthcoming talking to you than some representative from the town. The compensation will be substantial. Well worth the few minutes you'll have to spend."

"Then the Association can save a bunch of money by spending their own minutes." Nessa is a little surprised at herself. She certainly could use a substantial amount of money, but this doesn't feel right. Not at all. She's a little insulted that her boss thinks she can be bought off. Normally, she'd be on board to be of assistance. If the information he needed were about a school matter, that is. The favor he's asking has nothing to do with helping students.

There are a few more moments of silence, but Mr. Bingham isn't giving up. "Ms. Martin, I know I interrupted your school work. Why don't you get back to it? And then tonight, think about what you could do with a bonus. We'll talk again tomorrow."

Vanessa is grateful to escape the uncomfortable atmosphere of the man's office. *What kind of school administrator tries to bribe a teacher?* Suddenly she can't wait to get back to her apartment and her *odd* neighbors. Even Gordy is less frightening.

All night Vanessa lies awake worrying about Mr. Bingham's promise that they'll talk again tomorrow. What the man really meant was, "Tomorrow you will tell me you'll be an undercover agent for the Association." How can she justify betraying her neighbors to assist some secret organization who have no-telling-what planned? It seems clear they want the Fancy Tramp for some reason of their own. Then she remembers the camouflage she saw in Bingham's closet. Wow. She doesn't know a lot about the Ku Klux Klan, but the Association feels like a first cousin. Respected man in the community has a costume that can hide his true identity. The whole idea is much more disturbing than the white grease paint worn by clowns.

Knowing she is unequipped to go against Bingham by herself, Nessa knocks on John's door at 6:30 a.m. Fat chance he'll be up and around. Surprisingly, the door opens right away. The PI is wide awake and dressed. "What's up, Ness?"

She hesitates a bit at the nickname she's never heard him use before. "I have a problem," she announces and invites herself inside. Sitting at John's kitchen table, she feels the comfort of being her usual self instead of Ms. Martin caught in a nightmare. "My principal is asking me to do something. Something you've already been hired to do."

"Ha," he responds without amusement. "They must have given up on me. I submitted my first report yesterday telling the Association I've found nothing incriminating. I said the whole assignment seems to be a waste of my time and their money. I should've known they wouldn't accept that as the final verdict."

"Apparently not. I guess they'll keep at it until somebody finds something. If I come up empty like you, I have a feeling, they'll use force to remove Monique and her renters. I suppose that means me, too. Bingham doesn't seem to mind asking me to eliminate my own apartment building. Where does he expect me to go?"

"I'm sure he doesn't care. You aren't important compared to whatever his agenda is."

Vanessa tells him about seeing the flash of camo. "You're a better investigator than I am," declares John. "In your short meeting, you came up with some real evidence. Do you think his secretary knows the kind of man she's working for?"

"I'm not sure. Beverly is super loyal to him, but I think she may be in love and blind about his real life."

"Too bad you and she aren't friends. Women like to confide in their bffs."

""Yeah...well. That's not going to happen."

John thinks a few minutes and then gets serious. "Okay. I know how you feel. That smarmy man makes you want to tell him to go stick his offer. But then he'll go on to maybe do something worse to push Monique out. Why don't you go along with his plan? Pretend to spy but don't give him anything that can matter. Maybe some fake news. In the meantime, you might find out more about who else is involved and how big this business is. I think they're likely to be careless what they talk about around you because you appear to be ignorant."

"Thanks," she says grimly.

"I said *appear*. You are on to them and will be soaking up everything. When the time is right, we'll go to the police."

Vanessa is grateful to hear him use the pronoun *we*. Still, she resents this intrusion into her career. She wants to concentrate on being a good teacher, a great teacher. But just as she's becoming immersed in the lessons for her high schoolers, she has to take on a whole other project.

"I'm not experienced at spy work. Are you suggesting I be a double agent?" She's read a few novels.

"Something like that. But this wouldn't be as risky."

"Well, I'm trained in education, not espionage. What can you tell me about what comes next?"

"You should get in writing what they want of you and how much you're going to get for your efforts. Will you get paid even if you learn nothing or only if you give them a lot of juicy material? And I'd ask for an advance, in case they try to skip out."

"Actually, getting money for this doesn't sound very tempting. I'd rather be a poor school teacher than a rich mole."

"I know how you feel, but you'll be able to protect our friends this way. The Association wants me out of here by tomorrow. They have no more reason to pay my rent."

"I don't want you to move! I'll be scared to death to be here without you."

"I really don't do much to keep you safe."

"That's okay. I feel like I can stand anything as long as you and I can talk about it."

"No problem there. We have cell phones. I hope I'm on your speed dial. I'll check in at least once a day, and I'll be available to you 24/7. Almost as good as being here."

"Not really. But if you're sure I should get mixed up in this, I'll tell them yes."

She's made a decision. Why doesn't Nessa feel better?

At ten o'clock that morning, she gets a text from David Bingham. *"Come to my office after bell. Don't chk with Bev."*

On her way down the hall, she pictures the flash of camouflage she saw through the crack in Bingham's closet door. This second visit to his office is a chance to be sure she wasn't hallucinating. Perhaps what she saw was a scarf or a hat with that pattern. Many people own those.

As expected, the door to his coat closet is closed. No more chances to get a peek. She'll have to see if she can arrange one. The principal opens with friendly banter.

"Ms. Martin. How are your classes going so far?"

"Fine," she answers. *I know that's not why you had me come in.*

"Glad to hear it," he says pleasantly, obviously thinking ahead to his next question. "I'm pleased you were able to make it this morning. My colleagues and I are very eager to know if you've decided to help the community by being an alert listener in your apartment building. Not that you aren't naturally alert. You know I'm referring to being particularly tuned in to incriminating background information about the people there. It's the kind of thing you'll recognize when you hear it."

"It doesn't sound very time consuming, so I'll try to do it," answers Nessa. "I'll need a written contract that states clearly what's expected, how I'll be compensated, and that I won't be implicated in any illegal goings on in the building. I'll want to remain uninvolved in whatever your business is with Lola and her friends. I'm an independent renter who can leave at any time."

"Oh, of course!" he answers hurriedly. "I'm grateful to you for making this commitment. Let me go speak to Beverly a minute. I'm sure she can prepare a satisfactory document while you wait. Will five thousand dollars for three weeks be suitable?" He smiles big, knowing his offer is very generous and that this beginning teacher isn't apt to refuse.

Nessa hesitates just long enough to appear to be weighing the wisdom of what she's about to sign. "I think that will be acceptable. Please be sure the dates of service are specified. Sometimes three weeks can turn into longer."

"You're a sharp young lady," replies Mr. Bingham. "That gives me confidence we're asking the right person. I'll be right back. Today's paper is there on the desk. Something to read while I'm gone."

Nessa can't believe her luck. She's alone in Bingham's office and only a couple of steps from his closet. She waits a minute, just in case he forgets something and comes back in. Finally she goes to the closet door and, praying it's unlocked, turns the knob. It swings outward. No camouflage is near the opening. It appears that whatever it was, is no longer in there. To be sure, she runs her hands over the three jackets in front of her. Apparently, the principal sometimes forgets to wear home his coat so has to bring a different one the next day. Over to the side of those is a plastic garment bag probably meant to hold something more valuable than everyday jackets. Inside is a suit. Understandable. But further over on the rod is a garment that looks like a jumpsuit. A one-piece heavy coverall made of camouflage duck. Nessa looks for only a moment to be sure she's seeing what she thinks she is, then zips the bag shut. She is stopped in her exit for a moment by something caught under the closet door. A closer look shows a single brown lady's shoe is lodged there. A good tug frees it so the door can be easily closed.

David Bingham enters just as Nessa is laying down the front page section of the Haven Herald. She's sure her eyes must register alarm, but the principal looks so pleased with himself, that her facial expression seems to be of no consequence.

"Here you go, Vanessa. Look it over, and if it meets your approval, just sign the two originals and leave one with Beverly. Don't hesitate to shoot me a text message if I've omitted any important points. If everything's in order, you can consider yourself on the job immediately."

"Thanks," she replies quickly. "Now I must get back before my classroom is full of students."

By the time she leaves his office, she feels like she's sold her soul to the devil. Beverly, at her post, looks like she has a comment, but holds her tongue. Vanessa has been wondering how much the lady knows about her boss's extracurricular activities. Quite a lot, evidently, if it was Bev who typed the agreement.

Five thousand dollars. She must keep reminding herself of the amount she'll be able to deposit to her account in three weeks. All she has to do is get chatty with the Fancy Tramp renters. That shouldn't be unpleasant since she likes them all and is sure they aren't hiding any dangerous secrets.

When it comes to delving into backstories and future plans of her fellow tenants at the apartment building, Nessa isn't as interested as she probably needs to be. She already knows enough to satisfy her own curiosity. Any queries beyond what they've already told her just don't seem appropriate. She prefers to get to know her friends gradually, to pace out the discoveries. That, she feels, is what makes getting acquainted fascinating. Just as she'd love to have more facts about John Harnden. She wouldn't have liked to receive a dossier on him when she first moved in. She looks forward to finding out new interesting tidbits each day.

Nessa reminds herself that her project for Bingham isn't to learn fascinating information about potential good friends. She's supposed to be digging for dirt. She needs to adopt the mindset of a scandal magazine reporter. What the Association wants her to uncover is something that would work for the cover of The National Inquirer. Something the average citizens of Haven will regard as reason to banish the newcomers from the town. If not to jail, most certainly to another part of the state. She wonders if the Association would resort to terrorizing Lola and company, making them run away of their own accord like Jodie did. Vanessa's new friends appear to be made of pretty sturdy stuff so Bingham will have his hands full.

Any way she looks at it, her job is a sleazy one. Even if there is scandal to be found, she isn't sure she can accept the Association's thirty pieces of silver.

16

From his office in Arbor City, John hears that Nessa has signed her boss's agreement. "I'll be glad to do anything I can to help you earn the five thousand. I know first-year teachers don't get big salaries."

The new collaborators conclude their first priority is to learn the original home of the Tramp's renters, to determine how they arrived. Someone must have been present when the group first came. The party John and Nessa witnessed on second floor confirmed the impression that the five assorted out-of-towners have always been a package. Monique seems to be a long-time resident, but it's unlikely the others hit town one by one and found the old mansion. They obviously were acquainted in a past life and, by prearrangement, must have shown up at the same time.

John and Nessa meet in front of a small white house which sits at the base of the steep rise that is topped by the unpainted Victorian rooming house. It is unlikely that any townspeople feel connected enough to that eyesore to refer to themselves as neighbors, but for purposes of investigation, this place will do. "These folks have a pretty good view of the apartments. If they were at home at the time, they probably witnessed the arrival of Lola and friends. Unless the little troop came on foot and approached from the woods in back. And why would they do that?"

"You don't have to help me with this, you know," Nessa reminds John. "You're off the case."

"Can't quit cold turkey. I'd just started to work up a curiosity about these people." Again, she's grateful to have a teammate to help with questioning. She realizes she looks young and unintimidating. She can't imagine anyone feeling obligated to divulge any information to her.

When I stand on their doorsteps, I'll feel like a young trick or treater. If I were them, I wouldn't tell me anything.

"Do people actually answer questions when a private eye asks?" Nessa wonders. "I mean you're not like a policeman who has the authority to arrest them."

"*Private investigator* sounds more official than it actually is. But most folks talk easier to me than to the police. I'm more like just another gossipy person, not somebody who can punish them for not cooperating. Thanks to TV, I seem more important than just some guy off the street, and in a certain few circumstances I can issue an arrest warrant. So can you."

At the white house, a middle-aged woman meets John and Nessa at the door which she opens just wide enough to stick her head through. "Can I help you?"

John speaks up. "Yes, Ma'am, I hope you can. We are conducting a private investigation and just thought you might have some answers for us."

"I didn't do anything wrong. And I don't know anybody who did." She starts to close the door.

"We know you didn't. We're not here to talk about a crime. I'm just curious about the house on the hill. Do you ever see what goes on up there?"

"I'm not a nosey neighbor. I barely look out my windows. What do you need to know?"

"Well, my friend and I were just chatting, and we got to wondering how the folks up at the Fancy Tramp got to Haven. There's been no sign of a moving van. We've never even seen a car parked out front."

"That's because I have it."

Nessa and John are stunned. They haven't expected to get their answer so easily. "You do? How did that happen? Are they friends of yours?"

"Oh, no. I only met the tall one. Named Lola or Lily or something like that. The van they came in was parked in the woods for a while. I could just see the back end sort of peeking out, which I thought was curious. And then one day she came by and asked me if I had room in my garage. Said she can pay $20 a month. I should've asked for more, but I can use even a little extra, so there it sits." The woman motions toward the sizable garage. I drive a two-door Cooper so I don't need much space for myself."

John tries not to sound too eager. "Interesting. Do you suppose we could take a look at the vehicle?"

The woman hesitates and twists the towel she's been holding. "Well...Lola, or whoever she is, told me not to mention it to anybody. Don't want her to get mad and quit paying me."

"We aren't trying to *take* the van. We just want to look. And we won't tell a soul. You can stay in the house so you won't be caught showing us. We're just a couple of harmless snoops."

"Well, okay, if you don't stay in there long. I have a few of my late husband's tools and other things I don't want to disappear."

"You're welcome to search us before we get back in our car," offers John with a good-natured grin.

It turns out Lola was wise to hide at least most of the big vehicle. Just a glance at it will tell anyone who cares to know exactly who its passengers were. Both sides of the van are painted in swirls of red and yellow with a picture of clown faces in the middle. Jaunty lettering spells out HAPPCO ENTERTAINMENT. It's the kind of automobile that plainly announces "The circus has come to town!" The most curious thing about it is that it's the only one. Circus wagons used to travel in caravans. How did Lola get one for her own use? John believes he's heard they travel by train these days. Maybe this vehicle is one that hasn't been used for several years. Perhaps it landed in a salvage yard, and the Fancy Tramp family saved it. The colorful little band may have no other connection to HAPPCO.

The doors to the van are locked, so John quickly snaps a couple of photos with his phone, and he and Nessa exit the garage. For the benefit of their hostess who is watching from her kitchen window, they both put their open hands in the air to show they are carrying no tools. John also gives the lady a thumbs-up thank-you.

"I hope you don't have to report the location of the van to the man who hired you," says Nessa. "The Association will use that information to justify putting Lola and her friends back out on the road. People these days are ready to believe clowns use vans to kidnap little children."

"I've technically been released by the Association. I have no obligation to tell them anything now." Then he grins at Nessa as if to say, *"Don't worry. I really don't want to help the Association close in on the circus folks. You and I are on the same side."*

This PI thing isn't such a hard job, Nessa decides. "Unless they're ordinary citizens who ran across it at the dump, Mr. Bingham made a good guess when he said our new friends came from a circus. They could very well be the clowns he's been so worried about. *Boy, will he be mad if he finds out they've successfully stayed hidden from his men for several months. Poor Bingham. It's so hard for him to stay ahead of all the odd people in this town.*

17

$\mathcal{N}$essa and the PI are sitting in a worn wicker lounger on the front porch, which overlooks the large down-hill lawn, now covered in leaves. They are contemplating the situation at the Fancy Tramp.

"This is such a pretty place," comments Nessa. "I wish there weren't any menacing men trying to spoil it."

"Yeah," agrees John. "Every time something beautiful exists, something evil wants to spoil it. That's the way it's been since the Garden of Eden."

"Are those the words of the former Reverend Smith?"

"Nah. Just the feelings of a dumb investigator." John seems to be seriously trying to analyze the situation in Haven. "You wonder why a guy like David Bingham can't be content with being a first-rate high school principal."

"Who knows? There's no way to understand somebody like him. He seems power hungry to me. He wants to control everyone who works with him, the students and even the townspeople. And he has such a nice face, good looking, friendly. I wonder if his family has any idea what a jerk he really is."

"They could be just like him," answers John.

Two people can be seen emerging from the woods in back of the house. "Looks like we have trespassers." But as the walkers come closer, Nessa and John see it's only Pike and a pretty blonde girl who must be the famous Melody.

"Are you guys enjoying the lovely fall weather?" asks Nessa. She's pleased to see Pike has followed her advice and asked his lady love to walk with him. So much nicer than riding in a car, especially if it has to be the flashy van hidden away in the neighbor's garage.

"Yeah. Hey you guys, this is Melody. My girlfriend from the store. Melody these are my good friends Pastor John Smith and Vanessa Martin who live here at the Fancy Tramp."

Nessa is proud of Pike for the gracious introductions. "So nice to meet you, Melody. Pike talks about you. Are the leaves in the woods getting too deep for walking?"

"Oh, no," says the girl, "it's nice in there. Except for the creepy watchers."

Nessa and John wait for Melody to elaborate, but she doesn't. "Should we know who the creepy watchers are?" asks John.

"I doubt if you do," says Melody. "They don't talk. They just seem to stand at attention with rifles or bats or some kind of weapons. I don't know if they'd use them, but it kind of ruins the walk when you see one of them up ahead, hiding in the trees like he's ready to jump at you. We just keep moving and try to ignore them."

"Good grief!" exclaims Nessa. "That sounds like the person who caused Lola to have an accident when I first came. Do the ones in the woods wear camouflage?"

"These do. And their eyes are covered with dark glasses. So it's hard to tell if they're people you know or not. That's the scariest part. You just don't know." Melody takes hold of Pike's arm for security.

"Guys who dress to keep from being seen are up to no good unless they're hunters, but no one can hunt inside city limits so the get-ups don't make much sense. Except for keeping the home owner from running them off. People don't expect hunters to be prowlers." John has been pretty disturbed by Melody's description. "Those men probably think the elderly women that own the Fancy Tramp won't give them any trouble."

Two or more miles of woods are part of Monique's property. She has the right to report trespassing. But John is pretty sure no one will care to follow up even if she does. "Maybe you two should walk in a public park just in case. Sounds like Monique's trees are infested with stalkers, and I doubt if anybody's going to chase them down."

"I don't think they're really stalkers. They could be my father's friends. Protecting me. They'd find me in a park, too." Melody's tone is resigned, like it's an old story.

John and Nessa are speechless. The poor girl seems to take for granted that dear old dad has friends with guns who may be tracking her every move. Nessa would love to ask if Daddy owns camouflage coveralls, but of course, she doesn't. After what she's learning about her boss, Nessa isn't keen to find out Melody's father also has connections to the Association. Everybody is someone to watch out for.

The pair make a striking couple, but Pike had better forget making any loving gestures toward Melody during their walks. Something tells Nessa that Daddy Dearest wouldn't approve of his lovely blonde daughter seeing a black man.

"I can give you a ride to Arbor City sometime," offers John. "That's where my office is. I know where all the good hiking trails are around there, and maybe your father's friends don't."

Pike brightens. "Hey, Mr. John! That'd be great. And while we're there, maybe we can visit Melody's sister. She could use some cheering up."

The situation is growing more and more interesting. Nessa comes right out and asks the girl, "Does your sister have family trouble or something?" She thinks perhaps her sister is older and married with children.

"No, Katrinka doesn't have a family of her own. She's nineteen, but she's still a child inside. Do you know the Maynard Home?"

John does, indeed, know of the Maynard Group Home. It's one of the few places in the state where mentally deficient young adults can live, with supervision. "Yes, I know Maynard. It's a good place. Has your sister always lived there?"

"Not at Maynard, but ever since she was four she's been in some kind of institution," Melody answers. "She couldn't assimilate at home. My dad has given up on her, but I like to stop in. She always looks like she recognizes me, and she can say '*Mel*'. It's just hard for me to find a way to Arbor City since I don't have a car. I've biked there a few times."

"Mel says Katrinka likes to laugh," says Pike. It's so typical of him to be excited by that fact. According to his thinking, if a person can laugh, they have some quality of life.

"Oh, yes," says Melody with a smile. "She laughs at the doll I gave her."

"Then I'll visit her and make her laugh even more. I'm good at it." Pike tells his girlfriend.

"That will be wonderful," Melody answers, giving Pike a look of adoration. "I'll tell the administrators what you want to do. They'll have to okay it, but I'm sure they will. There isn't enough laughter in that home."

After the young couple have moved on, Nessa continues the thought. *Even though it houses clowns, there aren't many laughs in the Fancy Tramp lately either.*

A clown is an angel with a red nose - Syke

18

$\mathcal{A}$ timid tap on her door stops Nessa before she can lie down for her Sunday afternoon nap. It isn't that she's so sleepy. It's a luxury she enjoys, a time for herself, an hour of escape from responsibilities and problems. School work waits for the evening. Besides, the weather is gloomy, cloudy and wet. The raindrops on the porch roof are a lullaby. For a short time. A knock on her door isn't surprising.

"Nessa!" She enjoys Pike's company, but he's starting to appear everywhere and not at the most convenient times. She opens the door, trying to look as groggy as possible.

"Are you busy? I need a ride to Arbor City. I can pay for the gas when I get money on Friday."

The young man has a way of making many things sound like emergencies. "Is it urgent?" she asks to be sure she doesn't give away her free afternoon too easily.

She motions him inside for what she knows will be a lengthy explanation. "Yeah, it's urgent. Melody got permission for me to do a clown act at her sister's home. A friend from work said he'd drive me, but now he can't. I think the kids are probably looking forward to it, and I hate to disappoint them. I could ask Lola about using the van, but she told us to pretend it doesn't exist. She doesn't want anybody to see it. So that leaves you, but that's okay because I think you'd really like to meet

Trink. She's smarter than people think. Like me." And he grins the grin which will ultimately make Nessa agree to anything.

She resists the temptation to give him a lecture on waiting until the last minute to ask for favors. Nessa can understand the problems when you depend on someone else. And his intentions are very good ones. She notices he's carrying his duffle bag which today, she assumes, holds his important props. "Well, okay, but only if you let me watch what you do. I haven't really seen a clown act that I can remember except on TV. My mom would never have taken me to a circus because she has a phobia."

"Oh, too bad. I'd love to have you watch. It's pretty short. Just don't tell anybody about it. Lola doesn't want many people to know what we do on the side."

That is how Nessa finds herself entering the Maynard Home on a Sunday afternoon with Pike and being met by four girls in wheelchairs. Pike does the introductions. "My real name is Michael, but today I'm going to pretend I'm Juggles. This is my friend Nessa. We've come to make you laugh." His words are simple and to the point, enough to get the fun started. The girls are definitely in a cheery mood.

"Is one of you named Katrinka?" A heavyset girl wearing a red sweater raises her hand and gives a yelp.

Pike goes to her and takes hold of her hand. "I'm a friend of your sister Mel." That was Trinka's cue to give a hug. The other girls, not wanting to be left out, insist on hugs as well. Nessa tries to blend into a huddle of adults on the sidelines. Her last-minute idea is to take out her cell phone and film the visit. She won't show anyone except maybe her mom who will probably throw the phone across the room.

A young woman who seems to be in charge of the event says brightly, "Welcome to our home! We can't wait to see your show. I have to ask, can you do what you do without putting on makeup? It's possible some of the residents will be frightened.

They don't always react well to people wearing heavy makeup or masks. To them the unknown can be scary."

Pike is polite but firm. "I'm sorry. My clown personality is named Juggles. I don't feel like Juggles unless I'm in makeup. That's just the way it works. But what I can do is put the makeup on while the residents watch. It kinda makes them feel better when they understand there isn't something strange about my face or that I'm not trying to hide anything."

The lady, whose nametag reads MEG, smiles. "That sounds like it might work. It's just a matter of building trust, I guess. I'll get them arranged in their places, and then you can start. I've just asked the higher functioning ones for this first time."

Nessa watches, fascinated, while Pike opens his bag and pulls out different articles of clothing – big shoes, baggy striped pants, a bow tie and a polka dot jacket. The illusion is that the small bag has no bottom. The items just kept coming. He exclaims and acts surprised at each one and puts it on over his street clothes. Then he sits in a chair facing the residents and looks into an imaginary mirror. Even though his hair always shoots out in all directions, he now produces a neon green wig that is even wilder. He passes the wig around so the residents can pet it, then plops it on his head. Even to Nessa, he's looking more and more like somebody besides Pike.

Taking a large pouch from his bag, he puts on the clown makeup while pretending to be able to see himself in the mirror. Juggles is apparently not a total white-face. When his look is complete, the white only appears around his eyes and mouth, but his eyebrows and smile are vividly colored and their shapes are exaggerated but pleasant. The cherry that tops off this delicious character is a round red ball. He hands it to Katrinka and helps her fit it down over his nose. She squeals in delight. Nessa is glad her mother isn't here. Pike has transformed himself. The result is both humorous and mystifying. To his credit, the makeup he's applied is not designed for a scary face but for a happy one. From the moment he "becomes" Juggles, he utters no sounds. All communication is in pantomime. Talking with gestures is nothing foreign to this audience, some of whom are deaf.

The teens, including Katrinka, are mesmerized. The staff, too, relax and get into the spirit of the entertainment. Juggles does, indeed juggle, as Nessa saw during Lola's birthday party. He also does magic tricks and physical comedy. When he tries to run from place to place, he always stumbles and has to catch himself which makes his audience laugh with glee. Sometimes he keeps juggling at the same time he's stumbling. Nessa, knowing how coordinated the young man always is as himself, finds those bits funniest of all.

After a manageable fifteen minutes, Juggles reverses his disguise, morphing back into Pike, his bag again full of all things magic. He even takes a wet wipe to his face. The young people are thrilled to see the familiar features of Pike emerge and clap to show their appreciation. More thank-yous and many hugs later he and Nessa are starting toward her car. "Thanks Pike!" says the girl in the red sweater with some difficulty. A closer look at her face shows she strongly resembles Melody.

"They're twins but Mr. Bingham does tell anyone," Pike offers under his breath to.

Pike's simple statement was a startling announcement to Nessa. She hasn't known Melody is the daughter of David Bingham or that Katrinka is her twin. Many things are making sense now.

"Doing that show was so sweet of you. You're really a good guy. And a talented one. Melody's dad should've been here."

"I'm glad he wasn't. Trink wouldn't have had any fun."

I remain just one thing and one thing only, and that is a clown. It places me on a far greater plain than any Politian. – Charlie Chaplin

19

Monday on her way into the school building, Nessa resists the urge to stop by Mr. Bingham's office and report, "I met your daughter Katrinka this weekend! She's a sweetie and she loved meeting Juggles the clown!" No, that's the way one would greet a normal boss and father. She simply says a few quick words to colleagues who are themselves scurrying to get to their rooms and appear busy. Nessa has noticed a couple of young HHS teachers she'd probably enjoy knowing, but it is understood that loitering to visit is frowned on in this perfect establishment.

Startled, Nessa looks up from her computer to see the principal walking into her room. For some reason, she's been operating under the illusion he is attached to his office, not able to wander into other parts of the building. How awful that she'll now have to look for him around every corner. "Good morning!" she forces herself to say. She's reasonably certain Bingham isn't stopping by to inquire about her classes, but she tries to pretend.

The man looks around, as if he expects to find something amiss. He even picks a book up off her desk and thumbs through it as though to be sure it's actually what the cover says it is. "I'm just making my weekly rounds to see how things are going. I like to keep my fingers on the pulse of the school. That way I know if problems are likely to arise before they do. Anything you need to ask me?"

Nessa can't think of a thing she wants to hear from him. She's still looking for an answer for Pike's reading problem, but she knows by now Bingham has no interest in anyone's learning disabilities.

"I keep meaning to give you my out-of-bounds list. I'll do that soon," he states in a relaxed manner.

Nessa is unconsciously straightening her desk. Every English teacher she's ever known had a messy desk. She swore she'd be different, but alas, it's already happened. "Out-of-bounds for what?" she asks, not really wanting to know his answer.

"Over the summer, I compiled a list of the topics that don't fit into our agenda. You may be disappointed in some of them, but once you've given yourself over to Perfection at all Costs, you'll understand my reasons. Students will consult the list before settling on a subject for an essay or a speech. We can't have them wasting their time promoting ideas that aren't acceptable. Civil rights for example." Nessa is sure she can guess the other out-of-bounds topics. It looks like she and the principal are sure to have conflicts throughout the year. No surprise there.

He finally plants himself in front of her desk where he can peer down at her and blurts out what she's certain he's really here for. "How is your investigation at the Fancy Tramp coming along? Have you uncovered anything I should know?" The question is a casual one, but his eyes convey desperation. He'd like to be able to control her answer. Unfortunately for him, he cannot.

"No. Nothing." It's true. Except for locating the circus van, which she's determined not to mention, she knows no more about her friends than she did when she was tapped by her principal to be a spy.

"Maybe you aren't putting forth enough effort." He continues to smile even though that expression seems out of place. He reminds her of Juggles with a wide grin painted on his face. *And the public thinks clowns are the only ones with things to hide.*

"Oh, I'm trying. I have to be a little subtle. Otherwise, everyone will clam up and not tell me anything." *Bingham is much too impatient.*

"I hired a professional investigator who messed around and wasted our money, and now it seems like you might not be much better. Something tells me, I'm going to have to take matters into my own hands and *force* those people out." He's still smiling.

"I don't think one citizen can force another to move, Mr. Bingham. Not unless the person is doing something to interfere with his rights. You'd have to take them to court. It would be expensive. I doubt you can do it without a high-priced lawyer." Nessa had a good government teacher in high school.

"Just watch me, darlin'. There are ways to do anything. And some of us don't have to consult attorneys. No one in this town will even blink an eye if those weird tenants suddenly go missing."

"*I* will! They're fine people. Good neighbors. As far as I've been able to find out, your Association isn't something anyone's even heard of. In fact, most folks don't think you personally have any authority at all except here at school." Nessa's intentions to remain respectful are out the window.

She forces her voice to remain cheerful, but Mr. Bingham is smart enough to know when he's being insulted.

"Those of us who are blessed with superior intelligence and foresight must lead. The Association will put Haven on the map. In fact, you might as well know, I'm planning to run for Mayor next election. My Association associates know they'll naturally have prominent positions in the local government. We'll make Haven the ideal place to live and work," he says smugly.

"That's great," replies Nessa. "And I'm sure the fine tenants at the Happy Tramp will continue to make outstanding contributions to that effort."

"Those *fine* people you're defending include a mindless man who's shown himself to be dangerous, an unemployable obese woman who's putting a strain on the first floor ceiling of an historical building, and an uneducated *colored* person who has no place in this all-white community. There are filthy cats living in the place and the only janitorial staff is an ancient woman who is incapable of even keeping herself clean let alone a three-story house. The property is going to wrack and ruin, and I won't watch it happen." His face has gotten progressively redder during his rant. The smile is fading.

It's clear Bingham and his cronies have done a lot of investigating on their own. She can't imagine what additional facts he expects her to come up with.

"No thanks to you, I'm now aware that these people are escaped clowns from the circus," he continues.

"Not *escaped* ones." He makes it sound like they engineered a breakout from a locked facility. They simply left. In the night.

"I believe I've told you that this city has had bad experiences with clowns. It was hard getting that stopped, and no one wants a repeat."

"You don't have to worry, Mr. Bingham. The folks at the Fancy Tramp are *former* clowns, real ones. The pranksters were mostly clueless kids. I face those every day."

"You speak of them like they're harmless, but did you have any experience with those who terrorized the country in 2015? Let me assure you, you wouldn't treat the matter so casually if you had."

Nessa keeps her voice steady. "No, I didn't run into any then, but I read the papers. I know what went on. We can't spend forever holding it against the legitimate ones in that profession."

"Once terrorists, always terrorists," says the man who currently controls an army of thugs spreading fear among the townspeople. "I'm going to eliminate anyone who has at any time caused trouble in Haven."

She can't let him think she's intimidated by his bluster. "What puzzles me is why you care so much. You aren't mayor yet and may never be. You don't own the Tramp property or live near it. And you have a whole high school to run. Maybe you ought to leave any evictions up to law enforcement people."

"Oh, law enforcement around here are getting used to doing as I tell them. The current mayor is ineffective so they recognize when a man with vision steps in. The councilmen are eager to get on board."

Taking a cue from Bingham, she continues to smile. She knows she's out of line. A first-year teacher doesn't call out her superior. Ordinarily. But it's rare that any teacher has to deal with an administrator who shows signs of being dangerously unbalanced. For the first time, Vanessa admits to herself what she really suspects. She's working for a madman. No one will ever believe her, least of all his secretary. "The way I heard it, the Fancy Tramp sat empty for many years before Monique bought it. Where was the Association then? They could've bought it fair and square."

"We didn't exist. We were organized after the house on the hill was purchased. Otherwise, it would have been our headquarters from our beginning. And everything in it."

Nessa could point out that they are late to the game and must concede the house belongs to Monique. But after a bit, she decides no good can come of further argument with Mr. Bingham. "I really do have to get back to work. I hope you'll excuse me. You can expect me to try harder this week to learn about my friends. I'll find anything there is to find." Having assured her boss, she presses the space bar to bring her computer back to life.

The principal closes their meeting with, "You've been too personally involved with those misfits. I need to move forward. It's time for you to get serious about your assignment, or I'll have to end our business arrangement. I've tried handling this in a civilized manner, but you're causing me to consider force." He takes his plastered-on smile and exits, thinking he's just had the last word.

Actually, his threats *have* given Nessa pause. She's wondering how long before she personally becomes the object of his pressures. How long before he decides for sure to treat her as the enemy instead of a member of his team?

If Bingham dismisses her, he'll never give her a good recommendation. What will she do for a living if she has to give up on teaching? *I know how the clowns must feel.*

20

Driving home after school, Nessa's mind is still whirling from her disagreeable morning encounter with Mr. Bingham. She knows she said too much. She may have subconsciously been trying to get out of the deal she recently signed. Nevertheless, in the back of her mind all day she's been scolding herself. *I have to learn to control my mouth. Otherwise, I'm going to bring disaster on everybody around here that I care about.*

She has become increasingly conscious that, while she's had Bingham's assignment in the back of her mind, her real motivation is toward something different. She is hoping to prove beyond a doubt that the people she lives with do *not* have big secrets in their backgrounds. She would love to know for sure they have never been involved in anything illegal.

Her thoughts return to the present when she drives into her space in front of the mansion. She finds herself parked beside a patrol car. She hopes the police presence doesn't mean there's been an accident in the house. Surely Bingham hasn't had time yet to cook up some disaster to get back at her for her smart comments. Unless he reached the end of his patience and sent people with guns to accomplish his ends. She debates whether to go inside to help her friends face the music or stay out of it. Convinced her temper has brought on some of their problems, she finally opts to go inside and see what she can do to help smooth things over.

She tells herself it's her home now so there's no reason to hold back from entering. *They're probably talking in another part of the house so I won't be able to hear anything, but I might need to step in if they try to take one of the tenants away or something.* Lola is standing just inside the front door, listening intently to what the officer is saying. She is wearing a bright yellow gauzy scarf tied in a bow on top of her head. It gives her a slightly dotty look. The woman is careful to appear conservative when on the street, but in the house, she reverts to her natural taste for the outlandish – haute couture for clowns. The policeman probably isn't impressed.

Nessa takes her time removing her shoes, slipping off her jacket, and hanging it on a peg.

"...so we just need to know where you folks came from. For our records. It isn't legal to allow just anyone to set up a business in town, and somehow we have neglected to check you out. How long have you been here already? A year?"

"Not quite," answers Lola in a shaky voice. "The house is paid for, and none of us has escaped from prison or an asylum or anywhere. I can't think there's any problem. Most towns___"

"Haven is not *most towns* Ms. Lang. We have a unique set of expectations for anyone we allow into our city limits. It's just a matter of passing the test. I'm sure you understand."

Vanessa knows she should stay quiet and go to her apartment, but she simply isn't the type of person to hold back when she has a question. "Officer, I couldn't help overhearing what you've been telling the manager. It surprises me, because I moved to town only weeks ago to teach your impressionable

117

youth, and I wasn't given a test. How is it that I escaped that requirement?"

"Ms. Martin," the policeman responded in a loud, firm voice, "You may not think you took a test but you did, even before you arrived in Haven. The decision had been made regarding your suitability from your written employment application and our investigation before you met Mr. Bingham. The others in this ... *establishment* have received no such screening." He turns away from Nessa then, dismissing her. "Lola Lang, I'm hereby issuing a summons for you and the owner of the house, a Monique Dubois, to come down to the station tomorrow at 10:00 a.m. to answer some questions."

"Oh!" Lola exclaims, and Nessa feels sorry for the lady. She has done nothing to feel guilty about but is being treated like a criminal. Without much doubt, she's going to be found unfit for her position at this wreck of a rooming house. *Doesn't the police force in Haven have anything else to do but harass a harmless woman in a yellow hair ribbon and floppy slippers?*

Lola has no choice but to promise to appear. Nessa will lend moral support, but she can't take the test for her. She doubts it would help if she could. Disaster appears to be a foregone conclusion.

"I hope I can remember my name," Lola worries. It's actually Lolanna Benedetti, but I haven't even heard it in a long time. Lola Bennet is what I use. That probably makes me seem like I'm trying to hide my identity.

"I doubt they even figure that out. Just skip the real name," Nessa tells her. She doesn't have much confidence in the local cops to get at the truth, and she knows the facts about Lola's name are the kind of thing Bingham wants her to report.

She loses no time calling John. "Lola is distraught! The Haven police just now left the house."

"What were they after?" he asks.

"It felt like Gestapo. I get the impression our men in uniform are part of the Association. They're basically set on an eviction. And they don't seem to need a legitimate reason. We have to help Lola and Monique!"

Clowns and elephants are the pegs on which the circus is hung."
P.T. Barnum

Clown Alley

"Did you hear on the news about HAPPCO?" Lola asks the small gathering in Ms. Sofie's front room. Since newspapers are luxuries and TV news is of little interest, each person shakes his head *no*. "They're going to be forced to close before long."

One or two issue audible gasps. One person says, "Oh, no. Is it because of us?"

"I don't think we're the only reason. Once Ringling Brothers threw in the towel, it started a chain reaction. Circuses can't afford to keep going. Attendance is down, mostly because of the times. People have too many kinds of entertainment now. The circus seems slow and tame. Also there's been some bad publicity about animal cruelty. Especially to the elephants."

"HAPPCO doesn't have any of that! Of course, we haven't had elephants since Maybelle died. The animals that are still there live like people."

"Just the same, animal rights folks think keeping creatures tied up is wrong. Our circus was never the same without my friend Maybelle. She seemed like a very happy animal to me. She loved performing. Just like we did."

"Seems like it might as well close if there aren't any wild animals or clowns. But guess I'm prejudiced."

"I think what's been missing is better oversight. People in charge of seeing that no animals or performers are mistreated."

"Hiring more staff would take more money. And that's what the circus doesn't have."

"I wish there was something we could do to help. What do you think?" Lola asks. "Should we go back? Maybe the distrust of white faces has died down. The haters have probably moved on. Maybe we can pick up where we left off and help boost attendance."

"I don't know. It's probably too late. Once you lose your audience, they find other places to go. We might get back to the big top just in time to move again."

"Life is pretty good here, and what would Monique do for renters? She rescued us. How can we thank her by just taking off and leaving her with a nearly empty apartment building?"

Pike is worried. "I hate to go now. Nessa promised to help me read Harry Potter, and I can't leave Melody!"

"I've met someone myself. And I like being the school janitor. I'm able to make people around there smile without wearing grease paint."

"I'm pretty overweight now for keeping up my act. It's hard to bend and stretch. And I don't want to leave this area before I know for sure Moe isn't still outside looking for me."

All the protests come at once, overlapping. "Okay! Okay!" Lola concedes. "It was just an idea. If we were even considering it, I'd want to get the van out of storage and have the oil and tires checked before winter. Circus season won't start for a few months. Maybe I can get hold of the administrators of HAPPCO and find out how the situation stands. I should be in a position to wrangle a pretty big raise for us if you all change your minds, since it sounds like we've been missed. Except the circus is temporarily broke. And my immediate problem is that I have to pass some kind of test tomorrow or we'll probably get a police escort to the nearest jail."

"What test are you talking about?" "Who's giving it?" "Do we have to take it, too?" The questions are coming fast, and Lola doesn't have answers.

"A policeman was here today and said we didn't get vetted when we first came to town. Apparently, Haven has some pretty strict entrance requirements. I had the feeling the officer was making them up at the time, just for us. They are going to try to trap Monique and me into saying the wrong thing. I'm sure *whatever* we say will be the wrong thing."

"Well, in my opinion, there're two facts you have to be sure you *don't* give out. That we're professional clowns and that we came from the circus. We all have to accept the fact no one except the elderly and some of the kids want clowns around anymore."

"Then I'll have to lie," Lola says dejectedly. "I don't think I ever have, but I know they're going to ask where we came from, and I think they already suspect the truth. What do I tell them?"

Ms. Sofie offers an answer. "We used to be entertainers, but the company we were with was shutting down so we had to find other jobs. It's all how you tell the story. Just avoid the C words no matter what. Don't mention *the circus,* and remember that any hint of *clowns* would sign our eviction notice. The whole town may have coulrophobia."

21

Lola and Monique are driving down the hill in Monique's ancient Ford Fairlane. Lola appreciates her cousin's willingness to accompany her to the station house. Monique, after all, is a long-time citizen of Haven, and she was never required to take an entrance exam. It's running a business the Association is apparently worried about. Lola realizes she's lived a major portion of her life on the outskirts of reality, but the idea of having to qualify to live in a sleepy little town seems like a preposterous idea. What about the criminal elements in places like San Francisco? Different cities must want different kinds of people.

Monique, it turns out at the station, doesn't get to go into the cubbyhole with Lola. She just gives her a hug and says to tell the truth. "You have nothing to hide, my dear," is her final advice.

The questionnaire is short and to the point. 1. Where was your last place of residence? 2. Why did you leave? 3. How many people came with you? 4. Why did you choose to relocate in Haven? 5. Are you financially able to care for yourself and not be a burden to the town? Unless they are trick questions, there are none that give Lola any trouble.

Avoiding the C words is easy. Monique's last place of residence was Manly, OH. Taking Sofie's advice, she explains she was forced to leave when her job with an independent company was eliminated. Four people came with her. Gordon Harcroft, Lionel Downs, Michael Pikeston, and Sofie Potter. She chose Haven because it wasn't a long trip and because she has a cousin, Monique Dubois, who's lived here for forty years and owns a large house. Lola is working as an apartment manager and gets her lodging and a reasonable salary that covers her needs. Her companions are employed as well. Lionel is a school janitor, Michael is a checkout boy, and she can truthfully say that Sofie knits cat cozies and sells them online under her own brand, Feline Fashions. Gordon gets disability payments, but otherwise, none of them is on welfare nor do they owe anyone in town any money. She signs her name to attest to the truth of her answers.

Lola hands the paper to the clerk just inside the front entrance. "The sergeant will be in touch very soon regarding your score," the woman says formally. Lola and Monique leave the building.

"Maybe we should go home and pack," says Lola. "But if I'm the most dangerous person who's ever applied to live here, this little city is a safer place than it seems."

Monique is totally baffled. "My brother used to work for the Haven police, and he never mentioned any vetting practice. The Association must be finding all kinds of ways to intimidate folks. I'm sure I'd never get accepted if I had to apply today. My name sounds too foreign."

The apartment manager answers the doorbell an hour later to find a friendly police officer standing before her. "I came by in person to let you know the committee found no disqualifying information in your test answers."

Lola breathes a sigh of relief. Maybe now they can all live in peace.

"*However,*" he continues, "there remains the fact that the Fancy Tramp is an eyesore in the town. Its ramshackle condition makes it unsightly, even unsafe, and since it overlooks the city, it's of major concern when it comes to tourism. There will need to be considerable money spent to bring the apartment building up to code. Do you think your landlady is prepared to do that?"

Lola is speechless. What tourism? This "ramshackle" condition didn't just now happen. Why wasn't Monique told about the problems when she first bought the place and opened the business?

"You weren't informed sooner because the building department hadn't yet conducted its inspection. Several properties will be receiving notice about improvements that must be made. In the case of the Fancy Tramp, the list is long. Monique has two choices. To make the needed repairs and upgrades or to sell the building at a salvage price to The Association who are prepared to take over the restoration and turn it into the new town hall."

The apartment manager's face crumbles. She has no comeback to these unreasonable demands. The city council, or whomever is calling the shots, knows very well Monique can't afford the improvements on their list. In fact, she's certain they'll make *sure* she can't. The whole ultimatum is very unfair, but what can they do? Certainly not call the police.

"I'll relay your words to Monique," says Lola sullenly. She's tempted to tell the man what she thinks of his stupid orders, but suspects he's only a messenger and doesn't deserve her wrath.

"I'll mail you the list of changes that need to be made," the man goes on almost apologetically. "You'll have a week to decide which route to take. If choosing to stay and fix, I must tell you that our banks are very reluctant to issue building loans to businesses who don't show sufficient potential. I wouldn't count on getting one. If you can find the money somewhere else, you'll have six months to get the work completed. Good day."

Lola is stunned by the man's announcement. She's still reeling from the news when Nessa calls during her lunch break. "I know it needs a few repairs. And it really needs to be painted," she admits. "It's just that it's so big. It would take a lot of paint. We're all too old to climb up high and do the job ourselves, and painters charge a lot. I hate to tell Monique. I know she wants to fix the place up, but she was hoping to save for a while before she starts."

Nessa sympathizes although she can't help but understand the town's opinion about the house's condition, especially since it's being offered as apartments. "Maybe between Pike and Lionel and John and me, we can get it done," she suggests without much conviction. None of them have many free hours. "Do you have any other friends?"

"We did. There was a whole community of them, but we've pretty much cut ties. I'm sure we're on our own. And I don't think Monique has any money left. She got a good deal on the house, but she had to add kitchens, bathrooms and even walls to turn it into apartments. To be truthful, I think she bit off more than she could chew. Old houses can be money pits."

"Well, let's wait and see what all is on the list they send you. Then we'll figure out something." Nessa knows the Fancy Tramp and its expenses aren't her problem. She can likely find another place to rent even if it's in Arbor City. But she'd feel awful watching her new friends lose everything and be put out on the street.

When Nessa arrives home after school, she encounters Lola and Monique who are sitting on the wicker love seat out front, huddled together pouring over a piece of paper. "Hi!" Nessa greets them. "Are you ladies looking at dirty pictures or something?" The idea is almost too preposterous to be funny, but she's never witnessed such rapt concentration.

"We're reading the Directives for Continued Ownership. Have you ever heard of such a document?" Monique asks. "It's from the Citizens for Haven Committee. This town has more organizations."

Nessa agrees, but isn't surprised. In fact, she expected the Directives to be longer than one page. She almost hates to read it. "They probably want you to paint the place, right?"

Lola is indignant. "And that's not all!" She turns the document around for Nessa to get a good look. The list is single-spaced and covers the page with three columns. "We can't even afford number 1!"

Vanessa feels their despair. The good ladies would be willing to go along with the town's demands, but this is a treatise designed to make compliance impossible. Besides a five-color paint job, they're being told to install all new windows (the house must have at least fifty), acquire insulation, replace the roof, rebuild the porch, pave the driveway, and the list goes on. To be honest, every one of the tasks needs doing, but not in six months. And most of the items aren't necessary to keep the property from being an eye sore. The paint alone would make a huge difference along with the replacement of several pieces of wood siding and maybe the front steps.

Nessa would give anything to be rich. "Do you all have any wealthy friends?" she asks hopefully. The three women just stare at her like she's speaking a foreign tongue. "Guess not."

The following four days are a marathon of worry. Nessa spends every free moment consulting the town newspaper and asking people at school about alternative places to rent. She's asking for her fellow tenants as well as for herself. Nothing has been promised Monique as far as the city purchasing the mansion. Naturally, the Association will steal it in the end, since the poor woman will be forced into selling at any price.

If such a take-over happens, Nessa is convinced the same long list of improvements will not be required of the Association before they can make it *their* headquarters. Of course, they're sure to have well-off members who'll be eager to modernize the place, make it look dignified and important. She's willing to bet that being true to its time period and personality will be of no consideration. As far as she knows, most of the movers in that organization are men, men who wear camouflage. Their tastes probably don't run to Victorian. The Fancy Tramp will be obliterated as thoroughly as if it were burned down.

During her one study hall, Nessa runs over ideas for raising great sums of money. As her extra teaching assignments include being leader of the basketball cheerleaders, she's going to need to develop some marketing skills, but the Fancy Tramp's lack of funds isn't technically her problem and probably shouldn't be consuming her prep time. Refurbishing a three-story building is not on the same level as buying new pom poms. In fact, it's a pretty impossible goal when the named project will directly benefit so few people. She knows no one who can offer man power. Unless she comes up with a creative approach, her students aren't going to be interested. And what could they do anyway? It will take profits from more than candy bar sales and car washes to make a difference for Monique.

Even rounding up free labor would be hard since Nessa's new in town and knows no one who might have construction experience. Her acquaintances are frighteningly unskilled. It's possible to *learn* to paint, install insulation, etc., but not within the time constraints they've been given.

For the first time since school started, Cotton stops in the English room during school hours. Considering her recent depression, he's a sight for sore eyes. "Hi there! How are you holding up?" he asks with a smile.

"If you're asking about my classes, I'm great. If you're asking about my apartment situation, I'm stressed."

"Monique showed me the list the town council gave her. I think she hopes I can do it all."

Nessa smiles sadly. "I'm sure you could if you had endless time and didn't have to hold down your job here. Any other ideas?"

"Not really. I know people who could help, but they'd want to be paid. They'd have to take time off from their other jobs to work here so you couldn't blame them."

"I know. I've been trying to think of any rich people I know in Chicago. I'll look online. Maybe set up a Go Fund Me page."

"That'd be a great idea. Lots of people in our profession would be happy to kick in, but the way things are going with the circuses, none of them have money to give."

Everything comes down to money. "Your rent isn't too bad, is it, Cotton?"

"It was reasonable when I first moved in, but I think somebody from the town council talked to the landlord because it went up last month. I'm going to have to move back to the Tramp. Maybe I've been using too much water or something."

"Oh, Cotton, I don't think you've done anything wrong."
Except be a clown.

22

For once, Vanessa gets to leave school at 3:30. On Fridays, teachers are exempt from staying an extra half hour to be available for students. Because of the stress of the ultimatum facing her apartment, it has been a tiring week. She almost beats the last teen into the hallway after the bell.

"Ms. Martin!" *You might know.* Beverly has something to say. Doesn't the woman ever leave the building? She can't be married. Or have any friends or family. Maybe she has a pull-out cot under her desk.

"I...er...can't really stay late today. I have an appointment," Nessa lies. She isn't in the mood for any more scoldings, bribes, or additional jobs.

"This will just take a minute," the woman says, her tone holding urgency. What has happened to the snippy receptionist who's been annoying Nessa every day?

She goes on. "I just noticed something, and it frightened me. I feel like I should tell someone."

That statement gives Nessa flashbacks to that first phone call warning her about the Fancy Tramp. "I'm not sure you should be telling *me*. Maybe the superintendent. Or the counselor. "

"I feel like telling *you*," the woman states firmly. "You might know what it means."

"Okay, we'll see. Come on back to my room where no one will hear us."

It's a baffling turn of events to be sought out by Beverly for advice. At the moment, Nessa feels like her well of answers is completely dry. Miss Birch sits in one of the student desks, facing Nessa. The hands holding her pen are shaking. Knowing there have been no catastrophes reported this afternoon, Nessa suspects she's witnessing a case of like niece/ like aunt. Beverly and Jodi are both easily traumatized. She sits quietly, waiting for the secretary to gain her composure.

"I was ready to leave school on time today, but at the last minute I remembered I hadn't straightened up David's office." Nessa recognizes Mr. Bingham's first name – which no one ever uses. "I always do that. Sometimes he gets so busy during the day and maybe has to leave early, and he just doesn't get things put away. So I do it. I like to help him as much as I can." Nessa resists the urge to hurry the story along. *Patience pays.*

"Well, I was making the rounds of his room tucking little things into their places, straightening piles of papers, and so forth. I never know what I'll run across. I mean, once I found a lady's shoe – a brown one ----just lying outside his closet. But he knows I'm very discreet. I simply picked it up and placed it on the shelf above his coats and never mentioned it."

"*Beverly, you're a sweetheart.*" Vanessa has thought a lot about that shoe. Even if finding it says nothing except that the principal must attack women on their bikes and keep their shoes for souvenirs.

"I was putting some pencils away and I opened his middle desk drawer without thinking – it's usually locked – and lying right there in front of my eyes was a gun. Mr. Bingham has a gun! At school! It isn't a long one like some men use for hunting. It's a short one like they use on crime shows." She stops and waits for Nessa's reaction.

"Wow," was all the teacher can come up with. She isn't as amazed as Bev expects her to be, just because she's been growing continually more suspicious of her supervisor. "What did you do?"

"I closed the drawer, of course! As quickly as I could. But I just couldn't believe what I'd seen. I mean, we have a strict, no tolerance policy about guns. It specifically includes administrators. How can David ignore that? He's the one who wrote it!"

Nessa has her own opinions about Mr. David Bingham's integrity, but she puts them aside. "He must have a very good reason. Perhaps he confiscated it from a student and is holding it to return to the parents when he expels the kid. Maybe Mr. Bingham himself has been threatened lately and feels he has to have protection."

"The students may wish they had protection, too, but guns are simply not the answer. I have to believe David agrees with me on that point. We've talked so often about making sure there will be no violence in this high school. It's part of his PP!"

"PP?" Nessa tries not to smile. Beverly is obviously quite serious, but it sounds like she's talking about her boss's urine.

"His Perfect Plan! Haven't you heard about it?"

"Uh ... no. He hasn't used that exact term. Perfect Plan for what?"

"The Perfect People who'll make up the Perfect high school in the Perfect town. His vision is positively inspired. I think he's been Chosen, and I'm so honored he's letting me be part of it all!"

What a bunch of mumbo-jumbo. I could sell this woman a thousand acres of swamp land. Nessa is still wishing to get away before 4:00. She can't wait to start searching for a different apartment. She considers telling Beverly her intentions but stops herself. It would please the woman too much. Instead, she shows interest in the secretary's tale about her boss.

"Does Mr. B. know you come in his room after he leaves for the day? Would he expect you to find the gun?" He could have a warped reason for trying to scare her or simply to make her sorry for being in his office.

"Oh, no. If I told him all the things I do for him, it would be like I was asking for thanks. I like to unselfishly give my services to such a brilliant man. He has no idea how I feel."

"Right. Well, don't mention anything about the gun. If it's left over from an incident today, it should be gone by tomorrow. Why don't you just wait and see if it doesn't take care of itself before we get too worried?" *Meanwhile, I'll find out if the darn thing is meant to be used on me.*

"If you really think that's best. It makes me nervous to think it's in the next room when I'm working."

"I think we can assume it isn't loaded. A brilliant man like Mr. Bingham would have emptied it immediately.

"You're right, of course. I should've thought of that." Beverly stands up to leave. "Well...er...have a nice weekend, Vanessa. I'm sorry I haven't been exactly friendly to you before today. I've had nerve problems, I'm afraid." She looks hopeful. Maybe Nessa wants to hear about them.

"No harm done," is Vanessa's reply. Already she is wishing they could go back to their old animosity. Being the secretary's friend could prove exhausting. She isn't ready to hear about any "nerve problems." Providing those came from the amazing Principal Bingham, Nessa is likely going to have some of her own. *I'm only twenty-two. Still in my carefree years. Why didn't someone warn me teaching can be so risky?* Then she tells herself that these kinds of situations aren't common. They must only happen in *perfect* high schools.

Throughout the evening Nessa ponders Beverly's report of finding the gun. In spite of the way she brushed over its importance when she first heard about it, Nessa is worried. Bingham has shown signs of being both paranoid and power hungry. Could he be arming himself for what he perceives as a dangerous reaction to the list that was issued to the owners of the Fancy Tramp? He has no reason to think Monique and Lola will come gunning for him, but he may think he needs to have a way to threaten them if they kick up a fuss. Apparently, his goons carrying ball bats don't make Bingham feel sufficiently protected.

Then again, she may have hit the mark when she theorized the gun was simply confiscated from a student. When that happens in other places, everyone is horrified. Nessa feels guilty hoping student possession is all they have to worry about this time.

Finally, she's free to regather the student journals she started to take with her a half hour ago. In spite of what she told Beverly at the beginning of the term, she finds she'd rather take schoolwork home with her than to come back on Saturday to do it. As she has before, she questions why English teachers have so much more out-of-class work than some of the other instructors. Maybe she should've thought harder about what lay ahead when she was making a career decision.

Finally, she gets together the amount of work that seems reasonable and starts for her car. As usual, hers is one of few still waiting. The other is a navy blue Ford she knows is owned by her boss. Walking away from it is one of her English Literature students. "Have a super weekend, Aaron!" she calls.

The boy looks startled to have her speak to him. Nessa has noticed before his being shy around girls, and teachers are even worse than girls.

"You, too, Ms. Martin," he responds, head down. She notices he's carrying a paper sack. Did he get it from Bingham? What the principal may have handed him doesn't bear thinking about. One thing they don't need at a perfect high school is a drug-dealing administrator. She puts Aaron and the sack out of her overactive mind.

Clown Alley

"This meeting is an emergency one. I was hoping we were past those. I'm afraid we've run into some of the same dangers as we had before we fled the circus. I guess it just shows you there are mean people everywhere. It's impossible to avoid them all.'"

"I haven't met any mean ones in Haven. I was just telling my babies last night that we've come to the perfect town."

"It should be, but from what I've learned today, we still have to be careful."

"It seems a lot safer than where we were before. At least nobody has attacked us lately."

"No, but it's just a matter of time. Cotton has reported men who've been following him to and from his house. They may be the ones who knocked him out when he was in Vanessa's classroom. Either they want to hurt him or scare him into leaving town. Both, I'm afraid."

"What do they have against Cotton?"

"It isn't him in particular. It's US. They want us gone for some reason. I've known this ever since they caused me to wreck my bike. I wasn't a random target. They were trying to tell me something– Leave town!" And Lola throws out her hands in a gesture of rejection

"But that was several weeks ago. They haven't bothered you again have they? If they were serious, wouldn't they have done something even scarier, like shooting at you or setting fire to the house?"

"Shut up, Pike. Don't scare Lola. Can't you see she's already shaking?"

"Fire or gun shots could be coming," Lola replies ominously. "Do you remember I told some of you that I couldn't find my shoe from that day I fell off my bike? Well, this morning it showed up in my mailbox! And there was a note sticking out of it that said, "Watch your step! The worst is yet to come!"

23

"Want to see a movie?" John asks on the phone after she gets home Friday. It seems like you've had a pretty rough week. The impression I get is you can use an escape."

He's received a lengthy email from Nessa naming all the improvements Monique is facing. He doesn't even know yet about the gun or about the student she saw getting something from Bingham. There are only so many problems that can be addressed on the phone. Best stick to one at a time.

"The only thing better than a movie would be an offer from you to do tons of construction for free. I know you're between cases and the moral satisfaction you'd get would be priceless."

"Right," John replies. "But you really don't want me to do that. I'm willing to help, but I don't have the expertise to supervise. A minion is the most I could be. I'm the kind who stands around and waits for directions."

"Can't you call people who owe you favors?"

"Nope. I'm pretty much the one who owes those. Plus, no matter how cheap the labor is, Monique is going to have to purchase supplies. Lumber, paint, tools. The cost will be way higher than whatever we're imagining."

"Maybe she could qualify for a grant. Money for restoring historic buildings. I've heard of cities getting those."

"Probably. But we'd need the town council behind the project, and they'd have to have much more time. Grants take months. And grant writers want to get paid."

Nessa is quiet. She's run through her supply of ideas. "What movie were you thinking about?"

"Well, at the risk of sounding cheap, there's a pretty good one playing downtown Haven. Afterward we can go somewhere for a drink. I have something to show you. It might help to hang the Association."

Phooey, she thinks. *The movie is only an excuse to talk about crime in Haven. Or... maybe crime in Haven is his excuse to talk to me. Best not to overthink it.* "What time?"

The comedy John has chosen doesn't require deep concentration. Nessa finds moments to steal glances at her masculine companion who, when he sheds his jacket, takes her breath away in a peacock blue short-sleeved shirt that shows off his buff arms. Her suspicion that he bought the shirt just for tonight is confirmed when they are driving away from the theatre, and she casually asks how he spent his day. "I went shopping for clothes, believe it or not. Thought it was time I showed you I don't have to look grungy. Farm and Fleet had some good deals."

Vanessa smiles. When a guy looks like John Harnden, he doesn't have to shop at fine places to get great results. "Well, you sure don't look grungy. *I'm* going to have to check out Farm and Fleet. I might need some overalls."

"They have more than farm clothes. I found some respectable things for work."

Nessa glances toward the back seat and sees several packages. "Looks like you bought out the store."

"Not really. My stuff is just big so takes more sacks than yours would."

Nessa smiles thinking that would be the kind of excuse a man would make to his wife who complained about his spending.

Haven's one spot that stays open after ten seems to be waiting for them. They park under a street light, and John surprises her by saying, "I don't think I mentioned that you look especially pretty tonight."

She isn't sure what to say. She's never noticed that John thought she was pretty at all, let alone *especially* so. "Thanks."

Before she can reproach herself for such an unoriginal response, the private eye leans over and kisses her. At first it's what she'd call a peck, but then it turns into an honest-to-goodness kiss, long enough for her to open her eyes and look to be sure it's John, and that she isn't fantasizing the scene. It wouldn't be the first time.

As he releases his embrace, her eyes fall again on the packages from the shopping spree. One sack shows something protruding, something that catches her attention. She looks away quickly. She must have camouflage on the brain. But she'd swear that's what she saw. Why would John dare to buy something with that pattern after all their concern about the evil stalkers?

Now he's hugging her again - tightly. Normally, she'd love that. It's nice, she'd think, for him not to just hop out of the car as soon as the kiss is over. The hug shows he wants to make the moment last. But her mind won't let go of the suspicious sack she's spied. Of course, camouflage is commonplace at F&F but still. The fact he hasn't mentioned it is not a good thing. She'd have expected to hear something like, "Guess what I found? You're going to hate me, but I bought a camouflage pair of coveralls. I promise not to wear them when I'm around you." But he hasn't said a word. Men don't always think much about clothes. Maybe he just needs a little encouragement. "What did you buy *me* at Farm and Fleet?" She uses a teasing tone so he knows she's flirting.

"Nothing there really looked like you. Unless you need socks. I bought enough of those for two."

Nessa doesn't reply. John is opening the car door. He is ready to go into Billy's Bar and Grill. She realizes suddenly that she's contemplating spending another hour or so with a guy who is hiding something from her. Not her idea of a pleasant evening. "You know what, John? My stomach isn't feeling so good. I promise it isn't the kiss, but I think I'm going to beg off going for drinks. I think I need to go on home, call it a night. We can continue our date another time."

She isn't proud of herself. The look on her friend's face tells her she's hurt his feelings. She didn't even give him a chance to explain. Nessa admits she's often impulsive, jumping to conclusions before she's thought things through. Just the same, her gut feeling about his secret purchase reminds her how little she knows about John Harnden. She originally believed he was a preacher, but he isn't. Maybe he isn't even a private eye. Is he preparing to join the school principal's dangerous group of community leaders? Has someone sold him on the idea of the Perfect Plan for Haven?

"I'm really sorry about this," she makes herself say when he drops her off at home. No matter how devious John is, he isn't stupid. She acts perfectly fine all through the movie and then abruptly gets sick. He has to know something's upset her. "I-I just can't imagine what it is, but there's been a bug going around school." (Isn't there always a bug going around school?) "Th-thanks for the movie."

"Sure. Sorry we didn't get to talk. I was looking forward to it."

"We'll talk later," Nessa says as she opens the car door and runs for the Tramp. At least John doesn't still have an apartment there. *That would've been awkward.*

She recalls, too late, his mention of something to show her that could hang the Association. She probably should've hung in long enough to see it. Being on her own has made Vanessa paranoid. Her first fear about a man she's been attracted to for weeks is that he's been lying to her. *Geez*. The things she's learning about her boss are making her suspicious of everyone. But she has to protect herself, be more safe than sorry. Didn't she already realize that John was too good to be true? Handsome, kind, smart. When does she learn the rest of the story? He may be going to try to get her to see the wisdom of the PP. He may ask her to be part of it. No way is she that enamored of the guy. Her feelings can change. Maybe John Harnden has been only a fantasy. Maybe he's belonged to the Association all along but just hadn't picked up his uniform. The thought gives her shivers.

Later, from the safety of her apartment, things look different. Without realizing it, she's watching the Late Show with the sound turned off. When reliving her unfinished date, she grasps the fact that she played the whole evening wrong. Running at the first sign of trouble accomplishes nothing. If she avoids John, she'll never know if she's right or crazy. If she plays along and listens to his thoughts, she can find out where he stands, and where she stands. Mostly, she wants him to tell her the truth. No matter what it is. She can see clearly that honesty is a top priority for her when it comes to romance. She can never commit to a man if she can't absolutely believe everything he tells her.

Of course, the truth thing probably should work both ways. She's recently told John she is sick when she isn't. Maybe she should reconsider her requirement of uncompromising truth. If it's as important as she's thought, then she probably should've admitted what was really bothering her. *I didn't lie,* she tells herself, *My stomach does feel pretty upset...AND if I let myself think about the kiss, it feels fluttery. How could I just waste a beautiful moment I've been hoping for for weeks?*

24

Watching The Tonight Show is a lost cause. Even the thunder and wind outside her window doesn't win her attention. Finally Nessa curtails her thoughts about John by starting a novel, one which isn't a romance. The weekend is always her green light to marathon-read with no worries about what happens if she doesn't get her seven hours of sleep. She's been known to keep reading with only one eye open just because she doesn't want to cheat herself out of even five minutes of her favorite pastime. Deep into a chapter of tonight's murder mystery, she becomes aware of a clunking sound. The creak of a door opening and closing is also part of the noise that's coming from the hallway.

Nessa remembers she's in a shared living facility. There are others in the building, but they aren't her concern. She needn't worry about any commotion outside her apartment. Her college dorm was the same way. Things went on in the halls and in other rooms, and sometimes people were loud. But she learned to shut out noise that came through the thin walls. She can do it again. Squeak, stomp, stomp, thud. Squeak, stomp, stomp, thud. The rhythmic sounds are noticeable, she decides, simply because they are new and because she can't positively identify them. Door opening, footsteps, and setting something on the floor.

Lola must be completing some housekeeping chore that's easier when no one is around. Or the Clean Queen could be doing her thing. So far, Nessa hasn't actually witnessed any of the scrubbing and mopping she was led to believe are Monique's specialties.

Still, no voices can be heard. Maybe Gordy is doing one of his ritualistic chores. Stormy nights may bring on restless activity from him. She doesn't touch her lock. It would be too easy to give the impression of an open door policy. Gordy would love it. She scolds herself for such mean thoughts about the poor sad clown. He's probably very lonesome. She wonders if the man he is now remembers his days as Lola's lover. Probably not. She isn't even sure he recognizes Lola these days. But she's obviously very devoted. Though they never married, she acts like a woman with a for-better-or-worse commitment.

The noises stop. Perhaps Lola has emerged and is leading Gordy to his quarters down below. How sad. She wonders if he chose to have an underground apartment. The atmosphere would be forever sunless in the basement, not conducive to any mental stimulation or happy thoughts. Perhaps Gordy is past having thoughts, happy or otherwise.

Trying to read is as useless as watching TV. Before she puts her book away and settles in to sleep, she has to satisfy her curiosity. As quietly as possible, Nessa swings open her door and peers into the hall. Her eyes go to the basement entrance straight ahead. A sliver of light comes through the door which is ajar. She can see Gordy sitting cross-legged on the floor in front of it. He is surrounded by fruit jars. *Many* fruit jars. The old blue ball ones. *Good grief! How old must those canned goods be? And who put them there?* She thinks it a pretty good bet that Lola or Monique don't put up preserves.

Gordy seems unaware of her presence. He is doing his best to focus on picking up the jars, moving them a few inches, then putting them down in different places. They appear to be heavy for the elderly man, but he's determined. Maybe it's his present version of chess. Lola could be staying away because he does it so often she knows what's going on. The man must have trouble sleeping. He isn't active enough during the day to get tired.

Suddenly, he pops to his feet, turns around, and goes back down the stairs. Nessa knows he may have gone to bed, so she considers taking the jars back where they came from. First, she waits in her doorway for a few minutes to see if he's gone after some more. Sure enough, the rhythm starts again. The footsteps have slowed to a trudge. She wants to tell him to leave them in the cellar where it's cool, but he obviously isn't paying attention to anyone or anything except the chore he is trying to accomplish.

Nessa almost shouts "Hurrah!" when she sees John come through the front doors and down the hall. Though glad to see him, she his dismayed to know Lola has neglected to lock the entrance of the building. "What are you doing here at this hour? I thought you went home a while ago."

"I knew I wouldn't sleep, wondering what happened between us tonight. I took a chance you were still up. I think I have an explanation coming to me. What did I do? Or say?"

"Oh, don't worry about it. It was mostly me being paranoid." Now isn't the time to discuss her unreasonable suspicions. "We'll talk later. There's another concern at the moment. I'm trying to figure out what's going on with Gordy. Do you see what he's doing?"

John looks understandably baffled by Nessa's change of subject. "Well, so far, all I can tell is he's bringing you some old canned goods."

"Do you think it's just something he does?" Nessa is getting concerned about who's going to clean up this pile of what is likely moldy fruit.

"You'd think Lola would've mentioned it to us," John answers as he watches Gordy come through the basement door with another jar. It's a miracle he hasn't dropped any on the cement steps.

"I think we should get Lola. This is the kind of thing apartment managers have to take care of," says Nessa. She's braver now that she isn't watching the scene by herself.

"What's going on? Am I missing some excitement?" comes Lola's shrill voice. The lady flicks on the hallway light to see for herself. "Lordy, Gordy! Where did you find all those?" She looks at Nessa and John, questioning.

"We don't know," responds the private eye. "We thought the jars were probably yours."

Lola is a sight to behold in her poppy house coat and her red hair sticking in all directions. But she seems awake and alert. It could be she's used to her sleep being interrupted by the clown from the basement.

"I've never seen them before. Bring me one, Gordon dear. Let's have a look to see if the food is edible or needs to be pitched. I'm guessing it's way old."

Gordy cheerfully hands her one of his jars. He seems proud to have something the lady wants.

Lola looks through the clouded dirty glass but can't make out what's inside. They haven't turned on the big chandelier and the entry's other overhead bulbs are very dim. "Pickles, I think. I don't want any, that's for sure." She tries to twist off the lid that is caked with rust. "I'm so weak. Here, John, help me. And careful. They're going to stink."

John, too, has trouble getting the lid loose, an indication it is corroded from years in the damp cellar. When it's possible to remove the Ball lid and ring, John cautiously sticks a finger inside. "This isn't food," he announces. "It's just paper. Oh, and something round ... coins." The ladies are silent, not breathing. Moving to the worn oriental throw rug nearby, John turns the jar over and lets the money spill out. Everyone is prepared to see someone's saved pennies wrapped for deposit. Instead, they are viewing a quart of bills with change mixed in.

"Oh, my!" exclaims Lola. "Somebody must have used it for a piggy bank. Do any of the other jars hold money? Maybe it's just that one." For some reason, the woman is whispering. It seems likely they are looking at money that has been hidden, that is a big secret. It has very probably been stolen, although coins from a bank would be packaged in rolls.

Nessa is optimistic. "If they went to the trouble to seal them up and store them, these coins could be valuable ones. We'll need to look them over good."

"You're right, but it could be a plant," says John, reluctant to put a damper on what could've been an exciting event. "Judging by the kind of townspeople you've been running into, it could be a way to get you all in trouble. To implicate you in a crime."

"Maybe the crime happened many years ago," speculates Nessa. "Maybe Monique is going to be the lucky recipient of some very old stolen cash."

They hastily look through the other jars, removing an occasional lid. Lola was partially right about the pickles. Approximately every other jar seems to contain those, but others are full of currency. One has to look closely and check the weight before opening the jars. They find paper money stuffed among coins of various denominations, maybe to disguise the tell-tale jingle of change. They'll need to take everything to a well-lit location to count and examine the dates.

"I'm on the edge of being ecstatic," says Lola softly. "But I'm afraid there's disappointment coming." She isn't used to looking on the negative side of things, so she adds sheepishly, "It's just a feeling."

John attempts to face reality. "Well, usually the law says that found money belongs to the original owner if it wasn't included in the bill of sale. Who was the owner before Monique?"

Lola thinks. "I was told that the house stood empty for many years before it went back to the bank, and Monique bought it for taxes."

John is used to thinking of alternative answers. "The mansion has probably been a place for teens to hang out to do drugs and have sex. Any unknown individual could've used it as a hide-out for money they robbed or had saved for some reason. Probably nobody would have any legal claim to it. Cash is hard to identify unless someone kept a list of serial numbers. I'd still proceed with care. Let's put it all in a safe place where the wrong people won't get their hands on it."

"I have to tell Monique, and do you think we should notify the bank? Or the police?" Lola asks innocently.

"Normally, I'd say yes, but in this town I'm afraid those are the last people you should tell about this. I'll check with an attorney in Arbor City."

A beam of light flashes across the front entry of the Fancy Tramp. Someone is on the porch trying to get their attention. By this time, Pike is on first floor and has helped Ms. Sofie come down as well. An early-morning party is unofficially underway. Even though all members of the household have reason to be exhausted, sleep doesn't seem to be an option. The miraculous discovery has pushed any thought of rest from their minds. Except for Gordy, all the apartment dwellers are awake and alert. But who is at the door? They have no neighbors close by to be disturbed by their noise.

John goes to the entrance and peers through the long narrow panes on either side of the double doors. Their frosted glass makes it hard to see. A powerful flashlight shines directly in his face. He cautiously pulls back the big oak door. "Who is it?" he asks.

"Police. Open up!"

Puzzled, John does as he's told. A pair of men in uniform face him with Glocks at the ready. "Anything wrong, Officer?" John asks the older of the two.

"I hope not. We're just on patrol and have been keeping an eye on your lights. This old house is usually pitch black during our shift. We're wondering if some emergency is taking place tonight. Does anyone need 911?"

The policemen push their way into the foyer and look around. Their eyes fall on the little group of tenants planted in front of the basement door. With no explanations uttered, the friends have collectively decided to guard Gordon's apartment. The cops will not be allowed to search the lowest level.

"Nobody's sick? Hurt?" Wide eyes stare blankly at the officers. "Okay. Guess we'll leave you alone. But we'd better not hear about anything illegal going on here tonight. It won't take much to put the lot of you right out on your ears."

"Nothing illegal here," John assures him. "We appreciate you checking on us, though. It's good to know our police are on the job."

The men in uniform stroll through the foyer once more, glaring at each person present. "I feel like we're missing something...." says the younger man. He grabs the nearby door knob to the basement and gives it a turn. With a loud squeak it opens a couple of inches to reveal total darkness and the outline of narrow steep stairs.

"Basement. Not a very nice place," offers John. Typically, the cellars of very old houses are dank and spooky. The police forego that part of their inspection and go out without pulling the door closed or apologizing for the intrusion.

"Nice guys," says Pike.

Lola is suddenly aware her friend Gordon isn't with them. She hurries through the basement door and down the steps. Gordy is sleeping in his bed below. Nessa and John have followed and all three are looking now at what has been a hidden door in the far wall of the room. There is no visible handle, no clue from the interior of the room that an opening exists. Something must have triggered the latch which has done its job for a very long time. A look inside reveals shelves typical of any fruit cellar, heavy planks framed with cobwebs. Gordon has brought out only about half of approximately twenty jars.

"Lola," says John, "do you happen to have a big lantern or some sort of light? We need to look around. There could be a note or label somewhere that explains all this."

Lola flies upstairs as fast as her yellow slippers will allow and returns with a very large flashlight. Again, all voices go silent as John shines a beam into every possible nook and cranny. Nothing.

The basement hardly warrants the name. It is some kind of extremely old dungeon crudely dug out without moving the house. The walls are made of ancient 2x4s rather than cement block. How does Gordy stand living down here? A door has swung out of the end wall to reveal what is obviously a secret room or safe, though all they can see are some shelves of canned fruit.

"I think sometimes buildings had places like this where the owners could hide from any dangerous intruders. Somebody apparently turned it into a fruit cellar at some point. And a private safe. I guess it could be used as a tornado shelter, too, but you wouldn't get me in there," remarks John.

"Me either! I'd rather take my chances on whatever was going on out here. I wonder what made it open up after all this time."

"Maybe the wooden door has shrunk to the point that our strong wind tonight loosened it. Or maybe Gordy has been trying to pry it open for a long time and finally did."

"The Association probably would use it to hide bodies."

"Don't talk like that," scolds Lola. "I want to be able to sleep if I ever get to bed."

Gordy's bedroom feels very private, but they all understand they must put the money back inside the hidden room in case some member of the Association pays them another visit. That group will make short work out of eliminating Lola and company if they know she's housing a fortune.

"If I make a long plank table down here to work from, do you think Gordy can resist moving the coins?" asks John.

"Oh, yes. If you tell him not to touch, he'll die before he disobeys."

Suddenly, Nessa feels a daughterly warmth for Gordy. A good man. As payment for his amazing discovery, she feels he deserves to be assigned to a higher level of the house. He shouldn't have to stay in a dingy cellar, even though she's glad he was doing so last night. "Do you think he'd be happier upstairs in a room with a window?" she asks Lola.

"If I thought so, that's where he'd live. When we first moved in, he picked this dungeon. You should've seen it at first. I don't think previous owners came near it except to throw their junk down here. Monique and I had to do a lot of moving discarded stuff just to make space for a bed. We did our best to make the room look inviting."

Nessa glances around at the circus posters on walls and the floor lamps placed to illuminate the corners of the room. The overhead light even has a clown face on it. The space has been decorated for a child's taste, so in some ways it is more desirable than the dingy upstairs. A television provides some mental stimulation for Lola's friend. Nessa tells herself that if she were in Gordy's condition, she'd definitely prefer these quarters to a rest home. The man seems secure and content. And she can see he is loved. The old guy doesn't have it so bad.

25

"You two can have the honor of totaling the treasure. I don't think I can count that high!" Lola calls back on her way up the stairs.

"The cashiers at a bank would probably be more accurate, but I don't think you want to let anybody know just yet what Gordy found. The total amount probably won't be anything huge, but there's a chance there are some rare coins in this stash.

"We'll need to get it all to some experts for the final count, but we should have a written record of what we send them"

"Right," agrees Nessa. "Until we get that done, the fewer people who know, the better."

After a short discussion, a plan is established. "John will rig up a couple of high intensity bulbs to hang above makeshift plank tables. A couple of uncomfortable wooden stools will serve as seating until something better can be found. Another weekend day means the appointed cashiers can devote their time to the task. They may need a couple of hours of sleep first, however. The idea is to find out for themselves the total of cash in the jars. They can also put aside any coins with dates that bear further investigation.

"I know people who collect coins, and from what they say, you really have to be careful where you have them appraised. It's common for the experts to say you have nothing valuable, and then offer to take them off your hands."

"I bet. Where will we find someone we can trust?"

"Monday I'll do some checking in Arbor City," John offers. "Besides talking to a lawyer, I'll visit my buddy Carl who runs a little shop for collectibles. I'd bet he has a price guide we can borrow. I won't give away our reasons. And I'll check online. You can find a lot of information about this stuff, and Carl can tell me which sites we should believe. It's important not to get starry-eyed about something before we're more informed."

John can't forget about the Association. Is it too good to be true they're ignorant of the collection's existence? "Don't you think the Association has heard if there's a treasure in this building somewhere? I mean, there are other big houses they could buy that wouldn't take as much renovation to make into a town hall, but they seem desperate to get their hands on this one."

"Good point. I haven't heard any legends about hidden money, but it sure is possible."

Gordy has awakened and sits on the edge of his bed. He is watching them intently. They get the sense he's doing sentry duty. He doesn't remember much and has probably possessed very little wealth in his life, but must instinctively realize that money must be guarded.

Impulsively, Nessa stands and places a hand on the old man's shoulder while speaking to John. "Did Lola ever tell you what Gordy did at the circus?" Nessa has been instructed to find out everyone's background, but this gentle man is impossible to interview.

"No," he answers. "She didn't even mention a circus to me. She just said he was the funniest performer she's ever seen, and when she got to know him better, he turned out to be the nicest. Handsome, too, she said."

"I bet he was. She must have loved him or she wouldn't be so willing to bring him along wherever she goes. He sure does limit her freedom."

"Right." John can't seem to look directly at Nessa during this exchange. "But everybody needs to be needed. He obviously needs her, and he's convinced she needs him, too. It seems like a real partnership."

There is a brief lapse of conversation. Talk of romantic devotion is awkward for Nessa as well as John. If she'd let their date night play out to its natural conclusion, they might have had a cozy relationship by now. As it is, they must pretend to be casual friends with nothing to worry them except a large sum of money. Gordy has no idea how complicated his simple discovery has made their lives.

Vanessa mentally composes an explanation of Gordon's usefulness to give to David Bingham. *"The man is Senior Assistant to Lola and oversees her finances."* Nessa smiles to herself. Gordy has earned a promotion tonight.

"Oh, my goodness!" comes an excited voice from the stairs. It's Monique. Lola must have told her about their find which, of course, may become hers. "I've always thought this house was a castle, and now it really can be!"

"Now Monique, don't get your hopes up," John cautions. "This money may belong to the bank downtown or to a church or a community charity. Some crazy employee might have stashed it here. Just because the building is old, doesn't mean the money has been here a long time."

"I'm sure you're right," she answers reluctantly. "But I've lived in Haven since I was born, seventy-five years ago. I don't remember talk about any robbery in all that time. And I was always in the know. Nothing like that would've gotten past me!"

John believes her. Even a small crime wouldn't go unnoticed in Haven. "It surely isn't from a bank or it would be packaged in units. These are just miscellaneous. They have to be part of somebody's savings or collection. If it's only a collection, it isn't very organized. Suppose they meant to arrange it all later. I mean, as soon as we know the exact amount, we can find out if it was ever reported missing." He feels compelled then to repeat his earlier instructions. "We just have to keep it quiet. Anybody could come forward with a fake claim. You know how important silence is, don't you?" He looks at Monique sternly. "I know it'll be tempting to tell somebody, but I say the news stays within these walls until we know the real story."

"Okay. My lips are sealed." And Monique squeezes hers together. It isn't often enough you see a woman in her seventies glow with happiness, but this one seems to have a decidedly rosy look beneath her tear-filled eyes. Nessa hopes John won't work too hard at finding the owner of the fruit jars.

Sunday afternoon John and Nessa are hard at work going through the money. They place the old-looking bills into stacks along with arranging the coins which they can only put into similar-appearing piles.

Lola watches the counting with growing interest. Gordy sits quietly at her side. One thing the man seems to possess is endless patience. He watches the cashiering process with rapt interest. One might think he was aware of the coins' values and adding them in his head.

No attempt is made to total how much the entire stash is worth, but it doesn't take a genius to see Monique is in possession of a not-so-small fortune.

When each and every piece of money has been accounted for, Lola provides a small trunk for storing it all for transport.

The empty jars are given back to Gordy who puts them under his bed. He seems exceptionally attached to the cloudy old things.

Ultimately, John ends up with the coins in his car. It will be his job to deliver them to his friend at Carl's Coins in Arbor City on Monday. After much discussion it has been decided the money will be safer with him than to take a chance on obtaining a police escort. Their luck, the officers from last night would be the ones assigned to the trip, and it is very likely those men belong to the Association who'd love to get their hands on the money.

Nessa realizes she and Lola are putting a lot of trust in the man who, just two nights ago she decided wasn't trustworthy. This same deceitful John Harnden has been using his work hours to find out about money he won't benefit from. He is volunteering to help a bunch of clowns he barely knows and a teacher who recently walked out on him. It just goes to show that reality is always shifting. What makes sense one day is nonsense the next.

"Why don't you follow me, Ness? Just in case I have car trouble or an accident, I don't want to have to take help from somebody who'll go through my vehicle."

On the surface, the windfall can spell an answer to the future for Monique and friends. With this lucky find to work with, they can't be evicted because of failure to comply with the inspection results. If the final count is as good as John has implied it might be, every bit of restoration can now be completed and workers paid, with money left over. But the police are bound to ask questions about where the payment is coming from. How are they going to be able to deposit a large sum into Monique's meager account without drawing attention? And it isn't likely they'll even get that far. Bingham's followers are sure to throw some legal wrench into the works and prevent Monique from getting to take possession of even a penny. Never mind the jars were probably used as banks during the depression and the owners and immediate relatives are dead. Or that they could be the spoils from a robbery or a raid that happened during another generation. Vanessa can imagine the Association creating a way to make Monique look guilty of something that took place when she was a toddler.

The financial find will ultimately be either a miraculous gift or a huge headache.

Still afraid there's some catch to the treasure story, John warns Nessa, "I hate to tell you my record for happy endings."

Nessa can't help but hope his record improves on a couple of fronts.

26

Sunday night. The end of an eventful weekend. The big house is quiet for now. All are worn out from the excitement of Gordy's discovery. But Nessa finds her mundane chores have waited for her. Tomorrow starts another hectic five days with students. If she doesn't clean the apartment and do some wash, those chores may have to wait another week. She can't imagine ever being a married woman with a schedule for those kinds of things. She seems to be stuck in student mode, get them done whenever the mood strikes or you're out of clean things to wear.

Washing clothes at the Fancy Tramp isn't the most pleasant of tasks. It's a sure thing that a new laundry room should be on the list of places for Monique to put some of her money. Fortunately, Nessa doesn't have to go to the basement or carry her laundry to another floor, but the converted back porch is dimly-lit and smells damp. It's the kind of place that makes you hurry your work so you can leave. When she was at college, she used laundry night as a time to study while listening to the machines. Often it would be a social occasion also, meeting up with friends and hearing the latest news. Lola's dumpy little room doesn't offer such activities. Vanessa dumps her clothes in the washer and switches the light off. Before exiting the porch, she looks out the screened wall. It's always a pleasure for her to view the expansive back yard and the woods. The landscape is very rural and peaceful, blotting out recent memories of noisy students and screaming administrators. She has the feeling she can escape those stressful issues through the back side of this old house.

Her attention is drawn to the one moving element of the scene. The tall figure of a person running. He appears to have emerged from behind a tree and is scooting stealthily around the side of the house. It all happens very quickly, causing Nessa to wonder if she imagined it. There is no reason for anyone to be in that area unless it's one of the camouflaged men doing whatever they do. She's never seen any of them so close to the building, though they may have noticed her tonight and come to get a closer look. A creepy thought. Time to return to her room.

While waiting for her clothes to wash, she sits on the couch and sorts through her English materials. Having talked Lola out of an old file cabinet from the back hallway, Nessa is excited to have a place for her "stuff". She likes to keep her personal teaching materials separate from those the school provides. If she should suddenly pack up and leave town, she wouldn't even need to stop off at her classroom. To accomplish this major organization project, she has spread the contents of two boxes across the couch cushions.

A scratching noise is heard coming from the other side of the outside wall. The front porch wraps across the front of the house and under her window so an animal could be playing there or even trying to get inside. Wild animals seem to be very comfortable around the Fancy Tramp. One day she found a squirrel pawing at her window sill, trying to get inside.

The sound is repeated. Nessa is alert now. What if it's Sofie's lost cat, Moe? She looks over the back of the couch. Heavy drapes block the view. Maybe Pike lost his key and it might be the rare night when Lola has thought to lock the entrance door. Nessa rises and goes to investigate. She's greeted with a hideous sight. An evil-looking white faced clown peers in at her. The features are obviously those of a mask designed for the cover of a Stephen King novel. She gasps and quickly closes the curtain. Her heart is beating fast. There are many possible explanations for the face if she can only concentrate for a minute. She certainly isn't going to panic.

Nessa checks that her apartment door is locked, then returns to the window for one more peek. The clown face makes a lunging movement toward her. Again, she pulls the curtain closed. The person may as well go home because she refuses to continue this game.

If someone is trying to make her afraid of clowns, it isn't going to work. She knows several clowns now and knows better than to suspect them of trying to scare her. This visitor is someone else, probably the someone she spotted running around the house. That person was taller than Bingham. Plus, her principal wouldn't have the courage to be sneaking around in the semi-darkness. It does sound like an idea he might have. It's been obvious he wants Lola and friends to vacate the apartment building, but there's no reason why he also wouldn't like to scare Nessa away. After all, she is unsympathetic to his goals and too hard for him to intimidate.

Bingham has brought up the creepy clowns from last summer on more than one occasion, so he would think of it. Not for the first time, she wishes John Harnden still lived a few steps away. It would be nice to have him here to help her make sense of the sighting. She was about to swallow her pride and call him to come to her aid, but a quick look at her phone tells her it's out of charge. Probably for the best. John won't want to make yet another drive to Haven. The prowler might even be gone by the time he can get here.

After a good half hour, Nessa, against her better judgement, goes to the window once more. Surely the boogie man is gone. No one can stand looking at a closed curtain indefinitely. But there he is. And he has the nerve to wave. *Thank goodness my mother isn't here!* She's sure she can outlast the strange figure, so she resumes her sorting. He may have been out there for hours already, as far as she knows. He may stay all night, but she won't know because she won't look.

Her student Aaron, who she saw talking to Mr. Bingham on Friday, is a tall young man. A nice kid, she has thought. Would he be carrying out a request from his principal to scare Ms. Martin? Aaron, like most teens, could use a little extra spending money. It wouldn't be hard for Bingham to hire him to carry out a simple Halloween prank. She thinks of the paper sack. A ready-made disguise had probably been inside.

Pretty amateur tactics, Mr. B., she's thinking. *You won't get rid of me that easily.*

Monday morning she gets to school early and ends up walking in with her principal. "How was your weekend, Vanessa?"

"Exceptionally good. And yours?"

"The same, thanks. I hope you'll be giving me some information this week. Can I count on it? Time is winding down fast on our deal."

"I'm doing my best," she tells him. "But I can't give you what doesn't exist." And Nessa makes a bee-line for her room. *What a lovely way to start a day.*

27

The bell rings signaling the end of fourth hour and the beginning of the second lunch period. Nessa leaves her room and makes her way to the faculty restroom. To do so, she must pass Beverly's desk. Nessa hasn't connected with her since their conversation about the gun at the end of the day on Friday. Now, Beverly is nowhere to be seen. She could be at lunch or perhaps she's waiting for somebody to give her the all-clear regarding the gun before she resumes her post. Probably not a bad idea, now that Nessa thinks about it.

Coming back from the restroom, she passes the reception desk again to catch Beverly backing out of her boss's office. A loud voice from the other side of the door tells the story. "And please don't let me catch you in here again when I'm not around. We must respect one another's space, Ms. Birch."

Uh oh. Nessa should have seen this coming. Beverly has let herself get so absorbed in Bingham's affairs she's forgotten that, in the end, she's only the secretary. Not a good time to chat about the gun. Nessa keeps walking, wondering where first-year teachers fall in the hierarchy of the Perfect High School. If she'd been caught looking through his coat closet, she'd have found out but might not have lived to tell about it.

Before the lunch period is over, Vanessa tries again. This time Beverly is alone so she dares to touch on the subject of her concern. "Did you get to check on the thing we were wondering about?" It would be risky to blurt out the words *gun* and *drawer*. Beverly is eager to report that "It's gone." Nessa smiles, trying to think positively. Her imagination is providing several possibilities she won't share with Bev.

"I thought so," she says. "So we can forget you saw anything." *I only have to worry about what I've seen. Camouflage outfits in all the wrong places. Money that belongs to no one.*

"Yes. I feel better now. By the way, my niece is going to be in town tomorrow. If we end up eating at the diner, shall I call you? You two girls might enjoy comparing notes about the English classes."

The woman is speaking like she never mentioned the reason her niece is no longer at Haven High. "Sure. I'd love to meet Jodi. Maybe she has some stories that will help me as the year goes along." *What am I saying? I've already lasted longer than she did. How can she advise me?*

Jodi fits the image Vanessa's imagination conjured up on first hearing of her. Petite, colorless and shy. No match for the goings on in Haven. "It's good to finally meet my predecessor!" Nessa greets the girl sitting at a booth beside her aunt. She sits down to join them, all the while feeling wonder that Beverly is actually out in the world having lunch.

"Yes. Hello, Vanessa," replies Jodi.

"Jodi is a secretary now, like me," Bev offers proudly. "I never thought she'd be interested but am glad she is."

Nessa is pretty sure the niece changed careers more to gain peace than because of any calling to office work. "I hope you like it, but I always think it's sad to lose teachers. Good ones are so hard to find."

Jodi blushes. "I'm afraid I wasn't one of the good ones. I was a wimp. The kids didn't listen to me. I don't think my voice is loud enough. They'd just kept right on talking among themselves and ignoring me. It made me tense, and I could tell they weren't learning anything."

"Oh, I think all us newbies go through that. Students can smell our fear and inexperience. By the way, didn't you live at the Fancy Tramp where I'm staying?" Nessa can't wait any longer to find out Jodi's version of the story.

There is a definite gap in the conversation. Mavis comes by to take their orders so Jodi gets a reprieve. It takes a while for the ladies to make their decisions, and then they wait until drinks arrive to continue. "Jodi lived on the first floor, didn't you, dear?" Nessa is impressed with how smoothly Beverly helped her niece get back on track.

"Yes. But I hated that place. It was dark and old fashioned, and there were all kinds of creaks and groans at night."

"Oh, honey," soothes Bev, "you hadn't been in many old houses. I lived in one like that through my whole childhood. I was sure it was full of ghosts, but I got used to them."

Beverly is actually defending the Fancy Tramp. Imagine that!

"Well, the Fancy Tramp has worse than ghosts. I saw a … something. I couldn't stay after that. I knew I'd lose my mind."

"Wow." Nessa can't imagine. She doesn't find Lola or even Gordy that scary. "What did you see?"

"I really can't say. If I were going to tell, I should've done it at the time." Jodi hasn't touched her hamburger. Nessa feels a little mean, ruining the girl's lunch and the visit with her aunt. But this matter could be important.

"My mother has a horrible fear of clowns," Nessa admits. "I know that's who runs the place. Did you see one of them in makeup? They have pretty lively birthday parties in the middle of the night."

"Well, you're partly right. I hate clowns, and nobody warned me the house was crawling with them. The door to the end apartment was standing open one evening, and I looked in and saw an old guy in white makeup beside the couch looking at a man who had a pillow over his face. The man looked lifeless. My instincts told me the clown had just finished suffocating him. Either that or the man was just a stuffed dummy. Maybe they were practicing a circus skit or something. I didn't dare hang around to find out. I just ran."

Neither Beverly nor Nessa knows what to say. Mavis comes by with refills. "Need anything else?"

No one answers her. What they need is to unhear what Jodi has just told them. "We're fine, Mavis," she says finally, dismissing the girl. They don't need for the waitress to start any rumors.

To get the full story, Nessa goes first. She's less shocked than Beverly. "Lola told me that Marvin suffocated, but she didn't say it was murder."

"Maybe she didn't know. The clown probably didn't tell anyone what he did. " Having at last spilled her secret, Jodi was able to take a bite of her sandwich.

Knowing the kind of person Gordy is, even in his present mental state, Nessa doesn't believe he's violent. "The clown could have just discovered the body. He might not have done anything wrong."

"Well, it looked wrong! It looked really wrong, and considering how I already hated the place, I just wanted to get away! It was too late to save the man's life, so I just saved mine."

"The thing to have done was to call 911 right away — maybe from your apartment if you were scared he'd see you." Nessa has no problem thinking about what she herself would've done, but realizes most people can second guess that when the crisis has passed.

"Oh, I know that. I've chastised myself every day since it happened. I was just so terrified. Seeing a clown was enough to paralyze me, let alone a clown looking at a pillow lying on a dead man." The young lady gave a small shudder and picked up her sandwich. "I can't talk about this anymore. I've spent a year trying to wipe it out of my memory, and now it's back."

Nessa could understand the young lady's panic, but someone should know. She was sure the words, *He was a vagrant so there wasn't any explaining to be done* pretty well summed up the apartment manager's attitude. "Still," she advised, "You should explain to Lola what you suspect. Let her decide what's to be done."

"I might tell her if I ever see her." Jodi is thoroughly enjoying her burger now, already putting the whole sordid experience to the back of her mind.

Beverly changes the subject. "Tell us about your job."

That evening, back at the Fancy Tramp, Nessa makes another attempt to sort through the tale of the asphyxiated Marvin. She's learned just enough from Jodi to increase her curiosity. Maybe she should become an investigator like John. A natural desire to dig for the truth would seem to be a requirement for that job.

Lola is coming through the basement door that leads to Gordy's quarters. Vanessa assumes she takes him food on a tray. Maybe they eat together.

"Lola, I have a question for you. I know you said there will be no investigation of the death of the renter who died mysteriously. But today I talked to the teacher who witnessed Gordy being there at the time it happened. If you knew he was, shouldn't you have reported it to the police?" Even as she asks, Nessa can figure out Lola's answer.

"Well, maybe. But I know Gordy would never have done anything cruel unless it was an accident. And the way the police treat us around here, I was sure they'd blame him. The poor man would probably be put in jail for the rest of his life, and he wouldn't even know why. I don't think anybody would be better off than if we just keep it quiet. Or I could be the one sent to prison, and I didn't do anything but try to make Marvin's stay here the best it could be even though he didn't have the money to pay rent."

Lola's explanations actually make a lot of sense. "Did Marvin ever give you any hints about his family? That's what bothers me. Somebody never knew what happened to him."

"He didn't say much except that his wife was glad he left. If I thought somebody somewhere was grieving, it'd be different. I don't think his passing changed the world much."

"Did you say he was a drunk? I wouldn't think you'd have taken him in if he was."

"I thought he might have been at one time. When he was here, he didn't have money to buy alcohol. But he seemed to have emphysema or some kind of congestion. I'd hear him coughing and wheezing in the night and hoped he had some kind of breathalyzer, but I'm not sure he did. I always thought he might have been gasping for air, and Gordy found a way to make him stop. He would've thought he was helping the man. There's no way to go back and have a do over, and the people at the Fancy Tramp showed him kindness in his last days."

Nessa had no reply. Sometimes life is not as simple as we think it should be. Right and wrong can get confused. Still, she wishes Marvin hadn't had a wife, because that means there might have been children.

28

Vanessa is late getting home following an after-school teacher's meeting. Usually, the front foyer is empty when she makes her way to her own door. Today a huddled form is blocking her path. "Pike! Are you waiting for me?"

"Yes, Ms. Martin. I'm ready to read. I've been through this whole book about Harry Potter, and I've read every word I know, but there aren't enough of them. I just can't make out the story."

"I'm sorry. I really am. I know I promised to help, but I've been dealing with so many important issues lately_ "She catches herself in the middle of minimalizing Pike's problem. His *reading* is an extremely important issue. It will affect his whole life. How dare she put it on her back burner. "I haven't had a chance to research how to help you. Listen, why don't you come to the town library with me tomorrow? We can see what they have on the subject of reading disorders and maybe I can learn how to teach you."

"I guess I can. I have tomorrow off. Didn't know I have a disorder." Pike seems a little deflated by the notion.

"That word sounds worse than it is. It just means, there's something that needs work before you can master the art of reading. It would be the same if you wanted to learn the piano and couldn't read music."

"No. That wouldn't be hard. I already know how to play the piano and the guitar even though I don't know how to read music. Lola says I play by ear. Wish reading books was like that."

"Me, too, Pike. But you have the desire, and that will make it easier. Meanwhile, come on in my apartment, and I'll read aloud for a while.

Pike shows definite signs of wanting to do the reading for himself. Sometimes while Nessa is saying the words, he runs a finger along the line like he's trying to match the words to what she's saying. When she gets too drowsy to keep going, she begs off. "More later. I'm sorry, but it's been a long day. As soon as I get you some reading help, you can stay up as late as you need to when the story's good."

"Yeah. I'll probably read all night," he says hopefully.

Nessa notices an attractive ring on his index finger. It actually has the look of a girl's. Maybe he and Melody are going steady though she doesn't think they call it that these days. "Nice ring," she comments.

"Yeah. Ms. Sofie outgrew it so she said I can give it to Melody, but Mel's afraid her dad will get mad if I do. I'm wearing it myself just to keep it safe until her dad sees I'm an okay dude."

The ring looks like an expensive one. "That was really nice of Sofie." Nessa wonders how long Pike will be wearing it before he gives it away. Fathers' opinions aren't always quick to change. Especially when the father is David Bingham.

At 8:00 on Saturday morning, Pike is at Nessa's door, ready to go to the library. She invites him in for some breakfast. "The library doesn't open until 11:00," she explains. "We might as well get fortified for this reading thing." They sit together at her tiny table with Kellogg's Frosted Flakes between them.

170

"Hope you like this kind of cereal," Nessa comments.

"I like pretty much any food. And Tony the Tiger reminds me of the circus."

Nessa sees an opportunity to give Pike a crude diagnostic test. "How do you know his name is Tony?"

"I've seen Kellogg's Frosted Flakes ads on TV, I guess," he answers.

"The words Tony the Tiger is written on the box. Can you show me where?"

Pike looks closely at all of the words in front of him, then points to the correct ones. "There."

"Bingo!" exclaims his new teacher, happy because the placement of the words is a couple of inches from the picture. "Do you see *Kellogg's*?"

Again Pike picks out the correct word. "How do you do that when you can't read?" she asks him.

"Well, I know what brand it is, and the brand would probably be at the top. Also I know it starts with a *ka* sound and ka is like in ka-ellogg."

Vanessa is getting excited. This boy is not a lost cause. She senses that his early schooling, limited as his involvement was, has given him some skills. Maybe Gordy helped as well. "Do you recognize the sounds of the alphabet?"

"I don't know. Like what?"

Nessa takes him through the consonants. He doesn't always recognize them if he sees them on a paper, but if she asks what sound does T make, or a K or N, he can logically give her the sound. Blends like TH or ST are unfamiliar. The vowels give him trouble. It's as though he hasn't been taught the difference in long and short sounds. But it is plain that the guy who plays guitar and piano by ear also has a talent for discerning the differences between sounds of letters.

Nessa ends up giving Pike what seems to be his first phonics lesson. They go onto her computer and find phonics songs that are natural instruction for his musical ear. Most of the lessons are geared toward young children, but Pike doesn't seem to care. Vanessa thinks his being a clown is an advantage. A clown, while he is as smart as the next person, is able to look at life through the eyes of a child. Dr. Seuss, for example, is great entertainment for Pike.

Halfway through the morning, they notice it's almost time to go to the library. "We can if you want," but we might have enough material online to get you going on phonics. I think you're going to master that real fast. Then by next week we can check out some simple books at the library. You can come down here for a half hour after school every week day, and I'll drill you. You're going to do this!"

Pike is beaming. "When you help me, it makes sense. At school I'd look at those words and not have any idea what they were. I guess I just let them scare me."

"Your old school might have been one of those who didn't teach phonics. Mom says it was a phase in education, I think. Big mistake. Another difference is that you're more interested now. You're motivated – because of Harry Potter and maybe because of Melody. And you've had more experience with sound from all your years of playing and singing."

"It would be nice if I had a computer to look up the things we just did, but I bet Ms. Sofie will let me use hers. She's always wanting to read to me, but I'd rather be able to read to myself. Or to my kids when I get some. I want to be more of a dad than what I had. Reading to my son would be a good dad thing to do."

"I am prouder of my title 'The Children's Friend' than if I were to be called 'The King of the World'."
P.T. Barnum

29

It has taken Tracy Martin only two weeks to find a reason to make another drive from Chicago. She has been cleaning house and has found some things she wants to throw away with her daughter's permission. There's Nessa's first prom dress taking up room in the spare bedroom closet. "Maybe you can sell it in Haven or give it to a needy student." Also, Nessa's old luggage has been sitting in the basement. "If you didn't need the suitcases for the move, why am I keeping them?"

Vanessa has more important matters occupying her mind these days. She can't imagine why she has to personally take a look at the objects in question. Her mom could easily have asked about them on the phone. When Tracy suggests they have lunch again at the diner, it finally occurs to Nessa that the house cleaning dilemma isn't really what brought her mother to town. Tracy is gambling that the attractive guy with the prematurely white hair eats there on weekends. And she's right.

He's even seated at the same table as before, almost as though he's making sure the friendly lady from Chicago can find him. Cotton's mysterious stalkers from last time haven't made another appearance. They probably found out what they needed to know the first time they shadowed him.

The three friends are back in Doug's Diner having a grand time talking and laughing over hamburgers and homemade chips. Doug's has listened to the new teacher's request and added a bean burger to the menu. Mavis always plops one in front of Nessa as though she's serving it against her will.

When the waitress picks up their empty plates and asks "Ya want dessert?" Nessa uses that as her cue to get lost. What pair wants a grown daughter hanging around the whole time they're trying to make time? The trouble is, she has the only car, and the weather has gotten a bit chilly to send them out walking. She should've thought ahead. "Oh, hey, I see one of the teachers from school over there. I should say hi." And she gets up and descends on the surprised math instructor and embarks on a lengthy chat about the state's proposed collective bargaining law, leaving her mother private time with Cotton.

On one level, Nessa concentrates on what her teaching colleague is saying, but in the back of her mind she's wondering about honesty, her newly discovered priority. Tracy doesn't know Cotton's former vocation. If she did, she wouldn't be talking to him. Is it Nessa's place to break the news, or his? Judging from the fact that Lola's friends seem to have agreed to keep silent about their past, Cotton isn't going to mention it. And Nessa's afraid to say anything aloud in this town where clowns have such bad reputations. Her words might put the man in danger.

After chatting as long as she can without becoming completely annoying, Nessa excuses herself and goes back to the happy couple. Except her mother isn't looking so happy. A little boy has come over to their table and asked Cotton for a balloon bear. Evidently, Cotton has given the child one of his balloon creations before. The former clown takes a blue balloon out of his pocket and starts to make one, but the boy's mother rushes him away. "Don't bother the man, Ricky!"

Tracy is horrified that Cotton is familiar with balloon animals. What adult male knows about those? Except a clown. "Does this mean you …?" Without thinking, she scoots her chair away from him.

Cotton quickly explains. "I learned how to make those when I was a kid. That little boy was in here the other day, and he was crying about something. His parents were having a terrible time with him. So I made him an animal, and the boy settled down. I can't stand to see children unhappy, and if a balloon will help…"

"I'm sorry, Cotton," says Tracy. "If I think somebody is a clown, I get unreasonable. I'm the type who sees them behind every tree. It's a sickness, really. That was very sweet of you to help the mother out even if she didn't realize that's what you were doing."

The hidden identity crisis is over for the moment, but Nessa is uneasy. Tracy should know the whole story about Cotton, but maybe not until she finds out what a kind and transparent person this janitor really is. *Truly though, there doesn't seem to be much of a future for mom with a man right out of her nightmares.*

That night, a call comes from her mother's cell phone. Presumably, Tracy is letting her daughter know she's safely arrived home in Chicago. The two have had this routine for a long time. A lot can happen on a four-hour drive. It's nice to have someone to check in with. "I'm back."

"Good," says Nessa. "Seemed like a whirlwind visit this time, but at least you got to see Cotton."

"Yes. You know, I did a lot of thinking on the way here. About how much I like him and how long it's going to take for us to get to know each other at this rate."

Nessa hears alarm bells. "So what do you want to do about it?"

175

"Well... You know that I've just been rattling around in this big house since you graduated from high school. I really don't need it. And my job ... every town needs substitute teachers"

"Okay. Give me the whole idea. Are you thinking you should move out of the city?"

"I'd need to talk it over with Cotton, but..."

"Good grief! You've only visited with the guy a couple of times. He's nice, but I hope you aren't thinking of moving in with him!"

"He hasn't asked me, so don't get all bent out of shape. I just thought if I became a resident of Haven, we'd have a little more chance to get acquainted."

Nessa is on high alert now. She feels like the parent in this situation. "Now, Mom. Don't make any hasty decisions. Don't put the house up for sale or anything yet. There are a couple of things you need to know."

"Okay. Hold on a minute until I get inside. Sounds like a lecture coming on."

Should the lecture wait? Nessa is afraid it can't. She wishes her mom were here with her. She might be going to need a hug. She decides to try the lesser of the deterrents first. "Haven has requirements before you can live here."

"What kind of requirements?" By her tone, Nessa can tell her mom isn't taking her statement very seriously.

"You have to take a test. Answer a bunch of questions about where you came from and what your intentions are."

"That's odd. Never heard of such a thing. But I'm sure I could pass it. I don't have any money problems or criminal record or anything."

"You never know what little detail will make them reject you. And..."

Actually, hon, I think Cotton is worth taking a little test. It's silly, but not a deal breaker."

"Mom, I think something else is. Cotton isn't what you think...." She pauses, then chickens out. She resorts to a fabricated excuse. "He's not the school janitor anymore. He lost his job. And so far, he hasn't found another one. He may soon be homeless!"

"I thought you knew me better than that. I'm not a snob. If he doesn't have money for a place to live right now, I can help. I can afford it. I'd just enjoy knowing a sweet guy who's fun to spend time with."

"Well, Cotton is all of that. But I don't think he's told you what his previous job was. Before being a janitor."

"No. We haven't had time to talk about our past lives. That's okay. Unless he's a member of the mafia or something."

Nessa says a silent prayer her mom won't faint. "I think his main profession was being a circus clown. He even wore white face."

Silence. It's unbelievable that this is so serious a matter, but Tracy's phobia means there's nothing worse she could learn about her new friend.

"But he's moved on," Nessa adds quickly. "He's no longer a clown. It's like being a recovered alcoholic or a born-again Christian. He's a new person."

Silence. Nessa debates whether to hang up and call 911 in Chicago. They'd send someone to check on Tracy.

Just before she shuts her phone off, she hears her mom's weak voice. "I think I knew he might be. After the balloon thing."

"Can you deal with that news? I can't stand it if you're all freaked out and disappointed."

"Well, nobody ever died from being disappointed. I just have to do a lot of thinking."

"Cotton is a great person. Give him a chance. Maybe you should see a psychiatrist."

"Maybe. Thanks for telling me the truth. I have to go now."

Knowing your mom is in crisis is a good reason to wake up early. Nessa feels responsible for the whole messy situation. She's always known Tracy's feelings, and yet she let her own fondness for Cotton cloud her judgement. She knows her mother probably wants to be left alone right now, but it's hard for Nessa to admit she can't fix the problem. For the first time, she wishes they lived in the same town. It's hard to take care of someone who is three hundred miles away. Especially if she doesn't answer her phone.

It takes five rings but finally, Nessa hears a faint. "Hello. Don't worry about me."

"I'm not worried. I just thought I should get in touch before school starts. Once my room fills up with teenagers, I can't think straight about anything else. Did you sleep?"

"No, but that's okay. I have today off. I think I've made a plan. I Googled coulrophobia and found the treatment."

"There's a treatment? Are there pills?" *Maybe they have pills for helping you stand a crazy boss.*

"No. Nothing that easy. It isn't a documented phobia, just one the internet came up with. They say you just have to be forced to be around clowns until you desensitize yourself. It's called Exposure therapy."

"Well, you've been around Cotton a few times and got along okay. What will be different now? He won't be dressing up so you can just forget about it."

"Yes, but I'll know. It would always be between us. I think I'm going to work on my problem here in Chicago. Go see a couple of circuses. At the hospital, I can go into the children's ward when the clowns are there. I'll find as many places as I can to *expose* myself__to clowns, I mean!"

"Well, you can try it. But stay away from the Stephen King movie IT. That clown isn't typical, and it isn't fair to let him make them all look evil. There're cruel Santa Clauses in the world, too, but you can still love most of them."

"It all makes sense when you talk about it, but phobias don't make sense. You really can't reason them away. I know that much. But I'm going to force myself to get over it. Do you think I should tell Cotton what I'm doing?"

"Maybe not right away. Listen, Mom, the first bell just rung for home room. I have to quit talking. Take it slow. You don't have any deadlines."

Vanessa has been home from school for about an hour and is still resisting the urge to check on her mother. She knows Tracy is a mature lady and will find a way to handle her conflicted feelings about Cotton. But what about him? Maybe she should admit that she gave away his secret, that she may have sabotaged his chance for romance. Then the ball will be in his court. He can approach her mom himself. After all, Nessa doesn't run a dating service. She hasn't even had good results creating a love life of her own.

"Hi, Cotton! How are you doing?"

"I'm fine. What's up, Nessa?

"Well... I just have to tell you something, and we don't get to talk much at work."

"Is it about your mom?" He's apparently felt this coming.

"Yes. She was so eager to spend more time with you that she decided she wants to move to Haven. So I thought it was time for me to tell her the whole scary truth about who and what you are."

"I thought I was a middle-aged man with white hair who enjoys cleaning the school and thinks your mom is the sweetest lady I know. Is all that scary?"

"No. And you've got it right, Cotton. That's who you really are. But even though I swear my mom is a very normal lady in other ways, she has one big problem. It sounds like something she should be able to control, but I'm not sure she can. When I told her you're a clown, I swear she stopped breathing. It's like giving a handful of peanuts to someone with an allergy. No matter how much she likes the taste, those peanuts are going to cause a bad reaction."

"I understand that. I've met several other people with coulrophobia over the years. Who'd have thought I'd fall for one of them."

"I know. It's really a sad thing. I'm hoping there's a way for her to conquer it. I'm pretty sure she's going to try."

"Nessa, you said I'm a clown, but I'm not. I'm a regular man. My character, Banjo, is a clown, and I'm willing to kill him. I've had a good run in the business, and it's been a fantastic life. But I've left it all behind me."

"I believe you. We just need to let Mom get used to the whole thing. She's working on a plan for her recovery. It's something for her to do on her own. Life will make sense again if you can be patient with her." If worse comes to worse, maybe Cotton can relocate to her mom's house rather than Tracy moving to Haven.

"I'll stay out of her hair until you tell me she might be ready to see me. I don't mind the wait."

30

Vanessa is again up and at work early. Yesterday she promised her Seniors a quiz over the story they were assigned, and she still hasn't composed the questions. The hallway is dimly lit so she's surprised when she almost runs into a male figure coming from the opposite direction. Her first instinct is to expect David Bingham. The man invades her sleep, why not her hallway? But she's happy to see the janitor's sweet face instead. He appears to be turning toward her classroom.

"Cotton! It's so nice running into you first thing. Do I have another ceiling leak?"

"Oh, no," he answers glumly. "I'm just stopping in to say good-bye." The man can't even look at Nessa directly. There's no sign of his usual smile.

"Well, come on in!" The students won't complain if she has to cancel the quiz. "Tell me what you mean? Where are you going?"

"I've been fired." He sounds stunned.

"No kidding? There has to be some mistake." She remembers fibbing to her mother about him losing his job. Could that have somehow brought this on? "You're a great custodian. I haven't heard of one teacher who doesn't think so!"

"It isn't my work that's got Mr. Bingham mad. He thinks I'm dangerous, I guess."

Nessa can't imagine a less dangerous fellow than Cotton. "That man doesn't think straight. What did he give for his reasons?"

"He found a gun in my desk drawer. I don't even use my desk drawer! I don't even use my *desk*. The gun could've been there since the last janitor for all I know. I've barely opened the drawer since I was hired. I don't have any need for it. The only thing I do, is take out a pen, and I don't have to open it very far to get that."

Nessa thinks a minute. "Someone could've planted the gun to get you in trouble. You'll need to speak up. Don't be scared into letting them believe you've done anything wrong. They're the ones in trouble. Even if you decide to change jobs, your reputation is ruined. You can threaten to sue!"

The young teacher is talking like she's had a lot of experience with the law when in fact, TV shows and novels are her only sources of legal information. She has never even *talked* to a teacher who's been accused of something she didn't do.

Nessa is thinking of the gun Beverly found in Bingham's office. The same one? "What was the principal doing going through your private space?" Searching a teacher's room without just cause sounds like harassment to her.

"He didn't say exactly. He just left a note that said *a routine search uncovered a loaded firearm. I'm sure you know that is grounds for dismissal. Please stop by the office and pick up your final check.* I don't know what I'm going to do for a job."

"Well, I'm going to look into this. It's got to be a frame-up. They didn't know you were one of Lola's friends when you were hired, but now they do. I have a feeling everyone associated with the Fancy Tramp is slated to be kicked out of Haven. He's so sure nobody will make a fuss about it, but he doesn't know me very well!" Not only is Cotton her janitor and friend, but he's been good to her mother. He deserves better than to be bullied by Bingham.

"I don't know. You might be putting your own job in danger. I sure don't want that. There's probably some other business in town who could use a caretaker. I just won't be able to use Mr. Bingham as a reference."

"Maybe the next place won't ask for one. And if anybody does, tell them to contact me. I'm good at sounding like somebody important. I'll give myself a promotion and write about all your good work! Now don't go anywhere. I'll look you up after I talk to Bingham. Maybe it isn't too late to change his mind."

When Cotton has gone, Nessa is left with the dilemma of how to report an unjust firing. The school board doesn't deal with the custodial help. They rely on their trusty principal to do the hiring and firing at that level. And as a custodian, Cotton doesn't belong to the teacher's union. Life just doesn't give some folks a fair chance. She expects the gun in question is still in Bingham's possession and has never been near the desk in the little office behind the boiler room.

If she had a class coming up next hour, Nessa would have time to cool down and plan her approach before rushing down the hall. As it is, she is propelled by her loyalties – to Cotton, to the picked-on of this world, and to clowns -- to march to the front office ready to speak her mind.

Beverly sees her coming and can sense her anger. "Mr. Bingham has someone in his office. You'll need an appointment for later."

Although the secretary is just doing her job, Nessa feels an urge to strangle her. "I have no free time except this period. I'll wait until the person in his office leaves." And she sits on a chair in a corner of the reception area with her eyes fixed on Bingham's door.

Beverly is uncomfortable. She picks up the phone. "Ms. Martin seems to have an emergency," Nessa hears her say. "Yes, sir," she then listens to the person on the other end of the line. She looks over at Nessa. "It will be at least ten minutes." Nessa nods but doesn't pick up a magazine. She simply sits and glares at Beverly. Losing focus could mean losing her chance to plead Cotton's case.

Beverly Birch looks at the clock as often as Vanessa does. The woman is likely dreading the confrontation she can see coming. She's afraid it won't be appropriate for her boss's Perfect Plan. She knows he probably expects her to put a stop to it, but the look on Vanessa Martin's face is making her lose her nerve. Instead, she offers, "Can I get you anything?"

"Yes," comes Nessa's decisive answer. "You can get me into the principal's office."

Just as both Beverly and Vanessa observe the long hand on the clock hitting the ten-minute mark, the office door opens. Mr. Bingham personally invites his English teacher to come in. "My dear Ms. Martin, what can be so important that you come to me demanding an audience? I'm a busy man, you know."

Nessa decides to ignore his pompous greeting and the obvious fact that no one from a previous meeting is leaving his office. She stands and walks purposefully toward him and waits for him to move out of her way.

As soon as they are inside where they can't be heard, she says her piece. "I've just learned that the most trustworthy and hardworking employee you have has been fired. And for what? A trumped-up charge of possessing a firearm in the school. I simply can't stay silent. Please tell me Lionel is mistaken.

Please say the cowardly note he found was a prank, not a notice from his supervisor."

Mr. Bingham's face has grown progressively redder during her rant. It has apparently come as a surprise. It's inconceivable to him that anyone would get in such an uproar about a custodian. *"He probably doesn't even know Cotton's name,"* thinks Nessa.

"Ms. Martin*!* I don't remember asking your opinion on the matter. If you want to be in charge of personnel, then get your own school. Meanwhile, Mr. Downs will learn that crime doesn't pay." And he opens the office door and waits for her to go.

"There are two janitors working here. How do you know the other guy isn't the one?"

"Because, my dear" he says in a condescending tone, "Tom Clark has been with the school for many years and nothing like this happened until Mr. Downs came along. Besides it was Down's desk where it was found. You can be sure the accusation wasn't made lightly. I know you are an enthusiastic beginner but please trust my judgement."

Nessa resists the temptation to tell him just what she thinks of his judgement. "Where do you expect Cotton to get another job if you make it known he's guilty of a crime?"

"Not my problem. He should go to a new town that doesn't have high standards. A school who doesn't protect their students. The townspeople here are going to thank me and so should Mr. Downs. I could turn him over to the police, but I'm being charitable."

Nessa can tell she's fighting a losing battle. Bingham will never acknowledge that he's manufactured the crime. His world is whatever he says it is. And after all, he's going to be a candidate for mayor so his accusations are going to escalate. "Thanks for your time," Nessa snaps as she exits the office.

"Okay, Cotton, I tried to reason with Mr. Bingham, but that isn't possible." She has stopped by the boiler area after school to say some going-away words to her friend. "You can find somebody better to work for. In fact, I may decide to join you."

"No, don't. This school needs you. They need somebody who is fair and caring. You can't leave the students at the mercy of Mr. Bingham."

"I might not have a choice. Every time I talk to him, I catch myself overstepping. One of these days, I'm going to step right off into unemployment."

"Speaking of unemployment..." He gives her a rueful smile.

While waiting in Bev's office, Nessa has come up with an idea. "I do have a suggestion for where you can apply. On my way here every day, I pass the Happy Turtle Preschool. They have a *help wanted* sign out front. Hopefully, it's a paid position. You'd be super with that age."

"Hey, that does sound tempting." And Cotton smiles for the first time today. "I'll look into it. Trouble is, they'll want references."

"Just let me know, and I'll find you some. Doesn't Ms. Sofie sound like a preschool's friend? Or, like I said before, I can fake a reference if I have to."

Nessa would desperately like to help this nice man. Life seems to be handing him disappointments he doesn't deserve.

31

"I've got some news!" John has called on Nessa's cell phone during lunch. From the sound of his voice, he's learned something positive. "I talked to my attorney and he's now on the job.

"Sounds hopeful, but what exactly does that mean? What's he doing?"

"Well, first off, he counted all the regular cash that was in the jars. It came to over $100,000!"

"Yikes! Have you told Monique? She'll go crazy!"

"No, I haven't. I kinda took it on myself to open a special account at the bank in Arbor City. It's under Monique's name but is called Building Fund. She needs to go give them her signature. We don't want word to get around Haven about what was in the house."

"Sounds like a good idea. But do we know Monique gets to keep it? Does your attorney know the law on those things?"

"He looked it up. Haven is a town with no specific ordinance on found money. He thinks she can just keep it, but suggests we be on the safe side and post a notice for about a week in case anyone claims it."

"Are you kidding? I think I'll claim it. How could you prove it isn't mine?"

"He'll publish it in an obscure place, and there will be things the claimant has to provide. The amount of the money, the place it was hidden and approximately when, things like that. I doubt anybody will have a convincing story."

"I wouldn't count on it. And what about the vintage coins, the ones that might be worth big money?"

"My friend at the coin shop in still working on researching them, and I think the results are going to shock us all. There won't be anything said in the ad about those. The person who comes forward will be expected to bring up the subject of collectible coins.

"It sounds kind of pointless to look for the person who lost it all."

"I know, but God's attorney will feel better if he gives it a shot. Meanwhile, the regular bills are enough to finance most of the improvements on the Fancy Tramp. I'll have to explain to Monique how that'll work. I doubt she's ever even heard of as much money as she has in her account now."

"Gee, maybe she'll decide to forget running a rooming house. She's rich enough just to have a nice retirement and let the Association deal with all the headaches of that old building!"

"True, but I don't see Monique handling things that way. Some folks are counting on her for a place to live and maybe being paid for some renovation. She'll want to help as many of the clowns as possible."

32

"Ms. Martin!" The principal's voice catches up with her just before she reaches the door to her room after lunch. "May I have a word with you?" Students in the hallway look surprised and whisper among themselves as Nessa makes her way back toward the administrative offices. Young people sometimes enjoy hearing teachers get reprimanded. Why should teachers get away with everything when the students don't?

Beverly has been watching but lowers her eyes as Nessa approaches. Someone is in hot water, and she doesn't want to be associated with it.

Upon entering Mr. Bingham's office, Vanessa gets in the first word. "Was it necessary to yell at me in front of the students?"

"What does it matter? It lets them know that the same thing will apply to them if they make any trouble."

"Is that what I've done – made trouble?" Sometimes she expects to be called on the carpet but not today. Today she needs for school to go smoothly.

"That's what I intend to find out. I'm very disturbed."

You got that right, Vanessa comments to herself.

"It has to do with Melody."

"Melody?"

"Don't play dumb with me. Your black friend has been harassing my daughter, and I won't have it!"

Nessa is speechless. Pike might be overly friendly and persistent, but he doesn't *harass* people. And if he did, how would Nessa be responsible? "You'll have to explain that to me, Mr. Bingham."

She wanted to say, *"And when you use his name you don't have to specify that Pike is black. I don't tell anyone I'm going to talk to Mr. Bingham, my white principal."* She does, however, still have a little control over her mouth so refrains from making her point.

"Sit." She sits. The man stands looking down at her. Once again she's the object of his I-can-control-you stare. She doesn't move or speak. *It's best*, she decides, *not to volunteer information*. Her supervisor is shaking, and the wrong words from her might cause an explosion.

A tap on the door diffuses the tension. Beverly peeks her head in. "Mr. Bingham, I thought you might have forgotten you're to speak at the coaches' meeting. I think they're waiting for you."

Bingham's facial expression goes temporarily blank. It's obvious he has no memory of a meeting. Nessa wonders if Beverly might be inventing one. Then he comes to and starts gathering papers and laptop to make his exit. "I'm sorry. You are excused. For now. We will have our session very soon. Count on it, Ms. Martin." He marches through the door, shutting it in her face.

Nessa knows how a murderer on death row must feel when he's primed for the electric chair but gets a last minute reprieve. She wonders if it wouldn't have been less painful to have gotten it over with. Nevertheless, on her way out of the principal's office, she smiles weakly at Beverly and whispers "Thanks."

Nessa has stopped by the secretary's office again during her free period. "Did Mr. Bingham say any more about why he was yelling at me this morning? I need to get prepared because the first chance he gets, I know he'll start where he left off."

"I think he was upset over a family matter. He doesn't confide in me about his personal problems."

"I'm sure you know more than I do about them," Nessa persists.

"All I know about his home life is that his wife never comes here. He has two girls. One is out of school and is a store manager somewhere. I've overheard him bragging about her. The younger one is a mystery. I think her name is Katrinka, but I only saw that on some online form. I asked once, but he gave me such a sharp answer I never tried again."

"I'm just guessing," says Nessa, "but I feel like his younger daughter's story could be a reason for his obsession with normal children."

"Oh, my. I wouldn't know about that. No, I wouldn't know, and I won't pry. I know not to pry." Beverly becomes absorbed in her computer, and Vanessa admonishes herself for saying too much. She should know by now Beverly won't risk her job by speculating on her boss's motives. Not after the dressing down he gave her when he found her in his office.

"Yoo-hoo! Nessa!" The greeting is loud and shrill and impossible to ignore. Everyone within ten feet turns and, no doubt, people in nearby classrooms are curious, too. Around the corner of the hallway comes a tall, outlandishly-clad woman with fiery red hair. Her showy makeup and frantic demeanor remind Nessa of Carol Channing in old movies she's seen. Trying to balance on three-inch platform shoes, the woman is huffing and puffing like she's just run a marathon. Nessa can't believe she's seeing Lola inside this building. *How did she even get through the locked front door?*

"Lola! Did you walk all the way from the Fancy Tramp?"

"No, I rode my bike, but I was scared the whole time. Afraid some man was hiding in the trees!"

"What's so important it can't wait until I get home from work?"

"Something has happened to Pike! No one's seen him today. Not at the house or at the grocery store. We need to send out a search party!"

Nessa makes a mental note not to tell Lola any secrets. The woman doesn't know the meaning of discretion. Or how to behave in a school that's in session. "Come on down to my room and tell me about it." And Nessa takes Lola's arm and practically drags her down the hall.

We might only allow normal students in the building, but it seems like I'm always counseling some adult who has abnormal concerns.

"Lola, I think you can relax. Pike is an adult. He can go where he wants to. Maybe you don't know that he has a girlfriend. He may have stayed all night with her. Maybe they're doing something special today. They could even have eloped. I don't think we should panic."

"I'd be comforted by that except he left his bag behind and his favorite book. Pike's a good boy. If he'd been planning to run away or even take a vacation, he'd have told us."

In spite of her own reassuring words, Nessa is starting to get nervous. She takes out her cell phone and hits John's number. The bell for class rings just as he answers. "We have a possible emergency with Pike," she informs him. "I'm going to let Lola tell you about it while I start class." And she hands the phone to her colorful friend, expecting her to take it into the hallway. Instead, Lola proceeds to let the whole room full of teens hear her conversation. "Hello, John! Pike has been kidnapped! I just know he's in trouble. We need your help!"

Immediately, the classroom is abuzz. Most of the students don't know Pike personally but are at least acquainted with the principal's daughter so are aware she is seeing Pike, a black guy, the only one in town. And he's missing. It's perhaps the most exciting thing that's happened in Haven's youth community for some time.

As soon as Lola ends her call, the offers start. "Want us to help look, Ms. Martin?" "I've got a car!" "I know where a lot of guys go when they're hiding from somebody!"

Vanessa is quick to silence the room. "We really appreciate your interest in our friend, but I can't let you leave school. It isn't that big an emergency yet. He's a very bright and dependable young man, and I'm sure he can take care of himself. He'll show up soon and have a good story to tell." As she's talking, Nessa has to fight tears. She's remembering how clowns seem to disappear from Haven without a trace. Most people in town aren't aware of Pike's background, but there are a few who are. And those are probably the same ones who eliminated the creepy clowns of 2015.

33

$\mathcal{A}$s soon as school is dismissed for the day and Vanessa is waiting the required half hour before leaving, she calls John. She needs to follow up the disjointed information he received from Lola earlier. "Do you know anything more about Pike?"

"No – sorry. I talked to folks at the grocery store, and they didn't have any ideas. Said he hadn't mentioned he'd be gone today. I even spoke to Melody. I'd been pretty sure she and Pike were together, but she doesn't know any more than we do. I'm afraid I scared her pretty bad. I talked to the neighbor who's housing the van, and she hasn't seen any strangers in the neighborhood. I even asked at the diner and chatted quite a while with Lola, Monique and Sofie. They're frantic but didn't give me any clues to work with."

"I wish someone knew where Pike's family are. I doubt he'd go there, but you never know. Maybe he's thinking of asking Melody to marry him and feels he should give his parents a head's up."

"You have a great imagination, Ness, but that doesn't fit what I know about the guy. I don't think he'd skip out on work for anything. Or leave without telling Melody. I think something or somebody caused him to go all of a sudden. Probably against his will."

"You're talking about kidnapping."

"Sort of. Or he could've been threatened – *Get out of Haven or else*. Maybe they said they were going to hurt Melody."

Sadly, Nessa doesn't find that a far-fetched idea. "What now? Should we say anything to the police? They can get help from other towns."

"Yes, but I don't trust them. Several officers belong to the Association, and they hate blacks and clowns. I should be questioning *them* about their guilt."

"I agree," says Vanessa, "but telling them the situation can't hurt. If they're in on it, they already know Pike's gone, and there's a small chance you'll get to talk to an honest cop. Even if there's only one of those."

"True. And I guess it would tell us a lot if they don't even report his disappearance to the Arbor City department. That would let us know we should concentrate on the Haven PD."

At four o'clock on the dot Vanessa dashes to the front entrance.

"Not so fast, Ms. Martin!" It is David Bingham. "I don't have time now to talk about the matter from this morning, but I do want to let you know that I'm aware you have personal friends visit you in your room from time to time. Today it was even during class hours." His voice is tight, as though he's attempting to control his temper. *Why did Lola have to be so loud?*

"I'm sorry about that. It was an emergency." She's speaking rapidly, hoping he'll take the hint and not keep talking.

"Kindly tell your strange friends that no emergency is reason enough for them to come barging into a classroom. The woman should've stopped in Beverly's office. I could report you to the school board for such a thing. I'll let it go this once, however, since I have urgent matters of my own to deal with. Are we clear, Ms. Martin?"

"Absolutely," Nessa replies, one foot out the door. On her way to the car she considers the possibility that Bingham's urgent matters are the cause of hers. Directly or indirectly.

She goes on into the house, hoping to see Pike's smiling face. She's gotten used to finding him sitting on the floor in front of her door with an open book in his lap. Even when she's tired, she can't resist the young man's enthusiasm for learning. They will struggle through a few more paragraphs of Harry Potter, and he will be able to clear up all the confusion of the day. Obviously, she isn't to be that lucky. Her friend is not in sight, but there is a figure sitting in front of her apartment in his spot. This visitor has long blonde hair. "Melody!"

"I'm sorry to surprise you, Ms. Martin. But I didn't have your phone number."

"That's okay, hon. I've been wanting to talk to you ever since I heard about Pike. Come on in."

Once they are settled on Nessa's couch and sipping from cups of hot tea, Melody lets her feelings show. Tears are quick to come when she says, "I'm so scared, Vanessa. I just know something awful has happened to him."

Nessa keeps her voice steady, trying not to convey her own fears. "Do you have a particular reason to think that, or do you just have a gut feeling?"

"Both. But mainly, I have a reason. Pike and I ate at the diner Wednesday evening. We haven't been hardly anywhere together, but we were hungry, and Doug's seemed like such a safe place to go. Well, when we came out, we ran into my father. He went absolutely ballistic. Pike had been so nice paying for my meal and everything, and then he got treated like a molester."

What a shame Vanessa was thinking. Mr. Bingham doesn't know when to be grateful. He has the nicest daughter, and Pike is every bit a gentleman. They weren't eloping when he caught them. Only having burgers. "Go on," she prompts.

"Well, Dad said he doesn't want to see Pike's ugly black face again. Not anywhere in this town! He said if he finds out Pike put his dirty paws on me, he'll have him killed. I doubt if he meant it. He just loses his head sometimes and says horrible things, even at home. He used to scare Trink so bad she'd have a seizure. Most people haven't seen that side of him."

"Melody, do you honestly think he might have done something to harm Pike? Or maybe to scare him into running away?"

"He might have hurt him, but more likely he'd have somebody else do it. Dad isn't a good fighter. He just talks tough. But he has a lot of friends who'd love to work some Afro-American over. Pike wouldn't run from danger even when he should. He'd stay and fight for me. To the death, I'm afraid."

Nessa is quiet. She looks down at her cup and notices how tightly she's gripping the handle. *What if Pike is lying somewhere while we're sipping tea?* "We have to do something. Tomorrow is Saturday. I can round up a bunch of my students to search. But I don't want to just wait around in the meantime. What about the woods behind the Fancy Tramp where you two walk? You said you might have seen some of your dad's friends in there. Is it possible they have a secret meeting place in the trees where they could be holding Pike?"

"I'm not sure. We haven't been very deep into the woods. It's starting to get dark already though." Her eyes get wide when something occurs to her. "What if it's a building with no lights in it? Pike must be scared. And cold. He doesn't even have a cell phone!"

"Don't worry too much about it. It was only a guess." There might not be such a building at all. But the more she thinks about it, the more she knows they need to check it out. "I'll call my friend John and have him meet us in the back yard."

197

34

John is still in Haven and more than willing to accompany the ladies into the woods. He has a flashlight in his car. While searching for another of those in the kitchen, Nessa and Melody unintentionally acquire a couple more searchers. Lola and Monique are eager to help. Lola even puts on sensible shoes for the job.

The wooded area is dense. They stay on a narrow path that indicates many before them have ventured through the trees, but there's no telling if the path was made recently or fifty years ago. If there was never a cabin back there, where have people been going? It could simply be a shortcut to the highway which is about two miles away.

"I don't think Daddy would be able to come this far," says Melody when they've walked for fifteen minutes. "He's claustrophobic, and I'm even feeling a little closed in right now. It wouldn't bother Pike though. Nothing bothers him. He just does what he has to do." That thought seems to give her courage, and she picks up her pace.

Nessa thinks Melody knows Michael Pikeston very well. If anyone can elude a bunch of out-of-shape businessmen, he can. She spies a piece of something that looks like cardboard sticking up from a pile of leaves and stoops to pick it up. Under the glow of her small flashlight, she sees it's an unfamiliar one but definitely a bookmark. It could be a clue deliberately placed where they would find it. She wonders if it's to show where Pike has walked or to reveal where he's been dragged. The leaves around it have definitely been disturbed. She puts the bookmark in her pocket and continues on without mentioning her find. It could be something discarded by a stranger and not significant at all.

"I feel like we should be putting glow paint Xs on the trees," says Monique. "What if we can't find our way back?"

"You're right. It's too dark for wandering around out here. Why don't you ladies go on back to the house, and I'll walk just a little further," says John. No doubt, he's been wishing he were alone.

Nessa understands that complete quiet and concentration are usually more efficient than chattering women who miss things. *Although, John walked right past the bookmark.*

"I'd like to stick it out, if you don't mind," says Nessa. "If you make me go to the house I'll just be holding my breath until you get back."

"I won't make you do anything." John still doesn't seem to be entirely back to his agreeable self since their disastrous date. "I just thought since it's getting dark, you might want to ..."

"Not yet."

Lola and Monique opt to go to the house and report to Sofie. She was feeling terrible about not being able to join them. She and Pike are good friends and her concern is genuine. "I'd be in your way and no good if you had to chase someone," she lamented when Lola and Monique left. Being obese causes her shame because she knows that much older women than her are fit enough to hike over trails.

"I'll stay at the house in case Pike comes back. I want to see him the second he does."

John and Nessa continue the search in silence, looking closely with flashlights at every rock and leaf they pass. Instinct tells Nessa if Pike left a bookmark on purpose, he wouldn't have stopped there. Especially when it was such a sure thing they'd be sticking to the path. She wracks her brain to think of what else he might have on him that he could drop. Sofie is sure he didn't take anything along, but surely... Then she remembers, *"Sofie gave me this ring. It used to fit her but now it doesn't. I'm going to give it to Melody someday."* It's unlikely he'd be able to make himself drop such a valuable keepsake in the woods, but if he was desperate...

Nessa mentally kicks herself for having let so much of their search go by without thinking of the ring. It would be easy enough to slip off. Even at her lowest weight, Sofie's fingers were probably thicker than Pike's. Nessa pictures a shiny gold setting, the single red ruby. If the ring fell on the ground with the stone facing up, it would be reasonably easy to spot. "Look for a ruby ring," she tells John.

"Oh, yeah? Wish I'd known when we started."

She makes no comment. She feels like asking him where his camouflage coveralls are, but catches herself. This mission is for Pike. Not for her to prove anything about John.

"Hey! Look!" Nessa lifts her head at the cry. She's been keeping her eyes on the ground. John is pointing up ahead. Hidden behind some bushes, is a crude shack. It is very small, almost small enough to be missed behind the thick growth of bushes.

"Oh, my gosh!" she says in an excited whisper. "We've found him!"

"Let's don't get excited yet," John cautions. "Even if he was here, he may be gone by now."

Or he might be dead Nessa thinks before she gets a grip and realizes they have no evidence of anything so grim.

Not knowing who they might encounter inside the little cabin, they approach carefully, treading lightly. It is quite dark now, and it occurs to Nessa that Pike's dark face and hair won't be easy to spot. She has no memory of what he was wearing when she saw him last. He often wears bright-colored shirts.

John knocks on the door. Not that he's expecting someone to step up and greet them, but it seems the thing to do, to warn whoever's inside they have company. But there's no response. Not even the scurrying of mice or raccoons. John proceeds to push on the door which gives way only about an inch. The impression is that the wood is swollen, and that no one has passed through for a long time. He slams his body against it and is rewarded by a squeaking that indicates the old hinges still work. There is, of course, no light switch, and the two windows are boarded shut so the only light is from their flashlights and large cracks in the walls. They sweep the room with their little bit of illumination, being careful to show the corners. They also walk over every inch of the floor to see if they bump into something __or someone.

"Nobody's here, but we should come back tomorrow when we have more light. You never know what clue might be lurking."

Nessa's disappointment is acute. She has felt a strong sense of being in the right place. Apparently, they're just too late. The front door of the little building has a porch area which amounts to four rotting 2x4's. Nessa's thin-soled canvas shoes feel a definite lump underneath. Her guess is that it's a pebble which would feel even worse inside her tennies. Instinctively, she bends over and picks it up. A dark red stone winks at her. "John! It's...it's the ring. Pike's ring! He's been here!"

John hasn't been around Pike enough to know what ring she's talking about but is happy about her happiness. "You're sure?"

"Yes! Yes! I saw him wearing it just a couple of days ago." They are both silent for a few minutes. The news is positive – most likely. But what comes next? A ring on the porch of a deserted shack doesn't tell them where Pike is now. It doesn't even tell them if he's hiding or if he's been abducted. Or if he's alive. Still, it feels better than nothing.

John and Nessa follow the worn path beyond the cabin all the way to the highway. No more clues are found. Their friend was in the area but isn't close by now. There's nothing to tell them he ever got further than the cabin.

"Pike wouldn't play games with us. He would have revealed himself by now if he could have. He's definitely in trouble."

"You could be right," replies John. "I keep expecting a figure in camouflage to step out into our path. Somebody who just stares and hopes to frighten us."

Nessa's nerves are shot, and her earlier intention not to start an argument has deserted her. "Is that what you thought when you bought camouflage last Saturday? That you could intimidate someone on the street?"

With no discussion, they've both turned around and are trudging back in the direction of the rooming house. John stops in his tracks. "Uh ... what?"

"You heard me. I saw your sacks from Farm and Fleet. I know you bought the camo coveralls. Just like I saw in Bingham's closet. Too much of a coincidence."

John stares at her. "Ha. I knew something's been eating you. Couldn't imagine what. You think I've joined the Association! Why would you believe a screwball idea like that?

Looking straight at John's handsome, open face, Nessa is pretty amazed that he's right. That's exactly what she thinks, though right at the moment her reasons seem pretty unclear. "I saw what was in your sack the night of the movie. Or at least I saw what color it was -- Camoflage." *Good timing, Nessa. If you're right, you've just given him a reason to hurt you and nobody's going to know, given that you're in the middle of the woods and everyone who'd miss you has gone.*

"You know, the best thing to do when you suspect a friend of something bad is to ask! I didn't know you saw what was in that sack or I'd have explained it. Jumping to your own conclusions without giving me the chance to defend myself is a pretty crappy thing to do!" John is mad, no doubt about it.

"Well, things haven't been so logical around here lately. And you've already lied to me once about your identity. I don't see why it's such a stretch to think you'd lie again. I don't really know you at all!" Nessa isn't about to feel guilty. Yes, maybe she should've given him a chance, but using that logic, she should've given Mr. Bingham one, too. Maybe the outfit in his closet was a Halloween costume. Maybe the principal is just a misunderstood dad. No one to worry about. She starts walking. Her first inclination is to go back to Chicago where life for her was much more straightforward. People in her neighborhood there minded their own business.

John is right behind her. "Okay. Now you've gotten it off your chest, and maybe I can't blame you. But just listen to me. I was at Farm and Fleet and saw those coveralls hanging there. Twenty-three dollars and anyone can dress up as a scary bigot. It crossed my mind that if I could disguise myself, I might be able to infiltrate their group. If I went where they were and kept a low profile, I might at least find out who some of the members are. It just seemed like a costume that might come in handy. If I were trying to trap the KKK, I might have to wear a pointed white head cover. I didn't have a definite plan. Private investigators sometimes have to resort to unconventional tactics. It was an impulse buy that I might never use. I thought you'd tell me it was too risky so I didn't mention it. Guess I was wrong thinking you'd worry about my safety." He looked so down-in-the-mouth Nessa found herself backtracking.

"I don't know anymore. I've just gotten to the place where I'm suspicious of everyone. Forget I said anything," she tells him.

"Right," he replies as he follows her. "That's so easy to do. Maybe you have a better suggestion of how to stop those pals of Bingham's?"

"Of course, I don't. You're the expert. All I know about is Shakespeare. We nerds have to depend on you people with criminal experience."

The walk back is a quiet one and takes much less time than their entry. When they emerge into the Fancy Tramp's back yard they are greeted by Sofie, Lola, and Monique. What an army, the overweight and the aged. *How on earth did Sofie get all the way downstairs and out onto the lawn?*

A few short minutes after they emerged into the back yard, Nessa notices that John is no longer nearby. She knows she should be curious, but her immediate reaction is relief. It's difficult to sort out her feelings about him and worry about Pike at the same time. John can take care of himself.

In answer to Nessa's unuttered question, Lola says, "I thought Sofie needed to be down here. She pretty much raised Pike and is very upset by his disappearance."

"You don't look happy. You must not have found him," comments Ms. Sofie when she catches up to her friends.

"We found a couple of things that prove Pike was in the woods, but he doesn't seem to be there now." Sofie might not want to hear that her young friend threw her ring onto an old board. "Of course, we stuck to the path. Nothing says he couldn't be among the trees on either side. If I can get some of my students organized, they can cover the area better."

"Well, I don't think you need to wonder if he left on his own. Pike always tells me when he knows he's going someplace. Ever since he came to the circus he's checked with me even if he was just going across the grounds. I don't think his real parents ever cared where he was, and he liked the idea that I did." After expending so much effort to get out of the house, the woman looks ready to collapse into tears.

In a crisis, it seems, Lola reveals her practical side. "I believe you're right, Sofie, but in this case he could've been protecting you by not saying anything. Those men who've infiltrated our woods are dangerous, and they have definitely targeted Pike. He might have gone off to fight them on his own. He would know you'd be terrified if you knew."

"Well, here we are, terrified anyway," moans Monique. She's pretty old for so much tension. Waiting and doing nothing is turning out to be more nerve-wracking than if they joined the search.

"Just the same, Pike will be more effective if he takes on those creeps without having us to worry about. We need to have faith in him," Lola instructs her group. "Keep your phones charged in case he calls. I don't know that he has a phone but he can probably get hold of one. He might need us to do something for him, and he won't feel safe notifying the police. Whatever you do, don't answer any questions from outsiders no matter how well-meaning they seem."

Lola's idea about the phones gives the friends a purpose, a possible way to make a difference so the overall anxiety level seems to decrease. Ms. Sofie leaves them with still another mission. "Before you go inside, please scan the area around here for a black cat – a blue ruffle might still be around his neck. He answers to the name of Moe."

A few people searched as she asked. Finding a missing cat might be more possible than locating a missing man.

35

When Nessa gets back to her apartment, Melody is again parked in her spot in front of the door.

"You haven't found him, have you?" Nessa's face conveys her answer, and Melody continues, "I've been thinking and thinking about where he could be. We talked quite a while after work yesterday. Pike was really worried that Monique is going to lose the house. He keeps thinking he can find time to do all the work it needs. He always wants to save the day. He doesn't have enough time or know enough about construction, but I think he was planning to find somebody who does."

"I hope that's it. Have you talked to your dad? You said earlier you were afraid he might be responsible for Pike's disappearance."

"I still think so, but I haven't seen him since then. I hope he's at home watching TV and not involved in this at all. Just by making phone calls, he can cause a lot of trouble. Someone told him that Pike clowned at the Maynard Home. He screamed that he's going to have to find another place for Katrinka. I hate that because he might put her far away from Mother and me. We're her only visitors."

"Nuts. I was afraid we were going to pay for that visit to Maynard. I wish he'd talk to the staff there and find out how much his daughter enjoyed it."

"What Kat enjoys doesn't matter to him. He doesn't even want people to know there is such a person as her. He's come right out and said he's embarrassed to have a mentally deficient person in the family."

"Ironic. In my opinion, your sister isn't the Bingham with the mental problems." Nessa is afraid she's being rude. She has just recently come on the scene and has no right to insult Melody's father in front of the girl. "I'm sorry. I shouldn't have said that."

"It's okay. I agree with you. I've known that about my dad for a while now. And I worry about Mother. She's found out she has very early signs of Alzheimer's. I'm the only one who knows. Dad is never going to be able to deal with something so devastating. He'll put her away somewhere awful and never mention her again."

Nessa is appalled. Granted, the family has more than its share of troubles, but Mr. Bingham may be the worst of those.

"I can't tell you how sorry I am, Melody...I"

"Don't worry. You have enough going on without my complaints. Can I do anything, or would you like for me to leave and get out of your way?"

"Oh, no. Stay here. You don't have to do anything, but if Pike comes back tonight, he'll want to see you."

"If," Melody answers bleakly.

36

The search continues after the supper hour. Some of Nessa's students have made their way to the Fancy Tramp and organized themselves to cover the hiking trails behind the house. There are so many circles of light jumping around it's hard to determine which ones belong to the good guys and which ones don't.

Nessa and Melody are sitting with Lola on the front porch. The women hate to leave Gordy alone and want to be available if Pike manages to call. Even if he gets hold of a phone, reception in the woods is poor.

A lone man approaches from the street below. He is dressed in a suit and tie, not typical for Fancy Tramp patrons. When he can be seen more closely, it becomes clear they are getting a visit from the distinguished high school principal. Nessa sighs. The night has enough drama without Mr. Bingham. "Go on inside, Melody," she says quietly to the girl at her side. Melody quickly obeys. Nobody wants a scene.

No greeting. No condolences about their missing friend. "I've been informed that an unauthorized school activity is going on here this evening." His tone implies he's ready for a confrontation.

"Nothing like that, Mr. Bingham," responds Nessa. "Just a few of my friends lending a hand. The kind of thing that happens in a perfect little town."

The dim light in the yard keeps Nessa from seeing her boss's reaction, but she can feel it. "What exactly are they lending you a hand with?"

Though it isn't any of his business, she knows he can easily find out what's going on from someone else. "One of the apartment residents is missing and lots of people want to find him."

"You mean the black fellow?"

"I guess you've heard. Are you here to pitch in?"

"Not on your life. I hope the kid gets lynched. He's become a threat to my happy home, and I've had enough. I'm only here to determine whether my daughter has gotten caught up in this mess. If so, I'll see she gets away safely."

Since Bingham knew about the "unauthorized school activity" and about the likelihood that Melody could be caught up "in this mess", he must know about Pike's disappearance. He may even have given an order to have him captured. Nessa is glad she can tell him, "I think Melody is around someplace but am sure she'll stay for the duration. She isn't going to want to go anywhere until they find Pike."

Bingham's face shows red under the yard light. "We'll see about that. She can't be allowed in those woods. There are men with weapons in there! Her mother is frantic that she'll get hurt. I had no idea my daughter was near here, or I'd never ..."

"Or you'd never have ordered your thugs to infiltrate the woods on Lola's property? I'm glad you admit to that, Mr. Bingham. You know, when you play with firearms, you have to be prepared for the wrong people to get in the way."

"Melody has been told not to come within a hundred feet of this brothel. And especially not late in the evening."

Oh, I've been very confused," confesses Nessa. "I assumed Melody is twenty-one years old. Old enough to decide her own curfew."

Lola has been quiet up till now, unusual for her. "I have coffee," she tells Mr. Bingham. "I'll get you some if you think you want to wait around to see Pike. I've decided he's coming back tonight. I just have a feeling. If he does, we'll be having a party! We may have to find something stronger than coffee!"

Nessa remembers Lola's birthday and realizes the often serious-minded apartment manager can be a party girl when life allows her a little freedom. Clowns, after all, enjoy people. And fun.

Ms. Sofie waddles around the side of the building. "Oh, hello, everyone! I can't be much help finding Pike, but I'm channeling my worry into looking for Moe." She looks hopefully at Mr. Bingham. "If you're going to be here awhile, perhaps you can keep an eye out for my precious little cat. He's actually an exceptional performer and very social. He's sure to show himself soon though he's probably frightened by all this hubbub tonight. He's black, but his ruffled collar is a fluorescent blue that shows up at night."

"I hate cats! I just saw a black one at the end of the drive. The dam thing was ready to cross my path. I took out my gun, and if it hadn't run, I'd have blasted the beast!" The idea of a bearer of bad luck sneaking up on him puts Bingham near collapse. Sofie ignores his bluster and persuades Lola to help her look for Moe   .

This evening amid a crowd of oddities is hard for a man of Bingham's sensibilities. His cell phone rings, interrupting his escalating anger. "Yes, Beverly," he answers impatiently. "I'm at that run-down old hotel where Ms. Martin lives. The place the Association is going to own soon" He listens to his secretary who is speaking loudly on the other end of the line. "I don't know. There are a lot of things happening. I'm not sure which one you want to hear about." He holds the phone to his ear for some time then says "Come if you want but don't know why you would," and then hangs up looking baffled by the activity around him. If he has ordered Pike's abduction, he is likely amazed by the fact that anyone else in town takes notice. A black person is a dispensable member of society. His absence should be of no more consequence than the fat woman's black cat.

Nessa has determined that Bingham poses no immediate danger, so she leaves him in the grass. In the back yard she surveys the activity. She estimates fifty high schoolers are swarming the area, and there seems to be a changing of the guard taking place. A stream of men in camouflage are ascending the hill while others emerge from the woods. Those who are leaving have shed their sunglasses and many are recognizable as policemen, store owners, etc. Most are carrying weapons and look somewhat embarrassed to be seen. Before their teenage children can pick out their parents, the men scurry down the hill to their waiting cars.

John catches up with one of the slowest, an overweight man breathing hard and making little headway down the slope. "Excuse me," says the PI, "I'm doing a story on this incident. May I ask you a couple of quick questions?"

The chubby guy seems relieved to have a reason to slow down. As John knows, a reporter sounds less threatening than anyone from law enforcement. The men in uniform might even welcome a certain amount of press. "A couple, I guess. I'm not sure I can help though."

"I understand you belong to the Association. Has that group orchestrated the vanishing of Michael Pikeston?"

"I don't know anybody by that name. We just patrol these woods. Our job is to protect the town from any and all invaders. If Pikeston is one of those, he's on our hit list."

John is speechless for a minute. *Hit list* sounds serious. "If you don't know for sure who's on the list, who do you take your orders from?"

"Sorry. I can't say. Just be glad somebody is watching out for the best interests of the town. And be glad for natural barriers like these woods. It helps us control who comes and goes."

"I don't understand who appointed you the keepers of the town and gave you the right to trespass on Monique Dubois's property. I'm afraid somebody could get hurt by you guys who are supposedly protecting us." To John, it appears the townsmen are like men who play war games. It's a way to feel tough and to imitate action heroes they idolize.

"Not if you're a legitimate citizen. If you don't pose a danger to Haven, you have nothing to worry about. My shift is over. I have to go." The man has recovered his breathing and takes off to follow his fellow soldiers.

Concern about Pike increases. Nessa wonders how hard it will be for him to get back to them if the guards of the town decide he isn't a "legitimate citizen".

37

The search continues with no noticeable lessening of enthusiasm. Beverly makes an appearance and is put in charge of keeping track of clues people find. She sets up a desk on the porch to direct newcomers to places that haven't yet been searched. Lola keeps making coffee and lemonade while Gordy hands the volunteers paper cups. Ms. Sofie has come forth with cookies from a mysterious stash she seems to have upstairs. Somebody must have called Cotton because he is taking part in the search. Melody is in the house, staying away from her father and his henchmen.

The excitement caused by Pike's disappearance is akin to a house fire. The late summer evening encourages many residents to come into their yards to investigate. One woman is approaching from the driveway, swinging a lantern. Nessa is surprised to recognize the neighbor who is renting Lola her garage. It seems the elderly lady has something important to say. She is panting from her uphill trek.

"I'm Mrs. Arnold. From down below." She points in the direction of the small white house with the large garage. "Where your van has been housed?"

"Yes! Thanks for coming. Is everything alright?"

"Well, no. Your friend, the detective, asked me this morning if anyone came around and took the big van in the last couple of days. I told him no one had. I mean, we don't keep the garage locked, but I was sure I'd have known if that woman Lola came after it. She'd surely have stopped at the house and said something. So I told your friend the van was still there, safe and sound."

Nessa waits impatiently for the rest of the story.

"But ... I just now went out there to look for this lantern and discovered your car isn't in the garage anymore! I couldn't believe it. I haven't had the Cooper out since Wednesday. The van was there then."

"That's interesting," Nessa agrees. "I was thinking we tried to open it that day the detective and I were at your house, and we found the van to be locked. Lola would be the only person with a key. She must have needed it." She remembers Lola saying she rode her bicycle to the school earlier today, but Nessa knows she wouldn't take the van with its logo out in public just for a trip to some place in town.

Mrs. Arnold is getting nervous, afraid of being blamed. "I didn't touch it. I barely let myself look at that big thing, and I wouldn't know how to open a locked car without a key."

"I know you didn't bother it. It had to be one of the people who lives in this house. One of them can't be located right now, and his friends have been worried. Now maybe we can all rest easy knowing for sure he drove himself away. It isn't your fault, Mrs. Arnold. We couldn't expect you to watch the garage every minute. He most likely took the van in the night. We appreciate you letting us know."

Nessa meets the manager coming from the kitchen with more coffee. "Lola, I've been wanting to ask you if you've taken the van out of storage. Mrs. Arnold says it's gone."

"Oh, my no! I don't dare let anyone see it. It has our logo painted on the side."

"Is your key missing? Because someone drove it away."

Lola turns around in circles twice, balancing the coffee pot, while she tries to decide where to look for the key. "Oh, stars! I don't exactly know where it was last. I'm sure I put it in a very good place. I'm not one to throw keys in the garbage or leave them in an old purse. I would've known how important it was, and I would've thought about it, and I would've put it where no one could possibly find it." Lola is coming up with no recollections.

Nessa and Mrs. Arnold are staring at the red-headed woman, knowing that in fact, she is wrong. Someone must have found it.

"Do you have a nail or a hook of some kind where you hang things like that? Lots of people do. Or maybe a trinket box or junk drawer where you put small things?" Lola shakes her head. "Well then, one of the renters must have borrowed it. Actually, you might have put it in a pocket and lost it where someone downtown picked it up." Nessa is trying not to get irritated. But reducing Lola to tears isn't going to tell them who took the van.

Melody offers a bit of information, "Pike always has one hanging on a chain around his neck. I don't know what that belongs to. He said he couldn't tell me, that it's top secret, and he can't take a chance on losing it."

"Oh!" Lola is smiling now. "Of course! I knew I wasn't to be trusted with it, so I gave the key to Pike! That dear boy is keeping it for me." Her eyes get even wider than usual as an idea dawns. "He has to be the person who took the van out of the garage. At least that means he's alive. Doesn't it? He couldn't possibly drive it if he weren't. "

Nessa can't wait to tell John. "Pike has the van! That's a really good sign, I think."

"Really? When did he take it?"

"We're not sure. Sometime after Wednesday. I'm surprised he didn't just tell us if he needed to go out of town."

"Maybe he couldn't. Maybe he isn't the one in charge. Someone may be forcing him to go somewhere. Or transporting him."

"What are you saying? Most people are starting to relax. Don't get morbid now!"

"The others don't know the things we found in the woods. If Pike were on his own errand and in no danger, I don't think he'd be dropping things for us to find. Especially not his valuable ring. He may have started out to pick up some acquaintance but got waylaid by the creepy camouflage guys on his way. If they tied him up or hurt him, they'd want to take him someplace away from here."

"Well, you sure are the pessimist. Do you think we should send everyone home? Just give up?" She isn't sure why she's so irritated at John. Maybe because he's right. She shouldn't have dropped her concern so fast. If Pike were safe like she's been telling herself, he'd have been in touch.

Along about four on Saturday morning, clouds have taken over and raindrops have started. Many of the young people begin to drift away. Because they've discovered no intriguing clues, they've been left with feelings of pointlessness. Searching just to be searching is not enough to sustain the interest of teens. Plus everyone is tired, and now they are about to be drenched.

"Find my daughter!" demands David Bingham. "Her mother will be fit to be tied if I allow her to continue this charade. Who cares where the black dude is? He's probably someplace warm, laughing at us."

Nessa has no answer for her boss. She's been wondering herself if the whole thing isn't an elaborate hoax. If she didn't know Pike to be such a responsible guy, she could've been convinced. Mr. Bingham obviously hates him but doesn't seem to have a clue what has happened to him.

Lola comes into the yard and rounds up her renters. "Come on inside, folks! Time for the Alley!" Nessa knows by now, those meetings don't include her. She takes a seat in the wicker porch rocker and watches the lightning. "Come on back, Pike," she calls into the air. "We've had enough excitement."

Instead of Pike, she is joined by her boss. It crosses her mind that other HHS staff would be stunned to know their principal has been up all night and now sits on the English teacher's porch.

"You know, if anything tragic happens tonight, you can kiss your career good-bye."

The man has lost sleep and is afraid for Melody, but Nessa still sees no justification for his extreme threat. "I'm just a renter here, Mr. Bingham. I didn't invite this emergency."

"Maybe not, but this kind of mixing of blacks and clowns and riff raff never occurred before you arrived."

A small black cat with a torn neck ruffle crawls up onto Nessa's lap, purring loudly. "Well, Moe! What a nice surprise! Welcome!" And though they've never met before, she gives the cat a big hug. "Where have you been since I've lived here?" Moe doesn't respond. "I bet you have a story if you could only tell it. I wonder if Pike will have a good one, too. I wish he'd appear as suddenly as you."

Nessa does the honors of taking Moe upstairs to Ms. Sofie. She's excited about surprising her friend but feels like she's betraying Moe. The poor cat wanted so desperately to get out of that big house that he jumped two stories and then existed on his own for two months. That should tell her that Moe gets claustrophobic. *We just assume a cat's phobia is no big deal, but those things shouldn't be taken lightly for anyone. Just ask Tracy.*

The knock on her door brings Ms. Sofie scurrying as fast as her chubby limbs can carry her. Upon seeing the face of her beloved Moe, she starts to cry. "Oh, my baby! I knew you'd be back. I never believed you'd left us for good." And she hugs him hard enough to bring on another bout of claustrophobia in the small animal.

Ms. Sofie faces Nessa. "Where did you find him? In the woods?"

"No, he just came onto the porch and crawled up on my lap. He couldn't explain, of course, but I'm wondering if he hasn't been trapped in a garage somewhere and just now got free."

"That sounds possible except the garage must've had lots of mice. He isn't a bit skinny. I guess he can stay fat on air. Just like his Mamma." Nessa pictures the desserts in Sofie's refrigerator which dispel that comparison.

She dares to offer a suggestion. "I was thinking maybe we can make some kind of fenced in yard out back so the cats can get some fresh air occasionally. That may help to keep any of them from wanting to break out of the house."

"Oh, you're right. I know how they feel, actually. Some days I want to hitch a ride on a bird that flies by my window!"

That scene is impossible for Nessa to picture. "Maybe after the renovation, you'd like to take my apartment on first floor, and then you can get outside whenever you want. It's just an idea."

"It's a good one. After being out in the back yard yesterday, I realized how much I like it. I promised myself that I'll start moving. I want to lose weight and join the human race. Maybe the babies and I can even get our act going again."

Nessa is pretty sure the small black performers won't be "babies" for that long.

Clown Alley

"I'm not sure how much you all know about Pike's disappearance. I just wanted to tell you that we haven't heard anything new."

"Do you think the camo men have him?"

"It's possible, but I don't know what they'd want with him. They'd be making themselves guilty of a federal crime without a reason. They haven't given anyone a ransom note or anything. We do know that he or someone who stole his key has the circus van. That big thing will be hard to keep out of sight."

"You know, it might be somebody we don't even know about. I hear every day about more folks who hate clowns – even circuses. It's like they've declared open season on the bunch of us. If one or two white-faces get killed, I doubt if anybody would bother to solve the crime. In fact, lots of folks wouldn't call it a crime."

"That is so wrong! I mean, all we've ever tried to do is make the world a happier place. We shouldn't inspire so much fear and hatred. I know there are mean clowns in the world, but there are mean teachers, mean farmers, mean school principals. It isn't fair we should all pay the price for a few bad apples."

"It's partly Stephen King's fault. If he hadn't created Pennywise..."

"You can't blame it all on one writer. People shouldn't be so easily influenced by a story."

"I say we hold our heads up. We shouldn't apologize for who we are, or go into hiding."

"Personally, I don't want to go back to clowning. I'd prefer to be a regular man who doesn't scare people. My friend Tracy will never be able to handle the fact that I used to be with a circus. It's like I have a terrible disability that she has to have therapy for."

"I'm sure she'll come around, Cotton. But right now, our main problem, besides Pike, is wondering if we can get all the improvements done to the Fancy Tramp before we're evicted. I'm happy to report that it looks now as if it may happen." Lola smiles broadly and waits for the news to sink in.

There are murmurs of amazement. How can they be promised something they can clearly not afford? If they took up a collection right now, they'd be lucky to come up with ten dollars among them. "Did you find a charitable carpenter who loves the circus?"

"No, I've never heard of anyone like that. But Monique has had a bit of good luck and might actually be rich! Or at least rich by our usual standards. We won't know exactly how much she has for a while, but it looks like there'll be enough to buy the materials and even hire some workers to get the restoration done!! And before winter gets here. Our fortunes are changing!"

"Oh, my!" Sofie exclaims. "I wish Pike knew. He would be thrilled."

38

"I'm so happy Sofie got her cat back. That gives me hope for a happy ending for Pike. Maybe we just have to give cats and people the freedom to come and go as they want." Nessa's philosophizing is coming late on Saturday when the search has been called off because of darkness.

John is free to go back to Arbor City, but it isn't like him to let a search lapse, even for a short time. "My profession is based on the idea that you do what can be done to speed up the process. We can't just wait around, and hope Pike will wander up the hill, safe and happy."

"It's funny. His parents must have felt the same way when he ran away from home as a boy. But Pike actually *was* safe then and surviving fine on his own. He's probably doing the same thing now."

"Well, just the same, I should be getting the word out more and see if I can get some leads. Twitter hasn't helped so far. I did get one phone call but she didn't have information. She wanted me to give *her* some. She didn't stay on the line long."

"What *did* you get, Mr. Detective? Her name? Her state?"

"No name. The caller ID said Arkansas. She only said that she's searching for somebody and was told I'd know all about him. Maybe she's talking about some other missing person. I told her she could send me an email or message me on Facebook, but she said she doesn't have a computer. Guess I just have to wait for her to call again. She was probably scared off when I told her how much I charge."

"I'm surprised you told her that so early in the deal."

"I usually don't, but it sounded like that was her main concern."

"What did she say when you told her how much?"

"She was pretty quiet for a while, but she didn't hang up. Probably trying to decide where she'll get the money. I'm hoping she'll call back."

"Did she have a cute southern accent? I'd take her case just to get to listen to her talk."

"She sounded like an African American. *And* southern. Soft-spoken, polite. Almost apologetic, like she feels embarrassed for needing my help."

"Hmm. Well, I hope she calls again. I feel like she could be someone we need to hear from. And I still think you have a fun job."

"Not sure *fun* is the word for it. I usually go with *interesting*. Doubt if you could do it. An investigator can't get personally involved, and I feel like that's impossible for you. You've gotten personally involved in the lives of every renter in your apartment building, and you've only known them since August."

It is nearly midnight when John's name comes up on Nessa's phone. "It's late," she answers. "No bad news, I hope."

"Don't know of any. I just wanted to hear your voice before I go to sleep."

"I'm sure that was it." She's laughing off his comment, but the truth is, part of her wishes he were serious. She loves the sound of his voice late at night. As long as it isn't an emergency. "Did your Arkansas gal call?"

"She did. She says she thinks she can probably pay me because what she's asking probably won't take very long. If it drags on, she'll just have to call it off."

"Wow. You don't have very good job security if people can just back out anytime they feel like it."

"Yeah, but I get a deposit to take care of that. And folks find out they don't want to stop once I give them a little information. Pulling out hardly ever happens. And they usually feel it's all worth it in the end."

"So who is she?" Nessa is highly curious. Any thoughts of sleep have fled.

"Her name is Mary Helen something. She's trying to find her son. He left home eleven years ago when he was only ten. Her husband, his father, wouldn't let her follow him, but the husband's dead now. I don't think her son even knows that."

"Are you sure she didn't give you a last name?" Nessa's instincts are shouting, *It has to be Pike's mother!*

"No, but I think in one more call, she'll probably be comfortable enough. I asked how she came to pick me. She said she'd heard on the news about a young man named Michael or Pike who disappeared from here. So she called information for Haven Chamber of Commerce, and when she reached them they told her about me. I'm surprised they have my name since I don't have an office in town. And don't belong to the Association."

"Don't you know who that has to be? A lady from Arkansas whose son left when he was ten?" Then Nessa remembers that John probably hasn't heard all of Pike's history. "She has to be Pike's mom! He told me she hasn't written for a long time. I'm sure he hasn't either."

"Really? Well, that does sound possible. Can you imagine parents who would just let their young boy run away without even trying to locate him. I don't know if I want to help her."

'Ah, come on. You don't know what kind of pressure she was under. I'd love to meet her. Pike has never mentioned having anything against his parents."

"Some circumstances are too awful to talk about. Anyway, the ball's in her court. I don't have enough information to reach her. She's going to have to be the one and will probably need to leave me a message. If Pike isn't back by morning, I'm going to see what I can find out. It might require some extreme measures. I might have my phone off for a while."

"Sounds like you're thinking of doing something risky. You sure you don't want someone along? I'd really like to help."

"Thanks, but I have to do this by myself. No girls allowed."

Nessa is on the front porch before dawn and looking down the driveway in front of the house, hoping to see the van. It hasn't returned, but there are several unfamiliar cars parked at the bottom of the hill. She hopes they are townspeople who are giving their mornings to the search. Though the woods has been pretty well covered, it doesn't hurt to look again for dropped clues. Other parts of the city are being combed as well. Though no one from the Fancy Tramp has called the police, she notices that one of the vehicles on the street below is a squad car. It is frightening to think it could either be friend or foe. The white car from the Haven Police Department certainly isn't a comfort.

224

She wonders what, if anything, is occurring out the back way. Lola is apparently sleeping in, but their yard could be full of helpful people who should be fed or at least given coffee. A glance out the large window in the rear of the house, lets her see camouflaged figures entering the woods. She has to face the fact that this little procession of Bingham's armed soldiers has probably been taking place every day since she's lived here. Even before that.

The impression she's had from the beginning is that the stalkers avoid arrest by carrying weapons of some kind that don't qualify as firearms. In the early morning light, she can clearly make out several men holding swords high as though they are part of a band of pirates. Are the swords even real ones? Is this a deliberate escalation? Is the fuss over Pike's disappearance putting the soldiers on some kind of red alert? Suddenly, the woods behind the Fancy Tramp look much more dangerous. And she is fearful for John as well as Pike. The PI didn't specify where he was off to, but intuition tells her, his destination is somewhere within that expanse of trees. It will be easier to worry, she decides, if she knows where John is and can keep an eye on him than if she stays behind and waits for news. She could simply have asked him where he was planning to go, but he'd have tried to protect her so wouldn't have divulged anything. She has no weapon to take along, but it's just as well. She wouldn't know the first thing about firing a gun so that could only end in tragedy. The best plan is to stay invisible and within a short distance from John. If she sees he's in trouble, she can at least try dialing 911. Hopefully, the emergency dispatchers aren't part of Bingham's team.

Nessa assumes it will help her mission if she dresses in colors that won't glow in the forest. Jeans and a dark green jacket will have to do. Camouflage would be ideal, but only John had the sense to buy some of that.

Taking off down the main path through the trees she stops every few steps to listen for voices. Her intent is to avoid running smack into a group of uniformed trespassers.

Getting braver by the minute, she turns off onto a less traveled trail. Realizing she is directionally challenged, she acknowledges the likely possibility she won't be able to find her way back and will be wandering in Lola's woods this time tomorrow. Having no crumbs like Hansel and Gretel, she periodically drops some change from her jacket pocket. Not a great idea, but at least squirrels don't eat nickels and dimes.

At last she hears male voices. Nessa quickly darts behind a large oak to listen. She can hardly believe her luck. The first words she distinguishes are those of her favorite investigator. She dares to peek around the tree. Indeed, she recognizes John, decked out in his camouflaged coveralls and wearing sun glasses. The glasses can't be much help in this sunless place, but their purpose must be anonymity rather than shade. With everyone's eyes covered, the men look very much alike.

"What next?" one of them asks. "That kid isn't around here. When the Professor said to shoot to kill, did he mean anybody we see or just the black guy?"

Nessa is disgusted that his minions call her deranged boss *Professor*. She wonders if that was his idea.

"Probably just the black guy. But I don't like it. I didn't sign on to become a killer. We could end up doing time, and we aren't even getting paid. I had to take the morning off to do this.

"My son has been part of the search. If he comes back for more, I don't want him to find out I've shot the guy he was looking for. Geez. Scaring is one thing, murder is something else. Even the creepy clowns last summer didn't go that far."

The men seem to regard each other impersonally. It must be enough that everybody is a member of Bingham's army. They don't seem curious about the fourth member of the party.

Finally, John sees his opportunity. "You know what?" he says gruffly. "I'm thinking I'm going to walk away. If Bingham wants killers, he can round up some convicts, somebody who doesn't have much to lose."

"You're really going to take off? Well, then, hell, I'm not staying. I could be deer hunting if I want to shoot something."

Nessa is holding her breath. She has her phone ready in case one of them gets suspicious of the extra guy. Her impression though, is that everyone in the group in fed up with Bingham's demands and starting to question what's in it for them. All they've been waiting for, is someone to take charge.

John waits a few minutes then takes the initiative. "So what do you guys say? Wanna split?" He looks behind him. There's nobody around to squeal." And he starts to walk away. "Coming?"

There is hesitation for one second, and then they hurry through the leaves, no one speaking. Nessa imagines each man is all of a sudden set on keeping his identity from the others.

After ten minutes, Nessa follows behind. *And I was mad at John for buying the camo!*

The arrival of a good clown exercises a more beneficial influence upon the health of a town than the arrival of twenty asses laden with drugs.
-Thomas Sydenham

39

One of the teachers from school put an announcement on email and on her Facebook page just recently, asking for information concerning the whereabouts of Michael (Pike) Pikeston of Haven, Iowa.

"I've gotten a bunch of comments but nothing definite until the last one," the teacher says excitedly. "It said they think Pike is on his way back and for us to be listening!"

"Listening? For what? Sounds of the van? I don't expect that old bus to make it very far before it starts chugging like a train."

In answer to their questions, the strains of a calliope melody can be heard in the distance. It reminds Nessa of Lola's birthday party. Happy circus music gradually enters their consciousness. Thoughts of a merry go round and wild animals make them look down the hill. Coming toward the Fancy Tramp is not only one van but also two wagons, each bearing the clown logo of HAPPCO Entertainment. Each is transporting individuals dressed in brightly-colored garb and waving balloons out the open windows and over the sides. In the driver's seat of the lead bus she can make out the smiling face of Juggles – red nose and all.

The sun shines brightly as the wagons pull into the yard, and clowns of all shapes, sizes and ages pile onto the grass. Along with them come ladders, cans of paint, bags of cement, boards, and many tools. Hopefully, someone in the group knows how to use those things. Nessa, John, Lola and all the gang are cheering loudly. No one in the neighborhood is allowed to sleep late. The clowns are on the job intending to restore the Fancy Tramp to its former glory and make sure the place remains the home of any misplaced circus folks who need a place to live.

"You scared us to death, Pike!" admonishes Lola.

"I'm sorry. Four of those dudes in camo captured me when I was walking home from work Friday. They tied me up for a few hours in the woods in a little shack, but I got away. Their knots were pretty sloppy. Then I sneaked back this way by taking the gravel south of town. I got the van and went to find some friends who found some other friends, and pretty soon we were ready to roll. All these guys are out of work and want to help!"

"Your friend could be in danger in Haven. People around here don't like clowns."

"I told them about the camo guys, and they aren't afraid. Most of them have faced worse in their lives."

"You did great, Pike!" says Lola. "We can't wait for them to get started. Lead me to the man in charge!"

"I'm him." I don't know much about construction, but I can organize the rest of them. Things will go fast."

"Just one little request, Pike," ventures Nessa. "Some people panic at the sight of a made-up clown. They have coalrophobia. So if you all don't mind, maybe could you be clowns with regular faces? Just while you're working on the house? I don't want anybody to panic and attack you."

"No problem, Nessa. We'll wash it off. There won't be any clownin' around now anyway."

"It might help create enthusiasm if you let your friends know Monique has come into some money. They don't have to cut corners now with materials. Lola will open an account at the lumber yard in Arbor City. They can just charge it when they need stuff. And, in the end, she'll be able to pay everyone for their work!"

"I don't get it." Pike can't believe Nessa is serious about a windfall of funds. "Where would Monique get money? Did she find a money tree?"

"In a way, Gordy did. It's a long story but truth is, The Fancy Tramp is in real good financial shape now."

"Well, Yippee! Heck, it seems like the world is looking pretty good. Wish there was some way to let my mom know that. She probably thinks I'm dead or something."

"Haven't you ever considered trying to find her?"

"Oh, sure but I've never had money or transportation. Or even a phone. So looking for her is kinda hard. Someday, I hope."

Nessa "Yes. You can't give up. Maybe you can get John to help you. He's good at locating people."

The young man's eyes light up briefly, before his face falls. "I can't get my hopes up. She lives far from here and doesn't even remember me. It's okay though. I miss her, but I just hope she's happy."

"I can't think a mother can be happy if she doesn't know what became of her son."

Pike brightens Someday maybe I'll do something that'll make her proud. Maybe I can even build her a proper house."

This is the first time Nessa's heard her friend imply anything about growing up poor. There's probably a lot about Pike's life she doesn't know. But the important thing is that such a good person has emerged from it all. His mom would surely be proud if she met him today.

40

Monday morning Nessa can't wait to encounter her principal. What must he be thinking after the events of the weekend? Beverly is at her post, smiling sheepishly. "Good morning! I want you to know I enjoyed helping you out, but today I'm feeling a little guilty." Nessa must look puzzled, so she continues. "I'm conflicted. I know it doesn't fit with Mr. Bingham's Perfect Plan."

Nessa laughs. "No, it's better than perfect. Anytime you have people working together to make other people happy, it doesn't get better than that. The best thing is I haven't seen a sign of armed guards for about twenty-four hours. I think a crowd of clowns is simply overwhelming for some of them. Is Mr. Bingham here yet?"

"I haven't seen him. I'm a little worried. He's never late."

Some banging is heard coming from the head office. Both women become still, staring at the door. David has entered from the back entrance. "Ladies. What are you standing around for? We have a perfect high school to run."

Nessa doesn't want to hear another of his rants about cleansing the student body or taking possession of the house on the hill. As expected, he starts in. "Have you all seen that wagon train of jokers that showed up to restore the Fancy

Tramp? What a waste of time and money. But I hope they can accomplish something because that will leave less for the Association to do when we take over. That punk Pike thinks he's a hero, but it won't be long until he gets run out of town on a rail. He doesn't realize how the townspeople here feel about that band of misfits he's a part of."

Nessa doesn't even have a comeback for such hatred. The only thing she can think to do is to take out her phone. "Mr. Bingham, I have something here you might enjoy watching. Maybe it will change your feelings about clowns." She quickly finds the video clip of Pike's performance at the Hartford House. It can't hurt. "I'll leave it with Beverly. I have to get to class. Just watch it when you have a minute. A family member of yours is in it."

Bingham's face shows fright. Up until his appearance at the apartment over the weekend, he's succeeded in keeping his personal and professional lives separate. As she learned from Melody on Friday, having his daughter in a group home for special needs is a source of shame for him and something he'd like to forget.

"Maybe you can remind him about the video and help him find it. I'll get my phone later," Nessa tells Bev. She has no secrets on it, and she can't resist giving him the chance to see Katrinka's interaction with Juggles. She wouldn't be surprised if the look of pleasure on her face is something her father has never seen. Hopefully, he has visited the Home a few times out of duty, but she can't believe he goes to any trouble to make Trink smile. When she thinks of the apprehension she feels when he enters her classroom, she can just imagine what his appearance would do to a girl who desperately wants his love.

Nothing is heard from Bingham throughout the day. No reaction to the video Nessa left with Bev. *He's a very stubborn man, so probably didn't even look at it. Then again, his curiosity*

232

may have gotten the best *of him.* Beverly stops in Room 106 after the last bell. She is delivering Nessa's phone. "Mr. Bingham says he doesn't have time to watch propaganda."

Nessa doesn't know if the secretary has been given the truth. "Did *you* watch it?" she inquires of Beverly.

"I must confess – I did. It made me cry. I'm guessing the girl in the red sweater is Melody Bingham's sister. That boy with the red nose was so good with her. I can't imagine her father wouldn't be pleased."

Nessa sighs. "I'm afraid that man is never pleased. Especially since Katrinka's happiness has never been important to him. I've heard."

Beverly still can't say an unflattering word against her boss. "Maybe he just has trouble showing his feelings."

41

$\mathscr{N}$essa is walking to her car after school when a taxicab pulls up to the curb beside her. She is startled to see the bright purple vehicle in Haven. She'd have said the town is too small to need taxi service. Bending down she sees that the driver is as much of a surprise as the cab. At the wheel is a diminutive black woman. Her puffed-out curly hairdo looks bigger than she does and sticks out from beneath a jaunty red hat topped with a bouquet of cherries. The impression is that she just stepped out of a storybook. A more clown-like little person would be hard to find.

"Excuse me," she greets Nessa brightly. "I'm looking for a man named John Harnden. I was told he might be in this town even though he lives somewhere else."

John's mysterious caller must have decided to make a personal appearance. Afro-Americans being rare as hen's teeth in this area, it doesn't take much to figure it out. "I can call him and tell him someone is looking for him. And Nessa takes out her cell phone.

John answers on the first ring. "Yeah. What's up? School out?"

"Yes," she replies knowing the cabbie can hear her. "I'm with someone you need to meet. Where are you?"

She listens to him answer, "Doug's."

"Okay. Be on the lookout for a purple cab."

John will save them a table at Doug's Diner. Nessa instructs the woman to follow her downtown and hopes Mr. Bingham will be nowhere around.

John stands when they enter and speaks to Nessa. "Who do we have here?" though he's sure to know the answer. Soon after talking on the phone to a caller they've judged to be Pike's mom, a black lady with familiar features is not a huge mystery.

Nessa is good at facial recognition and has already convinced herself that her driver is the spitting image of Pike – or vice versa. John chooses a booth at the back of the diner that invites conversation.

"I'm John Harnden. Am just guessing, but could you be the Mary Helen I spoke with on the phone?"

"You're right! I thought it would be a lot harder to find you. This must be my lucky day!"

Nessa loves her spirit. "It must be ours, too. John didn't even know where you lived, so we couldn't go to you."

"Well Little Rock is a long way to expect you to come."

"Little Rock, Arkansas? You got a cab to bring you this far?"

Mary Helen laughs. "Oh, it brought me alright, because I own it. It goes where I say."

Nessa and John exchange amused glances. Doesn't everybody's mom own a taxi? "How long can you stay?"

"That's the catch. I have to be back on my route on Monday so after a few hours here, I'll have to drive straight through like I did today."

Vanessa is impressed. Pike must have inherited his spunk from his mom. "I'm surprised you even thought of getting a job as a cab driver. I wouldn't have."

"Well, I had to do something when Marvin left me. He took our car. We owned the cab free and clear, but he couldn't drive two cars. He was sort of running from creditors, and I guess he didn't want to draw attention. Plus, I don't think he could've passed another physical for a chauffeur's license. He had a bad heart and emphysema."

"Marvin?" Nessa has perked up at the mention of the Fancy Tramp's only possible murder victim. However, any thought of whether Mary Helen's husband could be one and the same must be postponed.

"Yes. Marvin. Marvin the monster, I called him. I don't know where he is now and am not looking. He's been gone for a while now. I don't even know if he's alive, and I don't care. He cost me enough years without my boy. Is Michael still missing?"

"No. Actually, he made it back, but we haven't got to talk to him much. We should probably let him know you're in town. We aren't sure what his feelings are. Sorry." No one dares throw the young man back into the situation he's spent half his life running from.

Mary Helen's eyes grow teary. "I never said I didn't want him at home. It was Michael's choice to leave." Nessa notices the lady's lower lip quivering.. "He tried to get me to go with him. I wanted to so bad. But I was scared. His father would never have let me leave. He'd have hunted us both down and killed us. It broke me in half to see my son go, but I thought at least Michael would be safe if he was out of the house. I think he understood. I don't expect him to hold it against me."

"That must have been so hard, letting a ten-year-old boy go out into the world on his own. So many bad things could've happened to him. How did you ever sleep nights" Nessa is

236

thinking of her mom who hardly let her child out of the house alone when she was ten.

"Oh, I never did. I missed him so bad, but he was supposed to go to my sister's house. She had six already and didn't have much money, but said he could live with her. Trouble was, a circus was in town then, and Michael volunteered to work for them, sitting up the tents, scooping poop, and so on. I think Michael must've liked what he'd been doing, so when the circus moved on, he hid out in a trailer or somewhere, and they ended up taking him along."

"No kidding?" comments John. From what he's gathered from knowing Pike, he must've been pretty clever about surviving, even as a kid. "Did your sister know what happened to him?"

"Not for a while, and she was scared to tell me she lost him, so I didn't know. Then when the circus got to their next town, he found a way to call her. He said he was fine and for her to tell me not to worry."

"Was he close by where you lived?"

"I didn't know. He wouldn't tell anybody where he was because he was scared Marvin would find him. The circus moved around a lot anyway. And Michael can't write letters, so I didn't know much of anything until I saw on TV that people in Haven were looking for him."

Nessa is a little reluctant to spring a mother on Pike. What if she hasn't told them the whole story, and there're bad feelings between mother and son? You don't play with people's lives when you aren't sure. "What do you think?" She is looking at John.

John hesitates but finally comes up with words for Mary Helen. "I guess we don't have a real reason to keep you from him. We can arrange for the two of you to get together. Pike can take it from there. We'll supervise, of course. Do you want to go up to the house and surprise him?"

"I don't want to give him a heart attack or anything, but a surprise would be fun." Mary Helen is beaming at the thought.

"We'll take my car. I'll pull into the driveway and let you out," offers John. "But know that if Pike seems upset by seeing you, we'll be filling your gas tank so you can get out of town. He's dealing with enough drama right now so doesn't need any more."

"That's okay," she replies meekly. "I don't want to get in his way or make him unhappy. I've never wanted to do that."

"Would Pike recognize the cab?" Nessa asks Mary Ellen before she climbs into her own Honda.

"I don't see how," the woman replies. "Marvin didn't have it when Michael lived at home."

"just the same, you may as well ride with me," John says.

They leave the taxi in the diner parking lot, and Nessa follows John's car up the hill. She doesn't want to miss the next scene, whether it's good or bad. John pulls to a stop at the entrance to the drive and his passenger climbs out. Both John and Nessa keep their eyes locked on the thin black lady in her red hat trudging up the gravel driveway to the mansion. Nessa prays they are doing the right thing. It hardly seems likely that sweet Pike will be rude to the woman, but who knows what bad memories will do.

Obviously, at least one of Bingham's goons has stayed behind. He blocks Mary Helen's path. John always marvels at the way those guys can materialize out of nowhere. Apparently deciding Pike's mother can handle herself, he motions to Nessa to stay in her car. She rolls down her window so she can hear and be ready to rush forward if needed.

"I'm sorry, Ma'am," the man in sunglasses is saying. "I can't let you on this property. You haven't been vetted."

"I haven't been *what?*" the little woman replies loudly. Nessa and John are discovering their new friend is feistier than she first appeared. "I don't think you know who I am. I've been invited here by a private investigator. Who are you?" She is standing straight, making use of every bit of her stature. The cherries on top of the hat give her an extra inch.

There's a short silence, then the man answers, "I am an agent of our future mayor. My job is to help clean up this town."

"Good! I like a clean town. Now please let me go up to the house. I need to see my son."

"This is a white city, Ma'am. Nobody in Haven can help you. Don't make me___"

"These people standing around here have been trying to find Michael Pikeston, a black boy. He's the reason for all the commotion. Now don't tell me I shouldn't be here. If anybody says that, it'll have to be him."

The camouflaged guard looks around for backup. He's apparently reluctant to manhandle a female on his own, even an African American.

We have a lot of agents. I can let you go, but you'll just get stopped again. And if Mr. Bingham comes by, you'll wish you'd listened to me." He keeps positioning himself in front of Mary Helen without touching her.

"I don't know any Big Ham but I'll take my chances," she tells him while shooting him fiery eye contact. "I've come a long way. Now excuse me, please." And Mary Helen brushes past the man on her way to the front porch.

Nessa and John in their separate vehicles exchange triumphant smiles. They can see where Pike gets his courage. Their earlier fears give way to joy as they watch Ms. Mary Helen approach the Fancy Tramp. She is a lady on a mission. Eleven years without her boy has led to this moment. On her own now, she can almost feel his arms around her. "Michael, I'm here! Your mama is here!" The guards watch with curiosity. Isn't she supposed to be frightened? They raise rifles in a threatening show of force, but all eyes are focused on the black woman and the young man who is running to meet her. Right behind him is a delegation of visiting clowns ready to protect him if necessary.

"Mama! Is it really you?"

"It's me baby! Come let me hold you!" and the camouflaged men along with the clowns, are forced to allow the most heart-felt hug they've ever seen. She isn't tall enough to reach Pike's shoulders but she embraces his middle with all her might then laughs when he picks her up. "You grew so tall!" she says with wonder. "I'm sorry it took me so long to find you," Please forgive me!"

"No sorrys, Mom! I'm just so happy you survived in that house. I've felt guilty about leaving you."

"Only thing you could've done," she answers and hugs Pike again.

He grabs her hand and pulls her toward the house. "I have somebody you have to meet!"

"Oh, my goodness! You could have a wife! Or a baby!"

"No, mom. No wife or baby. I just want you to meet Sofie, the woman who watched over me so I wouldn't be alone." There was really no way for him to explain that situation without making his real mom feel guilty for not being there.

Mary Helen doesn't reply. She is still getting used to the idea that her son had no contact with family. Her original idea to leave him with her sister didn't work out, so naturally, he had to grab onto a stranger. Hopefully, not a perverted heathen.

Mary Helen looks around the mansion with its columns and high ceilings and utters a whispered, "Oh, my!" To the Association, the apartment complex is a dilapidated eyesore, but to Mary Helen her son is living in the lap of luxury. She looks very small climbing the big staircase. Pike taps on the door of Sofie's apartment and gets the usual response, "I'll be there as quick as I can!"

Finally, the door opens and there she is, the woman who has been Mary Helen's stand-in for eleven years. "Well, hi!

Come on in. The boys are sleeping." Four little black bundles are lined up on the couch.

"I'm Pike's mother", Mary Helen offers. To her credit, she has no obvious reaction to Ms. Sofie's size. "I understand I need to thank you."

"Sit right over here." Ms. Sofie gestures to the recliner. "I can't imagine what you want to thank me for. I've been his friend since he first came to the circus, but so have lots of people. That's why he was able to round up three vans full of friends. Your boy is much loved."

Mary Helen beams. Maybe she and Marvin didn't ruin his life after all.

42

Sunday evening Lola throws a welcome back party. Pike is safe and sound, and although she doesn't announce it, the owner and managers of the Fancy Tramp are in a fine position financially to proceed with renovations. The house is spilling over with clown construction workers who are eager to get started. And as far as anyone can see, the uniformed men are gone from the property. Everyone has something to celebrate.

The ballroom is alive with calliope music and sounds of folks who are not only happy about the project ahead but happy to see each other. It's a reunion to top all reunions. There are costumes and noise makers and popcorn.

Surprisingly, Nessa is able to hear her cell phone over the din. She sees the name KYRA come up on the ID. It's her old friend from Chicago calling again, perhaps to bring a spot of fun to what she's convinced is Nessa's boring life in the boondocks. Finding a corner in the hallway, Nessa says Hello. "What is all that noise?" shouts Kyra.

"I'm at a party!"

"'Again?" Their last conversation was after the dinner party in Sofie's apartment. "Don't people around Haven ever get serious? Or is life as a teacher pretty much fun and games?"

"Oh, I've had plenty of tense times here, too. But when you're with good people, the happy times always seem to follow.

"So I don't need to tell you about an opening for an English teacher downtown Chicago – great pay?"

There are squeals from inside the ballroom. "I'm going to have to get back to the others, Kyra. I'll call you real soon when I have time to give you the scoop! And no, I'll pass on the Chicago job."

From outside comes the booming voice of Mr. David Bingham. No one notices his shouting over the clamor of the celebration. Only Gordy has come downstairs to find peace in his usual quarters. He's still wearing a black top hat, something Lola has provided to put him in the party spirit. He stops in the foyer and, unbeknown to any of the guests, he listens to the loud threatening tone of the principal's voice coming to him from the front yard.

Nessa has come out of the ballroom onto the upstairs landing. She opens a window to hear the shouting more clearly. Her boss must have been drinking. He doesn't deserve to be acknowledged. Let him yell his lungs out. With any luck, someone will take him away.

"Come on out here you cowards! You think you're so smart since your black Bozo returned. Well yuk it up! This house is not going to belong to you much longer. You can't put on enough makeup to hide your freakiness, and freaks aren't allowed in this town. Haven answers to me you sniveling bunch of hippies! I'm dead serious. Your day is over, clowns. You're all going to die!"

Nessa hears the front door of the Tramp open and rushes to the top of the staircase in time to catch a glimpse of Gordy going outside. Just before his exit he grabs Lola's fly swatter from its hook by the door. He is ready to defend his friends. A gunshot is his reward.

A scream that Nessa recognizes as her own accompanies her all the way downstairs. People from the ballroom follow the scream, but everyone is too late. Gordon is sprawled on the porch floor still clutching the fly swatter. Lola falls on top of the sweetest man she's ever known.

David Bingham runs for his car, but many witnesses watch him flee, the smoking gun in his hand. The soon-to-be former high school principal is immediately surrounded by police officers who are likely in the neighborhood at his own bidding. The last view Bingham has of the Fancy Tramp is of a house that has been totally occupied by clowns. The front porch is covered with them, and the man on the floor whom they are praising is someone he calls a freak. The principal exercised his superiority by taking out the most vulnerable man in sight, but doing so didn't win him any points with the townspeople.

Unlike Bingham's prediction, the citizens do, indeed, notice. And with his death, Gordy has succeeded in foiling the principal's Perfect Plan.

I had a friend who was a clown. When he died, all his friends went to the funeral in one car.
–Steven Wright

Clown Alley plus Friends

A memorial takes place in the ballroom of the Fancy Tramp. All of Gordon's friends, including those who traveled a distance to take part in the renovation, are present. Everyone except Vanessa, John and Mary Helen is dressed in full clown costume and makeup. The males, in a show of respect have removed their hats no matter how important they are to their characters.

Clyde from Illinois begins the proceedings by offering a meditation. The robust man with green hair and wearing polka dots sheds some tears as he begins. "We want to offer a tribute and memorial to our brother Gordon Harcroft. In his day, this gentle man was a clown to top them all, and we know, God, that you remember. He loved you, he loved his circus family and he loved the people he made laugh. He was the sort of human being we all aspire to be. In recent years he had no memory and little understanding of who he was or what was happening around him. But to the end, he remained loving, helpful and fine. We will miss his sweet presence every day. We know Gordy would want this prayer read on his behalf because it expresses the way he felt about his profession. We've selected Pike to interpret it for us."

Nessa is startled. Pike has been working on his reading, but recent drama in his life has slowed his progress. She holds her breath, hoping he isn't going to stumble so much the prayer will be ruined.

Evidently, Pike is familiar with the reading. Just like song lyrics, he can remember many of the words and, along with the hints he gets from the letters, he pulls it off. After a little throat-clearing and a couple of coughs, nobody could ask for a more moving presentation.

"As I stumble through this life,
help me to create more laughter than tears,
dispense more happiness than gloom,
spread more cheer than despair.

Never let me become so indifferent,
that I will fail to see the wonders in the eyes of a child,
or the twinkle in the eyes of the aged.

Never let me forget that my total effort is to cheer people,
make them happy, and forget momentarily,
all the unpleasantness in their lives.

And in my final moment,
may I hear You whisper:
'When you made My people smile,
you made Me smile.' "

Listening to Lola's sobs is heart breaking and beautiful at the same time. John takes Nessa's hand. She isn't sure how serious their relationship is at this point, but she's sure about one thing. If it continues to grow as it has so far, she hopes their feelings have the same future as they've witnessed at the Fancy Tramp. Perhaps she and John will have the sort of love Gordy and Lola had, one that endures through everything. A love that is only made stronger if the day comes when they can't communicate. A love that remains even when their memories are gone.

At the end of the service, Lola dries her eyes and tells everyone, "Gordon would be so thankful and honored for the number of caring folks here today. You were his world, and he's up there, listening for our laughter so let's have some fun!"

A slide show follows, projected on a sheet at the front of the room, reminding the funeral-goers of scenes from the circus including the sad-faced antics of Uncle Bo (aka Gordon).

Mary Helen sits at the back of the room and smiles broadly every time Juggles lights up the screen. It's like getting a few minutes of her boy's youth back. She was allowed to enjoy him for ten years, but he was born for the circus. If he hadn't left home when he did, he might have missed the chance to ever be part of one. And that would've been a shame.

43

Beginning of Fall Semester

Vanessa is walking out of the initial staff meeting with the new principal, Jared Porter. First impressions are good. He is pleasant, well-spoken and most of all he has just declared his belief that "Education at HHS is for all students, regardless of race, creed or ability."

The idea of a perfect student body has a nice ring to it, but Nessa is ready to try her luck with even the most disadvantaged and imperfect students.

She stops by Beverly's desk before going to her classroom. The woman isn't smiling, but then, she has never done much of that. Nessa notes that Beverly's earrings are new, a good indication she's directing her interests toward someone besides David Bingham.

"What are your plans, Bev? I hope you're staying." Her words aren't entirely honest, but Nessa senses the secretary needs encouragement. After all, *she* didn't shoot anyone.

"I'm hoping Mr. Porter will want me to. I feel pretty foolish for not having better intuition about David. I won't make a mistake like that again."

"Don't take on his guilt, Bev. You were just being a loyal secretary. Most administrators deserve our admiration. Bingham was just the rare one who didn't. I'm sure Jared Porter will be a much more worthy boss. I have a really good feeling about him."

As if on cue, Bingham's replacement appears from his office behind Beverly's desk. His sincere smile gives both ladies a lift. "I'm a single guy, and I haven't found a good apartment to rent in Haven. Do either of you have any suggestions?"

Bev smooths her hair and offers, "I'd love to help with any other questions you have, but Vanessa can give you the best advice about housing."

Nessa is eager to advertise. "Oh, yes! I live in the Fan__, the colorful Victorian on the hill. North side of town. It's called Gordon House. Hopefully, they have a vacancy. There's a sign out front with a clown face on it. I hope you don't have a phobia."

"Oh, no. A clown face tells me the owner has a sense of humor. I'll check it out. It sounds like my kind of place."

ACKNOWLEDGEMENTS

Bushels of thanks to my super beta readers Kristi Paxton and Jayne McKinley. Writing would be a lonely process without the input of friends. Their perspectives and encouragement kept me going!

Thanks, too, to Jerry Thordsen, clown name Jericho, who is a member of my writers group. He loaned me articles about the profession, and through his gentle, loving personality proves that real clowns are, indeed, worthy of our affection.

DISCUSSION QUESTIONS

1. Do you think you could cope with working for a person who has way different beliefs and values than yours? Do you think your obligation to your boss ends at the doors of the workplace? Should Nessa have resigned as soon as she learned what Bingham's educational philosophy was?

2. Did you notice a similarity between the way the clowns of two years ago bullied the town and the ways the clowns are now being bullied? Are clowns getting what's coming to them?

3. Do you know anyone with coulrophobia? Do you find it hard to sympathize? Do we all have phobias?

4. Did you feel sadness at the demise of the circus? Do you think clowns will continue to be with us?

5. How would you describe Nessa? A) a naïve new teacher who'll put up with anything just to have a job (b) a spunky young woman who isn't afraid to speak up for what she believes (c) an idealistic female without good judgement. Do you expect her to become an exceptional teacher for Haven High?

6. Is a man who lies about his identity a bad bet for a love interest or does John's profession explain the ease with which he can invent or hide facts about himself?